MOUNTAIN SECRETS

NICOLE GARDNER

Publisher: Hawthorn Hill Books

Cover Art: BY THE BROOKE DESIGNS

This book is dedicated to Julie, Misty, and all my Keesler AFB girls. I will always cherish the memories of being stationed there with you!

But truthfully?

I wrote this one for myself.

Reader Note

This novel contains brief descriptions of domestic abuse and discussions of PTSD. It is my hope that I've handled both of these topics with the care they deserve.

Chapter One

Wilhelmina

Past

My heart pounded so hard I felt sure that the very sound of it beating against my chest would wake him and betray me.

If he woke, I was dead.

The thought should have terrified me, but it didn't. Instead, it calmed me. One way or another, I would soon be free.

Hearing no movement from him, I slipped my legs from beneath the cool sheets. I froze for just a moment, my feet hovering above the cold tile floors.

Nothing.

I lowered my feet to the floor, closing my eyes as my toes touched the tile. The cold that snaked up my body was welcome. I didn't need it to wake me—I had been wide awake for hours, counting down the very seconds until I made my move. But it sharpened my senses and reminded me I was alive.

Yes, I was alive. And if everything went according to plan, I might actually have a chance of staying that way.

Hope began to rise and unfurl like a seedling sprouting from a seed. I had spent too long in the dark, buried, without hope. But if I could survive just one more night, I would rise. I would bloom, and I would live again.

With one timid step, then another, I slowly crept away from the relative safety of the bed. Step by step, my feet silent on the frigid floor, I walked toward my future—or toward my doom. Only time would tell.

Unable to risk turning on a light in the pitch-black room, I relied on my hands to guide me safely. The room felt like a gauntlet of sharp angles and hard wood furniture, all waiting for me to trip or stub a toe —all fatal errors if they woke him.

After what felt like hours, I found the doorknob. This was the moment of truth. With my heart thudding in my chest, I cracked open the bedroom door. I barely dared to breathe, afraid the noise would wake him. But all remained still. Slowly, I pulled the door open as little as possible, slipped through the gap, and pulled it closed again. Then I waited, with my heart pounding even harder.

I had a thousand excuses ready if he woke up. I could pretend I was hungry and had gone for a midnight snack. I could say I had forgotten to wipe up the crumbs after lunch and wanted to get to it before the mess spoiled his breakfast. Either one would get me a beating, but I would live.

I didn't want to live anymore though. Not like this, anyway.

When the seconds turned to a full minute without any sounds of movement from him, I took my next steps forward, quicker this time, grateful for the bit of light that allowed me to see my way. Daniel had insisted on blackout curtains in the bedroom, but not in the rest of the house. It was enough to help me move just a bit faster without the worry of bumping into something. I had memorized every possible creak in the floor and could do this part in my sleep. Down the hallway, then the stairs, through the foyer, into the back kitchen—I moved silently, every step practiced and purposeful.

I didn't dare turn on a light in the kitchen, but I didn't have to. I had chosen tonight in part because the moon was full. The glow through the windows was just enough for my eyes, long adjusted to the dark, to see everything they needed to see.

My heart quickened. Now came the dangerous part. If I took even one more step forward, there would be no excuse to save me. Fear washed over me at the thought.

Just breathe. Be brave for just a little longer.

I crept into the large walk-in pantry off the kitchen, where I had hidden the first set of things I needed. Faded jeans and a t-shirt, rolled up and hidden behind storage bins. A pair of slip-on shoes tucked out of sight, beneath the bottom shelves. A thick wad of cash in a plastic bag, hidden inside the box of cereal he never ate.

It was all here.

I slipped into the clothes, then wadded up my silk nightgown and threw it into the trash can. That one act of rebellion gave me a thrill—and the courage to keep going.

I braced myself before tiptoeing out of the pantry, half fearing I would find him standing in the kitchen, just waiting for me to come out so he could punish me.

Kill me.

But the kitchen was still empty, and hope rose again—hope that I might actually survive this.

Time to move quickly. There was no way my absence would go unnoticed much longer. But that was okay. I just needed to take a few more steps.

Breathe.

I crossed quickly to the dining room and opened the bottom drawer to the hutch. Weeks ago, I had hidden a backpack beneath the tablecloth and napkins that were reserved for Christmas, knowing he would be unlikely to look there any other time of the year. The backpack held more cash, as well as the few personal items I couldn't bear to leave behind. I quickly tucked the money from the pantry into the backpack and took a deep breath.

It was time to wake the monster.

Daniel's security system had been the hardest part of the plan for me to figure out. He had changed the code so I couldn't disarm it, and if I opened even the smallest window, it would alarm him.

The only choice I had was to use it. But that meant everything had to go perfectly. If he caught me...

But I couldn't think of that now. This was no time to think about what could—what *would*—happen if I got caught. Success was the only option.

I went back to the kitchen and slipped my hand inside the backpack, pulling out the letter. I had written it weeks ago, when I first planned my escape—before he started locking me in the house. It was a simple suicide note, telling him I'd rather die than live with him another day and explaining how—and where—I would drive my car over the cliffs. The note was short and to the point. I hadn't bothered wasting words, knowing they wouldn't matter anyway.

He had never cared how I felt on any other topic, and this one was no different.

I put the note on the counter and walked to the back door, knowing as soon as I opened it the alarm would sound and wake him. I had calculated a sixty-second head start—sixty seconds for him to wake, jump out of bed, and run downstairs for the kitchen. It would take another sixty seconds, at least, for him to run back up the stairs for his car keys. He wouldn't find them though. Not quickly anyway. I had made sure of that.

Five minutes would be enough, if everything went according to plan.

Five more minutes and I would be free.

I paused, closing my eyes and taking a deep breath before opening the door. My hand trembled. My body felt unwilling to cooperate, knowing the pain that would come if anything went wrong.

But I was no stranger to pain.

I took one more breath and turned the deadbolt, feeling as if the sound thundered through the house.

Then I opened the door to my own future.

The alarm wailed through the house. I knew that Daniel would fumble out of bed before realizing I was missing. He would be furious. It didn't matter. I shut out all thought of him and began to go through the part of this plan I had only been able to practice in my head these last few weeks.

If only I had been brave enough to go through with it before he started keeping me trapped in the house, with either him or a "bodyguard" to watch me! Everything had been planned, everything prepared. I could have done this in the daylight, could have escaped with plenty of time to spare. His new rules—and the cruel muscle he had hired to "protect" me—changed all of that and made escape that much trickier. But there wasn't time to think about what could have been. This was the hand I had been dealt, and I was going to play the hell out of it.

I grabbed the spare set of car keys I had tucked inside a rain boot in the garage after the first time he took my keys as "punishment," sensing it wouldn't be the last time he trapped me.

My beloved car was waiting for me. I tossed my backpack onto the front seat and jumped in, reveling in the feel of the engine as it roared to life. This car had been one of my greatest pleasures. It gave me a new thrill now, knowing I would use it to gain my freedom.

The door to the garage flew open as I backed out. There stood Daniel, the image of rage, glaring at me with eyes full of shock and hatred.

I didn't stop.

I hit the gas, knowing he would come after me all too quickly. Once he realized I had hidden his keys, he would stop looking and go for his second set, kept locked in a safe to which he had never given me the code. It wouldn't take him long.

Just five minutes. I only needed five minutes.

I sped down the highway toward the coast and the treacherously curvy roads that would be my savior. The thrill of driving again, of being in control and taking the curves as fast as I dared brought part of me back to life.

One more uncurling of the seed of hope inside me.

The bright moon and stars lit up the night, but I barely needed them now. I knew the exact spot I was looking for. After all, I knew this road like the back of my hand and had rehearsed this in my mind a thousand times.

I could only pray that real life played out the way it had in my imagination.

As I approached the spot, I grabbed my backpack and slipped it over my shoulders. Then I let the car gain speed and set the cruise control, hugging the curves tightly until I reached the right one.

I unclicked my seatbelt, said a prayer, opened the door—and flew.

My body slammed against the pavement. It didn't matter. I had felt worse a hundred times before. This time, the pain only felt like freedom, as I watched my beautiful car career over the cliff and into the sea. I pulled myself up and ran toward it, unable to deny myself one look over the edge. There she was, tossing in the turbulent waves, sinking under the water.

Freedom.

Tears sprang to my eyes. I was alive. I was safe.

And now I needed to run.

I sprinted toward the cover of the trees, ignoring the pain in my body. He would be here soon, looking for me. I had to hide.

As I raced toward the tree cover, I heard the unmistakable sound of his souped-up engine coming. My heart nearly stopped. He hadn't given me as much of a head start as I had expected.

When tires squealed and his car door slammed, I didn't even turn around. I just kept running, even as I imagined the anger on his face when he looked over the edge of the cliff and saw my car. Maybe it was better this way. I wanted to laugh now, imagining his shock as he watched what he thought was me sinking into the sea below.

His precious prize, his *possession*.

Now I only belonged to me.

One painful mile later, feeling more battered and bruised by the second, I crept up to the little blue cottage where I hoped to find refuge. The sight of it brought tears to my eyes. It was a beacon of peace, sitting there underneath the starry night sky. I knocked on the door, praying Suzanna was home. It was the one part of the plan that was entirely up in the air, since Daniel had taken away my ability to contact anyone. If she wasn't here, I had money, but nothing else.

If she was here, I had a fighting chance.

The seconds felt like hours until I heard her coming to the door. When she opened it and saw me on her steps, her eyes went wide with shock.

"You got out," she whispered like she didn't quite believe it.

I nodded. Then the tears came and wouldn't stop.

"Oh, honey." She pulled me inside and wrapped her arms around me. "Can you stay the night?"

"No," I said, shaking my head, still struggling with the tears I had held back for what felt like years. "I can't take the chance. For your sake and mine. If there's any chance this didn't fool him, your house is the first place he'll look."

"I understand," she said, swallowing hard.

"Do you still have it?"

"Of course I do," she said. "I've prayed every day that you were still alive and that you would get out."

"Thank you." Relief washed through me.

Suzanna, my former housekeeper, was the only person in my life I could truly trust, the one person I had asked to help me in my escape plan. She hadn't been the only person to see the evidence of what Daniel had done to me, but she was the only one brave enough to offer assistance. I owed her more thanks than I could possibly give, and I wouldn't put her in danger for anything.

"You've got some nasty scrapes," she said, looking at my arms where they had met the pavement on my jump. "Let's get you cleaned up and on your way. Are you hungry?"

"Yes," I admitted. I had been too nervous to eat all day.

"I've got peanut butter and jelly," she said, laughing. "That's about it."

"It sounds perfect."

Suzanna set me up with a sandwich and pulled out her first aid kit so I could clean up. Then she retrieved the bag she and I had filled what felt like ages ago, when we were first planning my escape—before Daniel had fired her and the rest of the staff, locked me in the house, and cut off all contact between me and the outside world.

"It's all here," she said.

I let out a breath, feeling hope grow even more. Inside the bag was more money, clothes, and most importantly: a fresh name. Suzanna moved in different circles than I did, and she knew how to get the kind of identification you needed for a fresh start.

I thanked my lucky stars that fate had brought her into my orbit and she had decided to help me.

"You're sure it's all safe?" I asked, needing to hear it again.

She nodded. "Yep. Name, social, driver's license, all of it. You're starting fresh. It will all check out, as long as nobody digs too deep."

I pulled out the wallet to look at my new name. "Willa Monroe," I said, letting it roll over my tongue. "I like it."

"It suits you," she said with a reassuring smile. "Where will you go?"

I smiled back for the first time all night.

"Anywhere I want."

Chapter Two

Cole

Present

My car rattled and sent up a cloud of dust when I turned onto the gravel road that would lead to my temporary home. It was pretty out here, surrounded by the pine and oak forest, with the late afternoon sunlight cutting through the trees. Every now and then, the trees would open up, revealing scenic overlooks of the valley below. If the road had been paved, I would have enjoyed the drive. Nice curves hugging the side of the mountain, gaining elevation with every twist in the road—pavement would have made it downright fun. But when a rock bounced off my windshield, I winced, slowing my speed to a crawl. Gravel roads like these weren't made for a speedster like mine, making me wonder, yet again, what I was doing here.

I was as free as a bird, without a single obligation tying me down anywhere. No more military orders. No more living at the whim of the U.S. government. For once, my life was my own, and I could go anywhere I pleased.

Yet somehow, I had let Emerson Jones talk me into coming back here of all places. Rosemary Mountain. A tiny mountain town that filled up with tourists every summer.

At least there weren't many people here during the winter. That was one thing it had going for it. And it wasn't like I had committed to being here for long. It was a temporary job and a temporary place to hide away while I figured out what the hell I was going to do with the rest of my life. I'd be out of here before tourist season ever hit.

I cringed again as I pulled into the driveway and spotted Emerson sitting on the front porch of the log cabin. I should have known he would be here to greet me. For some reason, I had thought he might just leave a key under the doormat or something.

But no, true to form, he was here to welcome me to town and catch up. Problem was, I wasn't really in the mood for conversation.

A wave of guilt washed over me. Emerson was a good guy, and he was doing me a solid. He had lined up this job for me and was renting his old cabin to me at a ridiculously low price.

Low cash price, anyway. The obligatory social interactions were another thing altogether.

"Hey, Cole," he said, raising a hand in greeting as I stepped out of my car. He was wearing a flannel shirt and cowboy boots, having apparently gone native since moving to the region.

I returned the wave but said nothing.

He jogged down the steps to me. "Need help with anything?" he asked as he clapped me on the shoulder.

"Nah. I didn't bring much," I said, heading to my trunk to grab the bags I had stowed there.

He made a move to help me anyway, but I had already swung the oversized pack onto my back, and I grabbed the smaller bag with my other hand before he could reach it.

Emerson followed me up the steps to the house, apparently not reading the signals I was sending that I just wanted to be left alone. That, or he was ignoring them.

It was annoying either way.

"Everything's the same as when you stayed here for the wedding," he said, passing me a key once we were inside. "Except that we got the chickens moved over to the cottage, so you won't have to worry about them this time. Also, Daphne left you a basket of cookies on the dining room table. They're from the local bakery. Good stuff."

"Tell her thanks," I said.

"Sure thing." He studied me for a moment. "She also wanted me to invite you over for dinner tonight."

I kept a poker face, despite my realization that the obligatory social price might be even higher than expected. In other circumstances, it wouldn't matter. Emerson and I had once been close buddies, living out our military dreams together. And his wife, Daphne, was a jewel, perfect for him in every way. She was smart, funny, and easy to be around. A few years ago, I would have jumped at their dinner invitation, eager to catch up with such a good friend.

But I had lived a lot of life in the years since Emerson and I had both been fresh to service, bright-eyed and idealistic with no real understanding of the horrors of war. He had seen tragedy too, up close and personal. Yet somehow, he had come out on the other side of it and created a normal, happy life for himself.

I wasn't there yet, and frankly, I doubted I ever would be. I had seen too much. Done too much. Failed too many people.

A normal, happy life wasn't in the cards for me. Not anymore.

Still, I knew how to play a part. "Thanks," I said, forcing a small smile. "What time should I be there?"

"How does six sound?"

"Sounds great. Can I bring anything?"

He shook his head. "Just yourself. No need for you to drive all the way into town to pick anything up. We've got it covered. Figured you could use this afternoon to unpack and get settled and not have to worry about grocery shopping or anything until tomorrow."

"I appreciate it. That's thoughtful of you guys." I gave him a smile that was almost genuine.

Almost.

"Okay then." Emerson studied me a minute longer, then clapped me on the shoulder again. "Hey, man, I know we didn't get to talk much when you came for the wedding, with everything going on. But I'm glad we'll get to catch up now. It's good to have you here. And Chief's really looking forward to meeting you. He's got the whole team excited about the training course you put together for us. I'm glad you agreed to come."

"Me too." It was a hollow statement. I didn't really feel much of anything about it, to be honest. But here was as good a place as any, I supposed. And at least I'd be doing something I enjoyed. I couldn't muster up his level of enthusiasm though, even to play a part.

Emerson shook his head, pressing his lips tight, like he was stopping himself from saying more. Then he left me alone in the cabin with my ghosts.

WHEN IT NEARED 1800 HOURS, I DECIDED TO HEAD OUT ON foot. I had seen too many men grow soft after getting out of service and was determined to make sure that didn't happen to me. If there was one thing I had learned, it was that danger existed everywhere, not just in war zones.

The sky was already growing dark as I hoofed it up the mountain. Emerson's cabin was on the same twisty road as Daphne's cottage—their cottage, I supposed, now that they were married. It was at the very end of the dead-end road, and the climb was no joke. I relished every moment of it, enjoying the light strain on my muscles. This, at least, felt right.

I heard Daphne's laughter as I approached the house. The couple passed by the window, with Daphne giggling as she swatted Emerson away from the tray of food in her hands. He kissed her, tugging on her long red braid as a distraction so he could steal a bite anyway. But she just laughed when she realized what he was doing, shaking her head in mock disapproval even though she couldn't contain her grin. He leaned down and placed a second kiss on her growing belly. I stopped, almost hypnotized as I watched the scene, with an odd pang of longing for the happy family they were building together.

What they had was a gift not many received.

I shook my head and put my poker face back into place before heading up the steps. Daphne answered before I even had a chance to knock, swinging the door open as my fist hovered in the air.

"Cole! Come on in," she said, smiling from ear to ear. "I just brought some appetizers into the living room. Help yourself, if you can grab any before my husband devours them all."

"Can't help it," Emerson said, popping another one into his mouth. "These are too good. You've got to try one, Cole."

"Thanks. Smells good in here," I commented, reminding myself to put on a smile.

"Thank you," Daphne said, returning my fake smile with one that lit up her whole face. "We have bacon-wrapped shrimp, garlic-stuffed olives, and toasted ravioli to start. There's a lasagna in the oven, and I'm going to pop in some garlic bread and toss a salad real quick."

"That sounds amazing."

Daphne just laughed. "If it is, you can thank Emerson. He's the real cook here. The shrimp and lasagna are all him."

I just raised my eyebrows and looked at Emerson in question.

He grinned. "Yes, but darling, you did open the jar of olives. And I'm sure your salad will be great."

She rolled her eyes at him before turning on her heels and heading toward the kitchen, but even so, there was affection in her eyes.

That odd pang hit again before I squashed it down. Some people were meant for the family life. I was meant to be alone.

"Have a seat," Emerson said, gesturing toward the couch. "Want a beer?"

"Unless you have something stronger." I removed my jacket before heading to the sofa and popping one of the bacon-wrapped shrimp into my mouth.

Emerson was right; they were great. Maybe I would learn to cook in my newfound free time. My therapist had suggested I find a new hobby, something completely unrelated to what I had done in the military. Something less likely to activate my nervous system and send adrenaline coursing through my body. Maybe cooking would be it.

Then again, I kind of preferred my old hobbies. And I had a real fondness for the feel of adrenaline.

"You still like bourbon?" Emerson asked.

"Yep," I answered.

"I've got one for you to try," he said, heading for the tiny liquor cabinet tucked in the corner. "Greg bought this for me as a wedding gift. It's supposed to be extra special because it was aged at sea, or something like that." He grinned. "Tastes about like their regular stuff to me, but maybe you'll be able to tell the difference." He brought the bottle over for me to look at.

"That's good stuff," I said, impressed. "I've actually had it once. Awfully nice gift."

"He's a nice guy," Emerson said. "I told him you were going to be here for a while. He said to tell you to give him a call if you're looking for work. Says he could use someone like you."

"I'll keep that in mind," I said as Emerson poured me a drink.

Greg, his best friend here in Rosemary Mountain, was also the county sheriff. I had served as backup for him at Emerson and Daphne's wedding when they were facing an unknown threat. Greg was a good guy, one I wouldn't mind working under. But I had no intention of going into law enforcement.

Problem was, I still didn't know what I was going to do, long term anyway.

Emerson handed me my glass and sat in the easy chair across from the couch, studying me. "You looking forward to working together again?" he asked, giving me an easy smile.

"Yep. Just like the good old days."

Emerson snorted. "Let's hope not."

This time, my smile was real. "Good point. Listen, I really do appreciate you hooking me up with the gig while I figure things out."

Emerson was a flight nurse for the local air evacuation team. He had talked his boss into bringing me on temporarily to conduct some advanced training simulations, teaching their crew how to get to some of the more difficult rescue sites. With more and more tourists flocking to the mountain every year, often doing stupid shit in order to get a cool photo for social media, the team was getting called on to conduct more complicated rescue missions all the time. Emerson had framed it to me like I would be doing them a favor.

I knew he was really doing me one.

"Gotta put all that expensive training to use somehow," he said, winking. He raised his glass to me. "To new beginnings."

"To new beginnings," I echoed. I didn't really see it that way though. The way I saw it, there were no new beginnings—only continuing. No matter what you did or where you went, everything you had done before was still there.

There was no real way to run from the past.

Chapter Three

Willa

I stared at myself in the mirror, checking to make sure everything was perfect—or at least presentable. My wild mess of hair was already trying to fall out of my attempt at a sophisticated bun. I blew out a breath, tucking in a few more bobby pins, hoping it would stay put and meet Janet's approval. My new boss was a picture of elegance, with never a hair out of place. But mine had a mind of its own. It simply wanted to be wild and free. Like me, I thought with the tiniest smile before my nerves took over again.

Nerves were nothing new for me. I lived with mild anxiety every moment of every day, always feeling like my new world could come crashing down around me at any moment. But this was a different kind of nerves—the good kind. The kind that accompanied a fresh start.

For the first time in years, I was starting a real job in my former profession. It was a gift beyond anything I had hoped for when I first wandered into Rosemary Mountain, hoping it would be a safe place to land for a few weeks at least. After months on the run, criss-crossing

America, never feeling far away enough from Daniel to truly feel safe, I wanted somewhere to catch my breath. I expected it to be two or three months at most, but somehow I had built myself a fresh life one step at a time. And somehow, that new life had turned into the kind of job offer I had never expected to have again.

Now, I desperately wanted to do an amazing job and make my new boss proud.

Yes, these nerves were new and welcome. But the old ones were there too. I reassured myself, yet again, that everything would be fine. My identification was secure. Suzanna had made sure of that, and it hadn't given me any problems yet.

Of course, until now, I had avoided the kind of jobs that did much checking on that kind of thing. Working for Janet Morrison—*Sheriff* Morrison's wife—was something altogether different. This would be a true test of my new identity. Anyone could see how protective the sheriff was of his new bride. I had a feeling he would run a background check on me the minute I turned in my paperwork—if he hadn't already.

"Just breathe," I told my reflection in the mirror. "If anything goes wrong, you can always run again."

I had done it before, and I would do it again if I had to.

I smoothed the fabric of my skirt, checking again to make sure there wasn't a single flaw. It was my own creation, a flowing silk skirt in the most glorious shade of crimson. I had paired it with a cream cashmere sweater, a luxury I hadn't felt against my skin in entirely too long. Cashmere simply wasn't in the budget of someone working temp jobs that didn't look into your background. The sweater was a gift from Janet to celebrate our opening. It was a thoughtful gesture, one that came with an unspoken reminder that she wanted me to look the part of someone who worked in an upscale clothing boutique. I got the feeling she didn't entirely approve of my eclectic thrift-store style.

The outfit was perfect. I bit my lip, unable to hold back the smile at my reflection. Willa Monroe, running the floor of an upscale boutique —a boutique that would feature *my* silk designs hanging beside the established designers Janet had sourced. It was a dream come true that I had once stopped hoping for. It felt like the world had opened up for me again, tempting me to start dreaming about an actual future that involved more than cleaning toilets in empty office buildings or wait-ressing at dive bars.

My smile wavered. I had learned long ago that hope was a dangerous game.

"Just breathe," I repeated, this time for an entirely different reason. *Don't get your hopes up. Don't dream of anything that might put you on Daniel's radar. Be content with a small life.*

With a deep breath, I slipped on my coat and wrapped my scarf around me, tucked my hands into my pockets, and headed out for the short walk to my future.

Janet was fluttering around the store, rearranging things we had already arranged three times the day before, when I walked in through the back.

"Oh, Willa!" she called out, putting a hand on her heart. "You scared me. I wasn't expecting you quite so early."

"I wanted to see if there were any last-minute details we need to take care of," I called back in answer, hanging my coat and scarf up in the little break room Janet had set up in the back.

It wasn't really quite cold enough for the coat yet, but even after a year of safety, I still felt the need to take certain precautions. I carried my old leather backpack instead of a purse, with a change of clothes and enough cash to buy a new beater car in the bottom, just in case I needed to run. If I drove anywhere—rarely necessary since I lived in the middle of town—I changed up my driving routes in case anyone was watching me. I wore flat shoes I could walk long distances in, and I wore a coat on even the mildest winter days in case the weather turned and I couldn't go back to my home.

Not one of those things had ever been necessary. Daniel believed I was dead. It had been all over the news, images of the grieving senator, the rising star in the political world whose life had been disrupted by the tragic loss of his beloved wife.

Those images sold. They were also a lie.

"I'm glad you're here," Janet said breathlessly, poking her head into the break room. Her eyes lit up when she saw me. "You look fabulous. Absolutely perfect."

"You look great yourself," I replied, smiling as I recognized the dress she was wearing.

It was one of mine, a long-sleeved silk dress in a gorgeous green that looked adorable with the suede boots she was wearing. Her hazel eyes sparkled with excitement. Her brown shoulder-length hair had fresh highlights and was straightened to perfection—unlike my own, which was already falling down again.

"Thanks," she answered, beaming as she glanced down at the dress. "I couldn't help myself. When I saw this one, I had to buy it. It's perfect for today. Besides, we need to show off how beautiful these pieces are."

"That was my thought, too. Now," I said, turning toward her after tucking my backpack away in the chest Janet kept for our personal things. It hit me that it was an odd little bookend. My life had once ended by pulling this backpack out of a drawer. Now, my new life was beginning by tucking it away in a drawer again. It was an emotional moment that sent me straight back into unwanted memories of the past before I shook myself and pulled it together. I straightened and took a deep breath, then plastered a smile on my face. "What do you need me to do?"

By the time Janet unlocked the front door, I had assured her every detail was perfect. The store was pristine, the displays were thoughtful and beautifully designed, our selection was chic and sophisticated, and we were ready to receive customers. I acted as the calm voice of reason, but truthfully, I was nearly as nervous as she was. The store was entirely her investment, financially speaking, but my whole future was riding on it. I was grateful for every temp job I had been given over the past year, but I wanted more. I had always been hungry for work that stimulated and excited me.

That hunger often got me into trouble. Had I not wanted more, I never would have fallen into Daniel's web.

But that was in the past. I had learned to be content with a small life. All I really wanted now was to stay anonymous and live out my days in

Rosemary Mountain, gradually feeling safer every day. That would be enough for me. But designing clothes and working in a boutique, while still small in many ways, was a thousand times more enjoyable than waiting tables and cleaning office buildings. If I could have a small life *and* work that inspired me, I would never want for anything else.

So, despite my calm appearance, I was as edgy as Janet.

"They're coming!" Janet called from where she was peering out the window. She had insisted that nobody come into the building except the two of us until everything was set up, but her family was scheduled to come see it all the minute it opened.

"I'll get the champagne," I said, hurrying to the back.

There were several bottles chilled in our mini fridge for both this initial celebration and to offer customers who stopped in for the grand opening. I had already prepared a tray with enough flutes for those of us who would be at this little gathering, and I quickly popped the cork on one of the bottles.

The bells on the front door rang softly. Then the front room was filled with excited voices, all proclaiming how beautiful the space was. My heart swelled. This was Janet's baby, but my fingerprints were all over it too, and hearing their excitement was gratifying. I smiled, took a deep breath, finished filling the flutes, and went to join them all.

Sheriff Morrison, a flannel-and-jeans-wearing man with a touch of silver in his hair, had swept Janet up in a tight embrace and was whispering something in her ear as she blushed profusely. Daphne, Janet's daughter, was making her way around the room with Fiona, Daphne's elderly neighbor and honorary grandmother. Together, they oohed and ahhed over every little detail, despite the fact that Janet was so caught up in whatever Sheriff Morrison was saying that she didn't even hear their compliments. Emerson, Daphne's husband, stood by the door with a proud smile on his face, his eyes following his wife. Next to him stood a man I hadn't met before—a man who instantly got my attention.

A man who, even from here, seemed deadly.

He wore a black long-sleeved t-shirt tucked into gray cargo pants instead of the normal flannel and jeans most men here seemed to wear in the winter. His posture was rigid as he stood with his legs wide and his hands clasped behind his back. Everything about him screamed danger

—except his eyes. Even from across the room, I could see the sorrow that lived behind them.

"That's Cole," Daphne whispered in my ear, noticing my stare. "He's one of Emerson's old Air Force friends. Want me to introduce you?"

The man's eyes met mine, and I nearly dropped the tray I was holding. He was gorgeous, yes, with smoldering dark eyes that matched his hair, scruff that made it appear he had simply forgotten to shave for a few days, wide shoulders, and muscles that belonged on a gym advertisement. But that wasn't what had me frozen in place.

It was the feeling that radiated off of him, a feeling that if we were all divided into two categories, either predator or prey, he would certainly fall into the former. His fierce intensity suggested he could kill a man with barely a flick of his wrist.

I had only known one other man with that kind of intensity, and I had no desire to get to know another one.

Despite my silence, Daphne took it upon herself to make the introductions, likely assuming I was just feeling shy. "Cole," she said, calling him over, "come meet Willa. She's the one who designed my wedding dress." Daphne bumped my shoulder. "Cole was one of the groomsmen. You would have met him if you had come."

There wasn't any reproach in her voice, although it made me feel guilty just the same. Daphne was my first real friend here in Rosemary Mountain, and I had skipped her wedding without explanation. But weddings meant cameras and photographs plastered all over social media. The danger was even higher at Daphne's wedding, as her involvement in an ongoing criminal case meant those pictures could easily end up on tabloids or gossip sites. I had changed my appearance somewhat, but I still didn't need photos of myself popping up online. You just didn't know who might see them and notice a resemblance between the Willa Monroe of Rosemary Mountain and the Wilhelmina Cavendish who belonged to Daniel.

An involuntary shudder rolled through me as I imagined what might happen if Daniel found me here, having defied him.

"You okay?" Daphne asked, narrowing her eyes.

"Fine," I said, putting the tray of glasses down to ensure I wouldn't drop it.

Emerson and Cole walked toward us, and I couldn't help noting the stark contrast. They were similar on the outside—both had dark-brown hair and brown eyes, and they both kept themselves in impeccable shape. But the differences stopped there. Emerson was relaxed and easy. Open.

Cole was the complete opposite.

He studied me, staring like he was analyzing a threat. I got the impression he saw the world that way and felt a momentary pang of sympathy for him.

It didn't last long.

"Willa Monroe, meet Cole Hawkins. Cole, Willa," Daphne said.

He continued to stare, silent.

"Would you like some champagne?" I asked, offering him a flute.

He took it and nodded his thanks, still staring at me. I shrank underneath it, feeling uncomfortable for a moment. Then it just pissed me off.

No one had the right to make me shrink anymore.

"Do I know you?" he finally asked, those eyes never leaving mine.

Panic rushed through me. Was it possible...?

"Nice pickup line," Emerson snorted, snagging a glass of champagne for himself. "Dude, we've got to work on your game."

Daphne rolled her eyes. "You've probably seen her around town." She turned her attention toward me. "Cole's been staying at Emerson's cabin for a few weeks now," she explained. "He's here doing some training operations for the life flight program."

"I see. How nice," I said, forcing a smile and calling on everything within me to stay calm.

"That's right, and I'm still hoping I can talk him into working for me." Sheriff Morrison joined us and grabbed a champagne flute to pass to Janet, who was beaming from ear to ear.

The conversation quickly turned to the boutique as everyone congratulated Janet on her excellent work. Fiona and Daphne took another walk around the room to make over everything, and I started to relax again.

Until the group dispersed and Cole moved to my elbow.

"What did you say your name was?" he asked, as intense as ever.

"Willa Monroe," I said. I began straightening a rack of clothing, using it as an excuse to avoid his eyes. I could feel them analyzing me even now.

"Are you sure we haven't met?" His voice was low and persistent.

"I'm pretty sure I'd remember," I said, unable to fake politeness for another minute, even for Janet's sake. "Hasn't anyone told you it's rude to stare?"

He continued to stare at me anyway, making me wonder if he was being purposefully defiant. But then he shook his head and averted his eyes. "Sorry," he muttered. "I must have been confused."

Chapter Four

Cole

As we walked down Rosemary Mountain's town square to the café Emerson and Daphne had picked for lunch, I stuck my hands inside my pockets and tuned out their chatter. I couldn't care less what Daphne thought of the displays or how proud she was of her mom.

All I could think about was Willa Monroe.

She had nearly taken my breath away when she'd walked out of the back room carrying that tray. Even at a distance, her beauty had struck me like a lightning bolt to the heart. She didn't look like someone who belonged in a small town. She was unique. Exotic even, with that lightly bronzed skin and wavy, brown hair that fell around her face in a way that made me think of legends of mermaids. Those pink cheeks and eyes so big they looked like they belonged on a doll. She was stunning.

But that wasn't why I kept staring at her.

Willa Monroe. Was it possible...?

"You've gotta get out of your head, man," Emerson said, clapping me on the shoulder. The touch instantly brought me back to the present.

"What did I miss?" I looked up, pulled out of my own thoughts.

"Daphne asked if you're going home for Christmas. If not, we'd love for you to celebrate with us. We're having a big meal at Greg and Janet's house. You're invited."

Christmas. Was it really almost time for that? I had lost track of time since moving to Rosemary Mountain. Not that it mattered. My days here were all pretty much the same anyway. "I'll be there," I said. "Thanks."

It had been years since I had gone home for Christmas. Didn't seem like there was any reason to start now.

I waited until we were seated and had ordered our lunches before bringing up the topic of Willa, even though I'd barely been able to think of anything else.

"How well do you know this Willa?" I asked, leaning on the table with my arms crossed.

A look of warning instantly crossed Daphne's face. "Well enough," she said, her tone measured.

"You sure about that?"

Emerson frowned. "What are you getting at, Cole?"

I shook my head. "Maybe nothing. Maybe something. How long has she lived here?"

"About six months," Daphne said.

"Where'd she come from?"

Daphne looked at me, then at Emerson. Some sort of silent communication seemed to pass between them before she turned back to me.

"Leave it alone, Cole," she said, her voice quiet but firm.

"Leave what alone?"

"Her. Just don't. Okay?"

"She went into business with your mom," I said, pressing the point. "From all appearances, she has full access to that store and everything in it. Probably full access to the financials, too. If she's not who she says she is, don't you think you need to know that?"

"No," Daphne said firmly. "We trust her."

"Trust is a recipe for disaster," I said, grabbing one of the rolls the waitress had set on the table.

Daphne looked to Emerson again.

"If Daphne trusts her, we all do," Emerson said, shrugging as if that were that.

I looked at each of them in turn. "You know something," I said, directing it toward Daphne. "Don't you?"

"I know you need to leave it alone," she said, not bothering to hide the edge to her voice.

"Okay." I nodded and dropped it.

With them, at least.

When I was alone in my cabin, I grabbed my laptop and started searching. It didn't take long to find what I was looking for: Wilhelmina Cavendish. Senator Cavendish's late wife.

I studied the pictures. There was no doubt it was the same woman, even though she had changed her look quite a bit. As the senator's wife, she had kept her hair blonde, straight, and cut in a sophisticated bob. She had often worn pastel colors that washed out her skin, downplaying that exotic beauty of hers. She had been thinner, too.

She looked a hell of a lot better now.

But either way, it was her. Unless she had a twin sister or a freakishly similar doppelgänger out there.

I snapped the laptop closed, shaking my head. Wilhelmina Cavendish had haunted my dreams for over a year. It had been my job to find her, and I had failed. Who the hell would have thought I would find her here, now, in Rosemary Mountain? The odds were astronomical.

Frankly, that was the only thing that gave me pause and made me wonder if maybe I was wrong. I was well aware of the tricks the mind could play on a person. Could my desperate need to find her have clouded my judgment? Made me see a stronger resemblance than there really was?

Maybe.

Maybe not.

I put the laptop away and paced the cabin, calculating my next move. I needed more information. First, I needed to find out if it really was her. Then, if it was her, I needed to figure out what she was doing here. Could she have amnesia? There were cases of that. Her car had gone over a cliff. The likelihood of surviving that was low, and a head injury wouldn't be surprising. Or she could have been without oxygen for a period of time before washing up on a beach somewhere.

Again, statistically improbable, considering the situation. But there was a chance.

I kept mulling it over, going with that line of thought. If she washed up somewhere and didn't remember who she was, maybe she had just started over the best she could. It wasn't entirely unheard of, even if that sort of thing happened more in the movies than in real life. If that was the case, the right move would be to contact the senator and let him know she was here so he could make arrangements to get her home safely and provide her the medical care she needed.

And in that case, I could collect the hefty reward he had promised for her safe return. A reward that would allow me to start my life over anywhere I pleased. I could open my own business and answer to no one. No more favors from friends. No more social obligations.

A tempting thought.

But there was also the possibility she knew exactly who she was and had chosen not to go back.

I would never forget Wilhelmina's haunted eyes the day I had met her—or her husband's rage the night she supposedly died. The rest of the world had looked at him and seen a grieving man. But I saw the hint of rage underneath it and wondered, even then.

I paced my living room, thinking that angle out. The way I saw it, her leaving on purpose could mean one of two things.

There had been rumors of the Cavendishes being involved in some less-than-legal backroom deals and schemes. Not uncommon for politicians. He had a certain level of protection, but that could always change at any time, and the country had become more eager to hold its leaders accountable. Maybe her crash had provided an opportunity to avoid jail time if some of those things came to light and her name was implicated.

Maybe the whole thing had been an accident, but she had jumped at the chance to start over with a new name.

A new name. I shook my head, realizing the implications. Surely Janet had conducted a background check before hiring her. If so, she had to have fake documents with this new name of Willa Monroe. That would surely rule out the possibility of an innocent case of amnesia.

On the other hand, this was Janet we were talking about—Daphne's mother. And if Daphne was willing to stick her head in the sand and not look too closely at Willa, Janet might have felt the same. They might not have checked anything at all, I realized, blowing out a breath of frustration. That would be easy enough to find out though, and it would give me a key piece of information.

If Willa had fled California to avoid criminal prosecution, informing law enforcement would be the right move—especially since she was involved with the sheriff's wife's business. If she was as dirty as her husband, she didn't need her hands anywhere near someone else's livelihood.

But there was also the possibility that she had fled to escape him. That he was the reason for the fear in her eyes.

In that case, the only right move would be to protect her from anyone finding out who she was.

And of course, all of this was dependent on her true identity. It might not even be her, I reminded myself. My gut immediately said I was being stupid for thinking that, that I just didn't want it to be her.

Or maybe I wanted it too much.

I simply didn't have enough information to make a decision. Not yet. But in the meantime, I was going to keep a very close eye on Willa Monroe.

A FULL WEEK PASSED BEFORE I HAD A CHANCE TO CHECK UP on Willa again. The training exercises I was conducting had kept me too busy for a trip to town. I appreciated it in some ways, as being out in the mountains and working with a team was helping me start to feel like myself again. But Willa was never far from my mind. I couldn't let it go until I knew what was going on with her and what I needed to do about it.

I pushed the door to the boutique open, mentally rehearsing my excuse for being there. Willa called out a welcome before she saw me. Her sultry voice filled the air like chimes in the wind, sending a pleasant tingle down my spine. But when she turned and saw me, all the warmth left her face.

Still, she was professional.

"What can I help you with today?" she asked, her tone cool but civil.

"I need to pick up some Christmas presents." It was true, although in normal circumstances I would have just grabbed some gift cards from local restaurants. Everyone liked food. No way to go wrong there. Gift cards were the safe choice, but shopping gave me a reason to be here.

"Okay, and who are we shopping for? Your mom, a girlfriend?"

She let the question hang in the air, and for a brief moment, I wondered if she was trying to find out whether or not I was single. The idea almost made me smile.

"Neither," I answered. "I've already sent gifts to my family back home. I need gifts for Janet and Daphne. Oh, and I guess Fiona too. They're having a big Christmas party at Greg and Janet's house."

Her professional smile immediately faltered, and a look of worry crossed her face. "Yes, I know. Okay." She took a deep breath, shaking off whatever my statement had brought up. "Sure. I can help you with that. Do you have a budget in mind?"

"It doesn't matter. Just pick something they'll like."

"Okay." She scanned the store, her lips pursed up in thought. "Maybe a nice scarf for Daphne. She loves them, and that one in the window will go perfectly with the sweater I knitted her. Fiona loves funky jewelry. There are some cute necklaces over here made with local stones. She'd love something like that, and they're fairly inexpensive. As for Janet..."

I waited while she bit her lip, seemingly deep in thought.

"Yes?" I finally asked when she didn't continue.

"Well," she said, letting out a little laugh, "I wish I could recommend something here for her. After all, I work partially on commission. But truthfully? She sort of owns everything here. Anytime we order in pieces, if she likes it, she'll order one for herself too. She advertises the merchandise that way. I think you should ask Daphne's advice if you really want to give her something thoughtful."

"Ah. I didn't think of that. Will do." I paused for a minute, trying to think of a way to ask her about her past. But before I could, she fluttered away.

"I'll just get the scarf and the necklace for you, if you approve of those," she called as she moved away from me.

I watched her movements, noticing they seemed nervous, like I made her uncomfortable. "Yeah, those are fine. Good ideas," I said, continuing to study her as she flitted nervously around the room.

She grabbed the scarf from the window display, then headed to the jewelry, never looking my way. "Unless you have a strong preference, jewelry wise, I would get this one for Fiona." She pulled a long silver chain with an orange stone pendant. "It's jasper, locally harvested. I've seen her eyeing it."

I walked over and looked at the necklace, noticing the tension in Willa's body as I got close. "Yeah, that looks like her. Good choice."

"I'll wrap these up for you," Willa said, easing away from me. "Then you'll be set, other than Janet. I'm sure Daphne will have some good ideas for you there."

"Thanks." I hesitated, then decided to go with my gut. "I'm sorry if I made you uncomfortable when I was in here last time, asking if we knew each other."

"Oh, it's fine!" she said too brightly, still avoiding eye contact. She slipped behind the register, putting a physical barrier between us as she began wrapping up the gifts she had selected. "I probably just have one of those faces. Or, you know, like Daphne said. You may have seen me around town."

"Maybe so," I said without committing to it. "Maybe not even here though. I've lived all over. Moved around a lot in the military. Daphne tells me you're a transplant to the area. Where did you live before you moved here?"

Her hand faltered, but she kept her face steady. "St. Louis."

"Oh, nice. Cardinals fan?"

"Of course." She handed the package she had finished wrapping to me, an obviously fake smile plastered on her face.

"Don't you wish Pujols would have hit seven hundred home runs before he retired? He was so close. Such a shame he missed it."

"Oh, absolutely," she agreed, nodding. "That was heartbreaking for all of us."

Liar. A true Cardinals fan would know he hit 703.

"Have you ever lived in California?" I asked, prodding again. "You look a lot like someone I used to know there." This time, I just wanted to see her reaction.

She kept that fake smile, I had to give her that, but she couldn't hide the way the color drained from her face. Or the way her pupils instantly dilated.

"I'm afraid not," she said, her tone still entirely too bright. "I've heard it's lovely though. Anyway, here's your other package." She turned to the register and punched in some things. "Your total is on the screen. We take cash or card."

I gave her a hundred in cash and watched the way her hands shook as she counted out my change.

She was definitely hiding the truth about who she was.

The question was why?

Chapter Five

Willa

I held it together until I was able to shuffle Cole
out of the store. Then I locked the door behind him, went to our break
room, and broke down into tears.

I was still sitting there on the couch when Janet arrived, bringing in
some fresh stock for the store.

"Oh, honey," she said, dropping her bags the moment she saw me.
She crossed the room and sat down, putting an arm around me. "What
is it? What happened?"

I looked at her through tear-filled eyes. "I'm so sorry. I don't want to
leave you in a lurch, but I think today has to be my last day."

Her head jerked back as she looked at me in shock. "Your last day?
Willa, what in the world are you talking about?"

How could I possibly explain it to her? I had never offered explanations when I left any of the other places. I had just dropped everything
and run. No guilt. I was easily replaceable at every one of those previous
jobs.

But here, I had made a commitment. Janet counted on me. I owed her something for that.

"I'm sorry," I repeated as fresh tears began to fall. "I'm so sorry."

"Willa," she said, her tone soothing. "Calm down now. Let's have a cup of tea, okay? Then we can talk this through. Whatever it is, I'm sure there's a solution." She patted my hands and rose to prepare a pot of tea on the little burner she insisted on having in our break room for just that purpose.

I nodded, grateful for a moment to try to come up with at least a partial explanation of why I had to leave. But a solution? There was no solution.

Cole Hawkins knew who I was. I had to run.

I had dried my tears and regained my composure when she returned to sit beside me, passing me a cup of tea.

"It's one of Fiona's blends," she explained. "An herbal tea for stress. Daphne swears by it, especially now. I thought it might help."

"Thank you," I said, taking the delicate china cup from her and inhaling the soothing aromas of chamomile and lavender. Fresh tears threatened to come as I thought about how kind Janet had been to me —how kind all of them had been. Even though I was very much the outsider to their little crew, I had come to think of them as the closest thing to family I had experienced in years. When I ran, I would miss every single one of them.

Except Cole. Just thinking of him turned my grief to anger. Why did he have to come here and ruin everything?

"Now," Janet said after sipping her tea. "What's going on?"

I looked at her and knew that, for once, I wanted to tell the truth. Having worked with her for weeks now, I knew her well enough to trust her. She had a good heart. And she deserved the truth from me, especially if I was going to leave her in a lurch.

"If I tell you," I said, "you can't tell anyone."

Hesitation crossed her face. "I tell Greg everything."

"But please don't," I whispered, shaking my head. "Not this time."

She put her cup down on the table. "So it's that serious, is it?"

"Yes."

"Okay." She took a deep breath. "You have my word. I won't say anything without your permission."

I took another sip of tea, gathering my courage. "Janet, first, I just want to apologize. I lied to you. I had to. I've had to lie a lot over the past year, but I never felt any guilt about it until now. Lying meant survival, and I can't be sorry for that. But I am sorry for not being honest with you when you gave me this opportunity. I lied to you about who I am, and I lied when I said I could commit to this business."

"Go on." Her face showed no anger. Just concern.

"My name isn't Willa Monroe. I mean, it is. It is now, anyway. But that's a false name. An alias. I'm not going to tell you my real one. You don't need to know anything that might put either of us in danger. But the short of it is that I faked my own death and started a new life. I've been running for just over a year now." Even as I said the words, they felt so strange to me. It was surreal to admit the truth out loud after guarding it so closely. The truth sounded crazy.

I took another sip of tea and continued. "Rosemary Mountain is the first place I've tried to stay. But Cole, Emerson's friend, recognizes me. He may not have figured it out entirely yet, but he will. He won't drop it. So I can't stay."

Janet stared at me for a long time before her eyes widened. "Oh my God," she said. "You're Wilhelmina Cavendish."

Now it was my turn to be shocked—she had recognized me way too easily. "You can't tell anyone," I said, practically begging.

"Honey, I won't. Just give me a minute." She kept shaking her head, staring at me, then at the wall in front of us. "I can't believe it's you. The world thought you were dead. I, of all people, should have recognized you from the beginning. I followed your career for years. You look different now, but still. I was so caught up in everything happening in my life that I never put it together, but I should have."

"I'm glad you didn't. But you see now why I have to run."

She turned to me and grabbed my hand. "Oh, Willa. Please don't."

"I have to," I said. "Daniel..." I didn't know what to say. Even now, I was terrified to tell the truth about him. The importance of maintaining his public image had been drilled into me many times, with painful punishments if he thought I had made him look bad in any way at all. My tongue felt like lead. I couldn't voice the truth even if I tried.

"You don't have to tell me," she said, her voice gentle. "I'm well aware that things aren't always what they seem. I imagine they must have been pretty bad for you to go to such great lengths to leave. From the outside, you had everything—fame, wealth, a gorgeous husband who seemed to dote on you. You were practically American royalty."

I nodded, grateful she wasn't forcing me to put it into words. But there was one thing I had to make clear. "He'll kill me if he finds out I'm still alive."

She let out a breath. "Oh, Willa."

"I have to run again," I said. "I don't want to. I don't want to abandon you and the store. Or leave Rosemary Mountain. These past few months have been such a gift. But it's too dangerous with people recognizing me."

She bit her lip, thinking. "Do you trust me?"

"Obviously."

"Then please don't run. Not yet. If Daniel really does want to kill you, you'll be safer here than anywhere else. Willa, your face was on the cover of countless magazines. This won't be the last time someone recognizes you. If you run now, you'll never be able to stop. I know you don't want me to tell anyone, but I promise you, you can trust Greg with your life. He would do anything to protect his townspeople, and you're one of them. You're an important part of this community, and not just because of me and the store." She squeezed my hand. "You've found a home here. I know what that's like and how awful it feels to think you'll have to leave it. Let us protect you so you can stay."

That same seed of hope that had begun to unfurl the day I left Daniel started rising again. I wanted so much to believe that it was possible to stay here, that with the sheriff on my side I might actually have protection.

But that hope felt dangerous. I had gone to the police once, the first time Daniel had beaten me badly enough to leave marks. All I had learned from that experience was that his money and name were more powerful than my story. Nothing had changed, and I had paid dearly for it.

We were far away from California though, and my interactions with Sheriff Morrison had all made me think he was truly one of the good guys. That tiny seed of hope was enough to make me at least think about things.

"I can't promise anything," I finally said. "But I do trust you. I'll think it over. If I'm going to stay though, we'll have to figure out how to manage Cole. I don't know if he's figured it out completely yet, but he's close. And I don't trust him."

Janet sighed. "Let me think about that. I don't know Cole well, either. I do know Emerson, and I trust him completely. Are you giving me permission to tell Greg?"

I hesitated for a moment. "Janet, I'm pretty sure I broke some laws. Faking my death, forged documents... There was probably life insurance money, too. Daniel will have collected that. I can't even imagine how much legal and financial trouble I'll be in for what I did. Your husband has to follow the law. If you tell him..."

She looked at me with empathy and squeezed my hand again. "Of course, I understand. I didn't think about that side of it. I won't give him any details then. But can I at least tell him you need protection? He'll take that seriously, even if I can't tell him why."

I thought it over, then nodded. I was putting all my trust in Janet, but something told me it was the right move. It was the same voice that told me to trust Suzanna, that she really would help me get out. That voice was speaking again, and I decided to listen to it.

"What about Daphne and Emerson?" she asked. "Again, no details. No name or connections. But if they know you need help, I promise they'll be on your side. You can trust them completely. And they might know how to manage the Cole issue."

Regret washed over me. It was one thing to confide in Janet. But Daphne was my friend, a friend who knew me only as Willa—fun, free, happy Willa. I liked being that version of myself with her, and I hated to ruin it by being marked by the past.

"I don't know," I said. "I mean, you may be right. We may have to tell them something in order to manage Cole. But it's been really nice to leave the past in the past. What happened with Daniel is humiliating. I hate for Daphne to see me in that light, to think of me as some stereo-typical abused woman hiding from a man she couldn't stand up to."

Janet's expression was an odd mix of empathy and humor. "I don't think talking to Daphne will change the way she sees you at all."

"I don't see how that's possible."

She just patted me on the hand again. "That's her story to tell, not mine, but I'll say this—Daphne probably already knows anyway."

Chapter Six

Cole

My feet pounded on the gravel as I turned my face to the sun, soaking up the rare winter sunshine on a mountain that had lately seemed as moody and gray as me. The air was crisp and cold, but the steep incline kept my muscles burning as I pushed myself to go faster. Harder.

But no matter how hard I pushed, I couldn't seem to hit that zone where my mind would shut off. All I could think about was the situation with Willa. After seeing her again, I was fully convinced she was none other than the Wilhelmina Cavendish who had supposedly drowned. Based on her reaction to my questions, I was no longer really considering the amnesia angle. It was possible her nerves were because she didn't have answers to my questions, but that's not what my gut said —and I was exceptionally good at reading people. It was a skill that had kept me alive more than once, and I'd stake my life savings on the fact that she was lying.

She had disappeared deliberately.

But why? The answer to that question mattered. If she had disappeared to escape the justice the Cavendishes deserved, it was my responsibility to see she didn't get away with it.

But if she had disappeared to escape *him*, that was a different story altogether.

I wanted to believe that it was none of my business. That it didn't matter. She had her reasons and I should just look the other way and leave the whole thing alone. It wasn't my job to get involved.

But I was involved, dammit. I had been involved with this from the very beginning.

Images from that night flashed across my mind. The bright moon in a star-filled sky. The murky water, eerily placid, hiding her car beneath the gentle waves. My team called to action, more sober than normal because of who it was. Or maybe I was the only one more sober than normal—the only one with a personal stake in it, a stake known only to me.

Two by two, we went into the water, racing against time. The equipment felt heavier than normal, but maybe it was the weight of knowing we were probably already too late.

More images danced in my memory. My underwater light hitting her car. The driver's side door open. The car empty.

I had expanded the search, looking far longer than protocol called for, because it was her. Eventually, I called it. We had failed our mission. Wilhelmina Cavendish was lost to the sea forever.

Or so I had thought.

I would never forget the look on Daniel Cavendish's face when I gave him the news that I had been unable to save his wife. The man had barely looked human. The polished senator disappeared, leaving a madman in his place, wailing in agony. Everyone around assumed that it was grief, and they surrounded him with support and pity.

But I had seen the rage beneath it. Rage that made me wonder, even then, if the woman with the haunted eyes had taken her life deliberately. If I had failed her not once, but twice.

The senator's story was that his wife suffered from terrible insomnia, that she couldn't sleep and had decided to go for a drive. He said he'd tried to talk her out of it, of course, telling her it was too dangerous to drive at night when she hadn't slept. She was wildly stubborn, he said —and I hadn't missed the flash of hatred in his eyes when he said it— and went anyway. He had followed her to make sure she was safe and watched her car go over the edge in horror.

I hadn't believed his story for a minute, though there wasn't a bit of evidence to disprove it. From all appearances, things had happened exactly the way he said they had. But that failed mission had been a turning point for me, a sign that I was disillusioned and ready for a new life of my own.

And now, in the craziest turn of events of my whole life, Wilhelmina Cavendish was in Rosemary Mountain, posing as Willa Monroe.

It wasn't my place to get involved. But I had never known how to walk away.

By the end of my run, I had formulated a plan. Why? I still didn't know. The best thing for me to do would be to just leave her alone to live her life in peace.

But with a face like that, I had a feeling peace wouldn't last. Frankly, I was surprised she had remained anonymous this long. If there was one thing I had learned during my years of service, it was that you couldn't count on peace lasting. You had to be prepared. Have contingencies.

I needed time to figure out the truth of what was going on and to plan my next steps. So the first thing I did when I got back was call to see if I could extend my temporary job by a few weeks.

Next, I called one of my contacts and asked for all the information he could dig up on Senator Cavendish, including any intel on whether or not the senator was about to be surprised with criminal charges.

"What's this about?" Pete asked, his voice guarded.

"You know better than to ask that."

He chuckled nervously. "I'm just saying, digging up information on a U.S. senator might not be the wisest move of yours."

"Since when have I been known to make wise moves?"

"Good point. How soon do you need it?"

"ASAP." I tossed my pen onto the desk.

"Got it. I'll do my best."

"Do better than your best. It's important."

We hung up, and I mulled it over.

I still needed to rule out the possibility of her being involved in his criminal activities. But I couldn't stop thinking about the fear in her eyes the night we had met. It could have been fear of what was coming —fear of prison, of losing everything, of scandal in the headlines.

But again, I was good at reading people. And even before I got the report from my buddy, I would have almost bet money she was afraid of Daniel himself. If that was true and she had fled to escape him, there would come a day when Daniel Cavendish found out she was alive. I felt it in my bones. A face like Wilhelmina's was just too difficult to hide. She couldn't blend in. She was born to stand out.

Fate had crossed my path with hers three times now, and I wasn't going to ignore that. Not this time. So I grabbed my jacket to go ask Emerson for help on the next part of my plan.

"A WOMEN'S SELF-DEFENSE COURSE?" EMERSON ASKED, HIS eyes wrinkled up in thought. "Yeah, I think it's a great idea."

I nodded. "I was thinking I could offer it for free. I just need a space to hold it."

"I'm sure Greg will let you use the gym at the sheriff's station," Emerson offered. "He'll love this. It's a great community service."

"I was hoping you'd say that. Mind asking him for me?"

"Not at all." Emerson picked up his cell phone and immediately dialed Greg's number, heading out back to talk to him privately.

Daphne studied me from across the room. "Why are you all of a sudden wanting to offer a free self-defense class?"

I shrugged. "Just seems like something that might be useful."

We both stared at each other, daring the other one to speak first.

"This is about Willa, isn't it?" she finally asked.

My eyes narrowed. "What do you know?"

"Nothing," she said with a face that indicated otherwise. "She hasn't told me anything, anyway."

"But you know something." It was a statement, not a question. The answer was all over her face.

She sipped her tea and gave the tiniest nod of confirmation. "What do you know?"

I wasn't about to tell her that. Daphne was a jewel, but she was also a woman. In my experience, women were gossips, and there was no way in hell I was going to tell her anything I suspected about Willa's past. In all fairness, I had never witnessed Daphne engaging in gossip like that, but still. Better safe than sorry.

When I didn't answer, she spoke again. "You can't tell anyone anything," she said with a warning in her voice. "It's not safe for her."

"I know that," I said, taking it as further confirmation that I was on the right track. "Look, will you just make sure she comes to the class?"

"I will," she said, nodding. "Although, your timing is going to make that more difficult than it would have been a few months ago." She rubbed her growing baby bump, looking at it with affection.

"Thanks." My voice was gruffer than I'd meant it to be.

"Why do you care, anyway?" she asked suddenly, cocking her head. "I thought you didn't like Willa."

"I never disliked her. I just have a hard time trusting people who lie."

"I get that. But sometimes people have a good reason for lying."

She had no idea how right she was.

Chapter Seven

Willa

I WAS A WALKING CONTRADICTION IN FEELINGS THE NEXT morning as I slowly made my way back to the boutique, lingering as I walked through Rosemary Mountain's beautiful town square. It was decorated beautifully for Christmas, with twinkle lights, window displays, and a large Christmas tree in the very center of town. The crisp air, bright sunshine, and happy smiles on everyone's faces made me feel grateful Janet had convinced me to stay in this adorable little town. I had fully expected to be in a crappy motel by now, somewhere as far away from Rosemary Mountain as possible. Being here—*home*—was incredible.

But on the other hand, I couldn't shake the worry that staying was a terrible mistake.

Janet had sent me straight home to rest the day before, telling me she would take care of the store. It was a kind gesture, but it had given me too much time to overthink our conversation. It felt good for someone to finally know the truth of who I was, but it was also terrifying.

And that was without even considering the Cole issue.

I couldn't figure him out. He was so persistent in trying to nail me down. Was he friends with Daniel? It was possible, oddly enough. As a senator, Daniel frequently rubbed shoulders with the armed forces—the ones with a little prestige behind them, anyway. I knew he even occasionally hired them, off the books, to handle some of his more sensitive matters.

Cole Hawkins was deadly, which made it even more possible that he and Daniel had crossed paths at some point.

We would figure it out, Janet had reassured me. I just hoped she was right.

JANET WAS ALREADY IN THE STORE WHEN I ARRIVED, bustling around with busywork, which was odd for her. Other than our opening day, I normally worked mornings alone. The instant relief on her face when she saw me showed that she hadn't been convinced I would return.

She embraced me, enveloping me in her warmth and the softness of her perfume. I closed my eyes, holding back a wave of emotion as I thought of my mother. Missing her was an ache that would never heal.

Janet let out a sigh as she pulled back, studying my face. "I'm glad you're here."

"Me too," I said, though I wasn't entirely sure I meant it. The safety I had felt in Rosemary Mountain had disappeared, and I wasn't sure it would ever really return.

"I haven't said a word to anyone yet," she said, "other than Greg. All I told him was that you might be in some trouble, due to no fault of your own, and that we needed to watch out for you. He already has patrols pass by here frequently, but he said he would increase them and to let him know as soon as you felt ready to give him more information. He wants to help."

"Thanks," I said, mostly meaning it this time. "I'm just not ready yet."

"I know." She gave me an empathetic smile. "We'll take it one step at a time."

"So Daphne still doesn't know, right?"

That funny look crossed Janet's face again. "I can't promise that. All I can say is that *I* haven't told her a thing yet. But I still think we should talk to her and Emerson about how to manage Cole."

"I will. Soon. I think I want to be the one to tell her," I said, deciding. "She deserves to hear it from me."

Janet smiled. "I was hoping you'd say that."

Our morning was busy with our normal customers plus a large group of ladies who had traveled to Rosemary Mountain for a women's retreat. They were all ecstatic to find out we had one-of-a-kind clothing pieces and local jewelry, and they nearly bought us out in their enthusiasm. They claimed to be Christmas shopping for friends and family back home, but I could tell they were going to keep at least half of it for themselves. Either way, it was good for the store—and good for me, personally, to see them delighting over the silk blouses I had made.

By the time they left, the store was in disarray, and Janet and I were both happily exhausted. She flipped the sign to closed and collapsed onto the loveseat, kicking off her heels.

"We deserve our lunch break today," she said, laughing. "We sold more in two hours than we've sold all week."

"It was a good morning," I agreed, automatically straightening displays and refolding the sweaters the women had left scattered over the tables.

The door bells jingled and I looked up to see Daphne.

"I'm ignoring your closed sign," she said, laughing as she unwrapped her scarf and smoothed her long, red hair.

"I'll allow it," said Janet. There was a softness in her eyes when Daphne came around, a motherly love I missed dearly. It brought a lump to my throat that I had to swallow down before saying hello.

"You're exactly who I wanted to see," Daphne said, rubbing her adorable baby bump. "I'm craving fried fish today. Fried everything, actually. Fish, French fries, hushpuppies—I want the whole lot. Can I treat you to lunch at the fish house, Willa?"

"Oh, I need to get things cleaned up here," I started to protest.

"No, you don't," said Janet, waving me off from where she was still reclining on the couch. "I'll take care of it. Go have a nice lunch."

"Okay," I said, lifting up my hands in surrender. "Sounds fun."

"Great!" Daphne beamed at me. "Want to ride together or take separate cars?"

"I walked here today, so together if that's okay with you."

"It's perfect. See you later, Mom! Want me to bring you anything back?"

Janet shook her head. "No, I'm good. Greg told me he would bring lunch here so we could eat together."

Ahh. So that's why she was eager to kick me out of the store. The thought made me smile. Sheriff Morrison and Janet were both still in that newlywed phase, and I thought it was adorable.

"Have fun," I told her.

"I'm sure we will," Janet said, flushing.

Daphne and I just exchanged grins.

"Let's get out of here and let those two lovebirds have their lunch date. The baby is starving."

"Alright, let me grab my coat."

I ran to the back room, put my coat on, and pulled my backpack from the drawer. Twenty-four hours ago, I had nearly run again. Instead, I'd stayed, and now I was having lunch with a friend.

Staying was a dangerous game, but I hoped with all my heart it was a game I would win.

The fish house was already packed, but they squeezed us into a table quickly. Daphne seemed relieved. The poor girl probably was starving, eating for two. She immediately dug into the hushpuppies they placed on the table, letting out a contented sigh like it was the best thing she had eaten in her life.

"Feel better?" I asked, amused.

"Yes," she said, her mouth still half full. "Sorry. I was going to puke if I didn't eat soon."

"Didn't you eat breakfast?"

"Of course I did. And second breakfast. It is what it is."

I looked at her with a mix of sympathy and envy. I had once dreamed of having children, of a home full of laughter and love. I had dreamed of daughters playing with their dolls, and a son who romped through the halls with his puppy, leaving muddy tracks in his wake.

Then Daniel hit me for the first time and I realized I could never bring children into his world.

"Are you feeling alright otherwise?" I asked.

She nodded. "Yes. Just starving all the time, really. Fiona says I'm as healthy as a horse, and the baby is too."

"Do you know what you're having?"

Her eyes went dreamy. "Yes and no. Technically speaking, we're keeping it a surprise. It makes preparing the nursery a bit of a challenge, and Mom's dying to know so she can start shopping for clothes."

I eyed her curiously. "That's the no, but what's the yes? Do you know and you're just keeping it a secret from everyone?"

She blushed as the corners of her mouth lifted into a tiny smile. Her hand automatically went to her bump, caressing it with a tenderness that made my heart ache. "I have a feeling," she said, seemingly choosing her words with care.

"You're very lucky," I said, pushing away the jealousy that stung my heart. "Emerson seems like a good man. He'll be a good dad."

"The best," she agreed. She opened her mouth as if to speak, then closed it again, apparently changing her mind about what she planned to say. "Do you want children someday?"

"It's not in the cards for me," I said lightly, keeping my eyes fixed on the plate of fried catfish the waitress had just placed in front of me.

Daphne was quiet for a moment. "Maybe you're wrong," she said, lightening her tone as well. "Maybe it could be."

"It's not," I said, closing the subject. Eventually I would tell her the truth—that legally speaking, I was still a married woman. I would never be free to move on and raise the family of my dreams. Even if my false documents held up, it was too dangerous. Daniel would kill them all if he ever discovered the truth.

"Well, changing the subject," she said before taking a long drink of her iced tea. "I have a favor to ask of you."

"Anything," I said. I meant it. Daphne had taken a chance on me when I had nothing, and she had connected me to her mother. I owed both of them everything.

"Will you come with me to a self-defense class this Friday evening? I promised to go, but I'm too nervous to go by myself, especially since I don't know how much I'll be able to participate."

My pulse immediately quickened. Of all the things she could have said, I never would have expected that. I'd assumed she wanted me to make her a piece of clothing or help with her Christmas list.

"A self-defense class?" I asked, keeping my tone light. I lifted my glass to at least partially hide my expression, sipping water slowly to give myself time to slip my poker face back on. It was a trick I had learned long ago at one of the many dinners I had to attend with Daniel.

"Yes. Greg's hosting it. A community outreach thing, you know. I promised to go in support. Please don't make me go alone."

"Of course I'll go with you," I said, swallowing hard. Despite what Janet had said about Daphne probably knowing something about my past, she couldn't possibly know the reality of the situation. It would be fine. In my experience, self-defense classes were useless anyway. It would likely be a boring lecture followed by some impractical advice for escaping situations that rarely actually happened.

The topic made me uncomfortable, but it was just one night. I could do anything for Daphne for a single night.

It would be fine.

The cold, gray hallways of the sheriff's station stretched long ahead of me, making me want to turn and run the other way. Nothing felt friendly or safe here. As a kid, I had been taught that police officers were my friends. They were the good guys, here to keep us safe.

That certainly hadn't worked out well for me.

It felt like a lifetime had passed since I had walked with confidence down hallways very much like these and told my story to someone I thought would help, only to learn that money and prestige mattered more than one woman's broken body.

But tonight wasn't about me. I was here to support Daphne because I had promised I would. No matter how much I wanted to run away from all of it.

And the moment I slipped through the door to the training room and saw Cole Hawkins standing at the front, I desperately wanted to run away.

THE BACK OF THE ROOM WAS FULL OF WOMEN WEARING sweats and yoga pants, all looking as nervous and unsure as I felt inside. Everyone except Daphne, of course, who was abnormally quiet but seemed serene as she took a seat. No nerves for her, at least that I could see. I was grateful she wasn't chatty though. Small talk felt nearly impossible here, in a room where I already felt trapped and miserable.

I pasted an appropriately serious smile on my face while Sheriff Morrison greeted us all and began the lecture, with Cole standing by in a rigid pose. He was always so uptight. Did the man even know how to relax?

The lecture wasn't terrible. It was good information for the majority of women—tips for how to avoid looking like an easy victim, being aware of your surroundings, and basic common sense.

Nothing that would have done anything to help me.

I had taken a handful of women's self-defense classes before meeting Daniel. They had done their job, I supposed, in keeping me safe on my college campus. I had known to never leave a drink unattended and to always let someone know where I would be and what time I would be coming home.

But these classes had never taught me how to recognize the kind of evil that hid behind a thousand layers of charm. The kind of evil that could give me the world and then destroy it as a punishment. The kind of evil that had charmed my own father into thinking I was the problem after beating me so badly that I'd ended up in the hospital.

Where was the self-defense course for that?

It didn't matter now though. Even as I clenched my hand into a fist, feeling my nails bite into my skin, I reminded myself that I was here. I was safe. And I was supporting a friend, who seemed genuinely interested in this information. For her sake, I would play along and pretend like any of this actually mattered.

"Well, that's it for the lecture portion of the course," Sheriff Morrison announced. "I'm going to turn it over to Cole, who will be leading the skills portion of the night."

Daphne sat up straight. "This is the part I was waiting for," she whispered. "I need to learn this stuff if I'm going to do any more private investigation. I know I won't be able to participate much, not with the baby. But I can watch and take notes."

"It's probably just how to get out of wrist holds," I whispered back. That had been the standard fare at the classes I had taken before. The one time I had tried that one on Daniel, he had simply laughed before grabbing me and hauling me to our balcony, where he tied me to the railing and forced me to spend the night out there shivering in my thin nightgown. It was January, and the temperature had dipped into the forties.

I had never tried to escape his hold again.

Cole's voice drew me out of my memories. He cleared his throat awkwardly, then began. "Everything Sheriff Morrison told you is correct. Following that advice is a good thing. But sometimes it's not enough. What then?"

He had my attention.

"Let's get real," he continued. "Most of you would be easily outmatched in a fight. I'm going to teach you some skills tonight, but I'd recommend you get a weapon. Lethal or non-lethal—there are plenty of options. Get a weapon and learn to use it. Practice until it feels like an extension of your arm. If you want any recommendations, see me after class. Tonight, my job is to get you comfortable with uncomfortable situations and teach you some ways to throw your opponent off-balance so you can get away to safety. Some of the things we're going to do tonight *will* make you uncomfortable. There will be some mild pain.

This could be triggering, especially if you've had any trauma in your history."

His gaze flickered my way, pausing briefly before he continued. I felt my face flush crimson.

"If you need to take a break or get some air," he continued, "do that. But if you can hang in there, please do. It's better to be uncomfortable here, where nobody is going to seriously harm you, and work through that than it is to just avoid it and then panic if something happens in real life. Everyone got it?"

There were nods and murmurs around the room as everyone whispered about what exactly he meant by mild pain. I was the only one who sat silent, frozen in place. Icy dread crept up my spine. I wasn't afraid of the pain—I knew how to endure that, and I knew that nothing he had planned for class could possibly compare to what I had suffered in the past.

But I was terrified I would panic and give away my secret. That felt more dangerous than anything else.

I didn't want anyone's pity. I also didn't want anyone else to have even one piece of the puzzle of who I was. It would be too easy to start putting those pieces together. It was already dangerous that I was sewing again and selling my work, even in such a small boutique. There had been too much publicity over our marriage. If anyone started connecting the dots between the Willa who made clothes in Rosemary Mountain and the Wilhelmina fashion designer who had caught the eye of a rising political star and got swept away in the romance of the century...

I was taking too many risks already. Marking myself as a woman with a past was just one more thing to add to the list.

"Are you okay?" Daphne nudged me.

"Fine," I said, swallowing down the panic.

Her eyes said she didn't believe me, but I faked a reassuring smile. I was good at that, having had plenty of practice.

Cole's voice brought our attention back to the front of the room. "First up, we'll practice getting out of some wrist holds," he announced.

"Told you," I whispered to Daphne.

She just laughed and shook her head. I relaxed slightly. Wrist holds were nothing. I could handle that.

Cole and Sheriff Morrison demonstrated the basic technique for us, then told us to pair up and take turns trying it on each other. The room filled with nervous giggles as the women all started grabbing each other and practicing the evasive maneuver.

"Which part do you want to do first?" I asked Daphne.

"Either one," she said.

"Okay, you grab me first," I said. It was a selfish request. I knew it would bother me more to grab and potentially bruise her wrist than it would for her to bruise mine.

She grabbed me, but as I started to twist and move out of it, she went pale and closed her eyes. I immediately stopped moving.

"Daphne. Are you okay?" I felt frantic. Such a simple thing shouldn't have caused an issue with the baby, but in a split second, she had gone from vibrant and happy to pale and pained.

Sheriff Morrison and Cole noticed too and immediately rushed to her side.

After a moment, she opened her eyes and stared straight into mine. "I'm fine," she said as she realized we were all surrounding her.

"What happened?" Cole said, his voice a deep growl.

"All I did was twist my wrist to get away," I said, starting to panic again. "I didn't mean to hurt her or the baby. I would never—"

"I'm fine," she repeated, reaching for my hand as she interrupted me. She gave Cole a warning look, then exchanged a long look I couldn't quite make sense of with the sheriff.

He seemed to get it though, as a shadow crossed his face and he let out a deep sigh.

"Maybe you shouldn't practice these," Cole said, still frowning. "Emerson will kill me if anything happens to you or the baby. And I mean that literally."

"Cole," she said, "I'm fine. I promise. Now shoo, both of you. We need to practice."

"Are you sure?" I asked. My heart was still pounding in fear that I had done something wrong, made some mistake.

"I'm sure. I'm totally fine," she said. She hesitated for a moment, then spoke again. "But are you? I wonder if I was wrong in asking you to come. We don't have to do this if you don't want to."

"I'm fine too," I said, putting on that reassuring smile again. "As long as you are."

"Okay. Try again?"

I nodded and held out my wrist for her to grab.

Chapter Eight

Cole

I circled the room, watching the class and giving pointers to some of the women. For some reason, I found myself avoiding Daphne and Willa, even though my eyes continually drifted their way. It was hard *not* to look at Willa. She was the most stunning woman I had ever seen in my life. The woman somehow managed to make yoga pants and a sweatshirt look *glamorous.* There was a reason the paparazzi had loved her and treated her like American royalty.

But it wasn't just her looks that kept pulling my eyes in her direction. Most of the women here were giggling, letting out nervous laughter as they attempted to get comfortable with the practice. It was to be expected.

Daphne and Willa weren't giggling at all.

Both women were a picture of fierce determination as they swapped turns grabbing each other and practicing the various moves I had demonstrated. They would both leave with bruises on their wrists. I only hoped Emerson didn't get too angry about that.

"Time for our next move," I announced, clapping my hands so all the women would stop what they were doing and focus back on the front of the class. "Now, this next one is a little more intense. You may feel uncomfortable. Remember, it's better to experience that here, where you're safe, than to first experience this kind of discomfort from someone who is truly trying to hurt you. Get comfortable with the fear so you can keep a clear head and do what you need to do if you ever face anything like this in real life. Sheriff?"

Greg joined me to demonstrate the next move in front of the class, a move where I backed him up against a wall with my hand around his throat and he showed how to get out of it by blocking my arm and shoving my head into the padded wall. There was more than one pale face in the room when we were done.

"We have to do that?" one of the women asked, obviously nervous.

"Only the escaping part. We'll handle the attacker part, because we want to make sure we're the ones taking the blows. I'd like for you all to practice this, even though I know it's going to feel uncomfortable. But if you can't handle having our hands on your throat, just say so and you can practice the move without us actually touching you."

Some utterings of relief went around the room.

"Make two lines," I said, pointing. "Either for me or Sheriff Morrison here."

I wasn't going to direct her, but I hoped Willa would get in my line. If my suspicions about her past were correct, she might have a difficult time with this. Greg was, by all accounts, a stellar guy. But he didn't know anything about Willa, and he might not know to be gentle with her.

Oddly enough, Willa seemed to have the same idea. Daphne walked straight to Greg's line, but Willa hesitated, then stepped into the line forming in front of me. Her eyes met mine, like she was issuing a challenge.

And there had never been a challenge I had been more ready to meet.

·   ·   ·

I expected the women to refuse to let us put our hands on their throats. That feeling could terrify anyone, even someone who was used to training in martial arts. But surprisingly, all the women in my line wanted the full experience. Some of them even surprised me by handling it well and performing the move better than I'd expected.

But then it was Willa's turn.

It was clear she was scared as she stepped to the head of the line. That bronzed skin was way too pale. Still, with a look of determination on her face, she walked to the wall.

"I don't have to put my hand on your neck," I said, my voice low. "I'll just stick out my arm and you can practice it."

"No," she said, her eyes flaring. "All the other women did it, didn't they?"

"Yes. But you don't have to."

She lifted her chin in a way that spoke of regal defiance. I ground my teeth. On one hand, I was damn proud of her. This was obviously uncomfortable for her, but she was determined to do it anyway.

On the other hand, I was cursing myself for this whole idea. At the time, it had seemed brilliant. Start a self-defense course, teach her to defend herself so she'd have a fighting chance if anything ever happened, assuming my suspicions were correct. Get a chance to watch how she reacted, to get a better feeling for whether she was a victim or a criminal evading the law. Win-win.

But now? Now, I had to be the one to attack her, and I suddenly regretted the whole damn thing.

"I'm waiting," she said.

"Okay." I stepped forward and lightly closed my hand around her neck, careful not to put even an ounce of pressure on it.

Even so, her eyes flew open in shock, her pupils dilated, and her pulse quickened underneath my hand. She stood, frozen.

I forced myself to keep my hand in place. "You've got this," I said, keeping my voice calm and quiet. "You know what to do. Use that left arm, get yourself some room..."

Her breath hitched as she stayed frozen. "I need a minute," she whispered, her voice barely audible.

I dropped my hand instantly. "Do you want to go sit down?"

"No." The answer was immediate and hushed, like she didn't want to draw any attention to us. I realized that, on top of everything else, she was embarrassed.

She closed her eyes and took a slow breath. "I want to try again."

"Willa..."

Her eyes snapped open, piercing me with their anger. "I said I want to try it again."

I nodded once, then placed my hand back on her neck. This time, she was ready. She threw her arm up, knocked me off-balance, and slammed me into the wall with more force than I would have imagined coming out of such a small woman.

"That's good," I said, feeling an unexpected smile break through. "Very good, actually."

"I'm sorry," she said, even more pale than before.

"Why?" I asked, chuckling. "You did exactly what you were supposed to do."

But my eyes narrowed as I really looked at her. If she had been uncomfortable during the exercise, she was downright terrified now. All the color had drained out of her and she was shaking like a leaf.

"Willa," I said, stepping forward.

But she instantly stepped back and threw an arm up as if bracing herself.

"Willa, you're okay," I said, stopping in my tracks. I held my hands up and backed off, showing her she was safe.

But she turned and fled the room, leaving everyone gaping.

Daphne started to follow, but I grabbed her arm.

"Let me," I said. "Please. This is my fault. I need to fix it."

She gave me a sympathetic smile. "It's not, but I get it. I don't know if she'll want to talk to you, but you can try."

I nodded and left to track down Willa.

CHAPTER NINE

Willa

I COULD BARELY BREATHE AS I RAN DOWN THE HALLWAY, straight through the doors, and into the parking lot. Only then, outside of the walls that seemed to be crashing in on me, could I finally get a deep breath. I dropped down to the cold front steps and hugged my legs into my chest, letting the tears fall.

It was just too much.

The whole night had brought up memories I wanted nothing more than to forget. Worse, I had humiliated myself by making a scene. Every woman in there was probably whispering about me. *What's wrong with her? Wonder what happened to her to make her freak out like that? She's been a mystery ever since she moved here, never answering questions about where she comes from. No family or friends. Must be running from someone, you better believe it.*

I wanted to vomit, imagining them all gossipping about me. It was a nightmare of its own.

But I hadn't been able to keep myself together in there to avoid it.

The terror had felt so real. When Cole put his hand around my throat, in my mind he had become Daniel. Reality blurred, like I was back there again. And the first time, I did what I always did—I froze, ready to take whatever he was going to dish out. But the second time... The second time, I fought back.

You don't fight Daniel Cavendish.

The sheer terror of having fought back, of him moving toward me after, of the punishment I would surely receive... It was too real. The past year had disappeared in an instant, taking me right back to life with Daniel like I had never been free at all. Maybe I hadn't. Not really. He still had a grip on me I didn't know how to shake.

"Willa." Cole's voice, low and gentle, interrupted my thoughts.

I felt relief and resentment all at once. Relief that he had brought me back to the present. Resentment that he wasn't giving me privacy when I had obviously run away for that very reason. I opened my mouth to answer but couldn't seem to utter a word.

"I don't want to scare you," he said. "I'm going to come sit by you. Is that okay?"

My back immediately tensed. I didn't want him anywhere near me.

He seemed to sense that. After walking my way slowly, he sat on the opposite side of the steps from me, giving me plenty of personal space. He kept his hands in sight and his posture relaxed and non-threatening. The gesture meant something to me.

He stayed silent, just sitting there in what felt like an attempt at support. That, too, meant something. It gave me time to breathe, to pull myself together. And something about his silent support gave me unexpected strength. It was the last thing I had expected from someone who normally made me feel so uncomfortable.

"I'm sorry for what happened," I finally said, breaking the silence.

"You have no reason to be sorry." His voice was low and deliberately calm, but I detected a hint of anger in his words, which made me instantly anxious again.

"I made a scene. I'm sorry."

"Who cares?"

The comment stopped me suddenly. Who really did care? Daniel would have. I had gotten in trouble many times for "making a scene," even if my "scene" was nothing more than disagreeing with him in public over something as stupid as the flavor notes in a particular vintage of wine.

Now, I only had to answer to myself.

But the reality was that I cared. I didn't want to be that person. Didn't want to appear weak. And it wasn't about Daniel—it was about me and who I wanted to be. Freaking out made me look like a victim, and I was working hard every day to prove to myself that I wasn't one. Not anymore.

"I care," I finally said, my voice soft.

He stayed silent for a moment, then forced out words that seemed as difficult for him as mine were for me. "Then I'm the one who's sorry," he said. He sighed and pinched the back of his neck, shaking his head. "Tonight was my fault."

"You were just trying to do something for the community. It's not your fault I couldn't handle it."

That silence settled in again before he begrudgingly offered me the truth. "I didn't do it for the community. I did it for you."

I sat back, surprised. "Me? Why?"

"An error in judgment," he said.

As I looked at him, it was clear he was beating himself up over it. I realized the hint of anger in his voice wasn't toward me—it was toward himself. I wanted to ask more, to find out why exactly he had orchestrated tonight for me specifically. But more than that, I felt the need to soothe away the guilt he was obviously carrying for what had happened.

"It's fine," I said, sighing. "I'm okay. You didn't do anything wrong."

"Didn't I?" he asked. The words hung between us like there were a thousand things behind them I wasn't seeing, wasn't understanding.

I started to ask him more, but before I could, we were interrupted by footsteps. I tensed again and noticed he did too.

"Oh, there you are," Daphne called out in relief as she came through the doors. "Are you okay, Willa?"

"I'm fine," I said, putting that reassuring smile back on. I immediately missed the silence with Cole, where I hadn't had to wear it.

That, too, had been unexpected.

Cole stood to his feet. "I better get back to the class," he said. "Will you ladies be joining us for the rest?" He directed the words as if they were to both of us, but he only looked at me.

I glanced at Daphne, who had a questioning look on her face.

"I think we better sit out the rest, don't you, Daphne? They're probably getting into some moves that might not be safe for the baby."

She nodded. "Totally. I agree. Sorry, Cole. Great class, but I think we're going to blow off the rest and get some cheesecake."

"Fair enough." He stood and offered me his hand, but I ignored it.

If there was one thing tonight had reconfirmed, it was that I never wanted another man touching me again.

Daphne was quiet as we drove to Coco's Bakery, her favorite spot to grab dessert, but I filled the empty space with mindless chatter about the store, fashion, and cranky customers. I didn't want to talk about what had happened or answer any questions about it.

Thankfully, she didn't ask them.

But when we sat down at a booth in the back, I looked across the table and saw fresh pity in her eyes. I hated it.

We placed our orders—strawberry cheesecake for me, raspberry and white chocolate for her, just like always—and made pointless conversation while we waited. But after our cheesecakes were brought over, I sighed, knowing I should just get it over with and tell her the truth like I had promised Janet. I had put it off as long as I could, but after the incident at class, it wouldn't be a big shock anyway.

"I need to tell you something," I said, using my fork to pick at the crust on my cheesecake. It looked delicious, but I didn't have much of an appetite.

"You don't have to," she said.

I was grateful, but she was wrong. "I owe you an explanation."

She shook her head. "Willa, you don't owe me anything. That's not how friendship works. I'm always here for you, and if you *want* to talk, of course I'm here to listen. But you don't owe it to me."

I swallowed the lump in my throat. Friendship was something I hadn't had much of since Daniel had come into my life, and I was grateful for hers. I only hoped what I had to say wouldn't change things too much.

"It's because we're friends that I owe you the truth," I said. "I lied to you all. I wish I could say I'm sorry for it, but I'm not. It seems like my past is catching up with me though, and I'd rather you hear the truth from me. What I can tell you of it anyway."

She bit her lip. "Then I owe you the truth, too."

"About what?" She had caught me off guard with that.

"I see things sometimes," she said simply. "It's called the second sight. I try not to—really. I don't want you to think I'm purposely invading your privacy. But sometimes your feelings and thoughts are so strong, so vivid, I can't block them out."

"What do you mean?" My heart rate quickened as anxiety flooded my body at her words. Surely she couldn't "see" my past... Could she?

"Like tonight," she said, avoiding my eyes. "I wasn't trying to look. I try to keep the door closed. But when I grabbed your wrist, I saw."

"What did you see?"

"Him grabbing you," she said, her voice pained. "You pulling away. Then him dragging you out onto that cold balcony. You shivering there, afraid. Willa, I'm so sorry."

I was shaking now. "You saw that? I don't understand. How is that even possible?"

Her face twisted. "I'm so sorry, Willa. Sorry it happened, and sorry I saw it. Like I said, I try not to. I would never deliberately infringe on your privacy. But it just happens sometimes. Especially now that I'm pregnant. Something about pregnancy seems to have opened up the floodgates. I wish I could block it all out, but I can't seem to anymore."

I shook my head in disbelief. "How long have you known about me?"

"I don't know much," she said as if that helped somehow. "But I've known a little since basically the beginning. When you were fitting me for my wedding dress, I lost my balance on the stool one day and reached out, grabbing you for support. That was the first time I saw a glimpse. I grabbed your shoulder and immediately saw him doing the same. Grabbing you. Hitting you." Her face paled. "I realized you were here to get away from him. Other than that, I've mostly managed to block it out when I'm around you. Until tonight. It all happened so fast."

I nodded numbly. In a way, it made things better. She had known from the beginning, yet she had befriended me anyway. At least I didn't have to worry about things changing too much.

She reached out and squeezed my hand. "I've been so afraid to tell you about my sight," she said, "because I didn't want you to think differently of me. I didn't want you to be afraid of me, or our friendship, or feel like I was spying on you. But if we're being open, you deserve the truth from me."

I squeezed her hand back before delicately pulling away. Touch had been used to hurt me so many times that it always made me feel a bit pained, even when it was from a friend. It was just one more thing Daniel had stolen from me.

"I didn't want you to think differently of me, either," I confessed. "This is the first little bit of normal I've had since... Since I left. But I don't know how much of that I'm going to get now."

"Why?"

I looked down at my napkin. "In your..." I trailed off, not knowing what word to use.

"Visions?" she supplied helpfully.

"Yes. Visions. In your, um, visions, did you see who my husband was?"

She shook her head.

I glanced around the room, making sure no one was close enough to hear. Then I leaned forward and lowered my voice. "I was married to Daniel Cavendish."

Her face stayed blank for a moment until she made the connection. "Wait. The senator?"

I nodded.

"Oh." Her eyes widened as her jaw dropped open. "I see. That does complicate things."

"To put it lightly."

"He thinks—"

"I'm dead," I said, finishing the sentence for her. I could see her calculating, thinking it through.

"Then you're safe," she said, stating it like a fact, even though I could hear the question hidden in it.

"I don't know that I am. Janet recognized me."

Her eyes widened even more. "Mom knows?"

I nodded.

"You don't have to worry. She won't tell anyone," she reassured me. "Her knowing won't jeopardize you. And neither will I."

"I'm not worried about either of you," I said. "But it's just a matter of time before it gets out." The utter certainty of it hit me with a weight that felt hopeless. "What if Sheriff Morrison finds out? I broke laws, Daphne. He can't overlook that. Worse, I think Cole knows who I am or is close to figuring it out. I don't trust him."

Although, even as I said it, I felt a stab of guilt. Something about tonight had changed the way I looked at him. He had obviously been trying to make sure I felt safe and comfortable when he sat close to me. And surprisingly, I had. It was unexpected and made me wonder if I was wrong about him.

She bit her lip again. "He warned us you weren't telling the whole truth. I thought maybe he was some human lie detector or something. I told him to leave it alone. Then he came up with this whole self-defense class thing and asked me to make sure you came. I got the feeling he was trying to help. But I don't know how much he knows. I'll try to find out."

"Do you trust him?" I asked.

She lifted her hands helplessly. "Honestly? I don't know, Willa. I have a hard time getting a read on him. He's so quiet and closed off. I get the sense he has a lot of deep anger hidden in there, and that makes me nervous. But on the other hand, Emerson trusts him, and I trust Emerson. There has to be good in there for Emerson to open up our lives to him. I get the sense that he's very loyal to Emerson and, by default, to Emerson's family. Initially, I thought maybe he saw you as a threat because he doesn't trust *you*. But now? I really don't know."

"Well, I guess that makes two of us," I said, forcing a quiet laugh.

Chapter Ten

Cole

I FELT LIKE A COMPLETE JERK AS I STOOD IN FRONT OF THE sheriff's station, watching Willa and Daphne walk away. My intentions with the class might have been good, but it had clearly backfired. If what I suspected was true, it was no surprise that the moves triggered her. But I guess I had expected her to be able to work through it. Feel some sort of empowerment. Learn some things that might help her out when the trouble I sensed coming finally made it here.

I hadn't expected her to run out and quit.

Knowing I had done that to her made me want to go after her and try to make things better somehow. But her body language suggested I would only make things worse, and I still had a class full of women waiting for me.

I trudged back to the classroom, even though my mind was a million miles away. It was a relief to see that Greg had carried on without me and was in the process of dismissing everyone for the night, with reassurance that we would hold another class soon where they could continue practicing their new skills.

It took a while to get everyone out the door, but when we did, Greg shook my hand and congratulated me. "That went pretty well, I'd say. Great idea to hold this as a community service. I appreciate you volunteering your time tonight."

"No problem," I answered. "Happy to do it."

"It's something I'd like to turn into a regular thing. We've got some extra money in the budget, and I'll gladly pay for your time if you want to keep leading."

"Sure. I can do that." The words came out like I was forcing them over rocks in my throat.

Greg cocked his head. "Something on your mind?"

"You probably keep regular patrols around Janet's shop, right?" I asked, answering him with a question of my own.

He nodded. "Of course."

"Good." It wasn't much, but it was something.

Greg studied me, then leaned back against the table, crossing his arms. "It's not my wife you're worried about though, is it?"

I shook my head but refused to clarify.

He gave me a long look. "Janet told me Willa might be in some trouble. Refused to say anything beyond that though, which isn't like her. She normally tells me everything, but she was adamant she couldn't this time. You know something about what's going on?"

"I might. But it's not my story to share. And at this point, it's mostly a hypothetical concern."

"That's the impression I got from Janet, too," he said. "I asked her if there was a specific threat and she said no." He looked to me for confirmation.

"No specific threat that I'm aware of," I said.

"But there might be?" He let the question hang in the air, continuing to push for information.

I took a deep breath and sighed. "You saw how she reacted tonight," I said, letting him connect the dots himself.

He nodded. "Yep. Classic signs of abuse."

"Right. I think I know the man who abused her," I said, choosing my words deliberately. "And my gut says if he finds out where she is, he'll come after her."

Greg frowned. "Maybe I should talk to her. Talk her into filing a restraining order."

I shook my head again. "That won't work in this situation."

"I'm well aware of the limitations. I know it's just a piece of paper that won't stop someone. But it carries weight behind it, and it's a start," he said. "If he's a danger, we need to start a paper trail. Start building a case."

"No, you don't understand," I said. "You're thinking like a cop. But this situation is different. If my suspicions are correct, the only reason she's safe right now is because he thinks she's dead. Filing a restraining order takes that safety away. And a piece of paper would be meaningless for someone like him."

He frowned again. "How do you know so much about all this when you just got into town?"

"Because," I said. "I was there when she died."

Despite feeling anxious for news about how she was, I forced myself to wait a full week before swinging by the store to check on Willa, thinking she might need space before seeing me again. When I arrived, Janet was working alone though, with Willa nowhere to be found.

"Cole!" Janet said, brightening. "I'm so glad you're here. It's perfect timing, actually. Would you mind helping me with something for a minute? I have a new piece of furniture out back in my SUV. I thought Willa and I could carry it in together, but she's out sick today."

"Sure thing. Out sick? Is she okay?" I kept my tone casual despite the acceleration in my heart rate. I wanted to pepper Janet with questions—how long had Willa been "sick"? Had she been in at all since the self-defense class, or had she been at home ever since? Had anyone checked on her? My guilt intensified as I imagined her holed up in her apartment, fighting off the demons from her past.

"Miserable, but okay," Janet answered. "I don't know why people have to get out and spread their germs when they're sick. We had customers come in the other day talking about how they had the flu. One of them sneezed right on Willa. Twenty-four hours later, she was down for the count."

"Oh man. That's rough." Even so, I felt relief knowing it wasn't the class that had her down.

"Fiona took her some soup and tea," Janet said, motioning for me to follow her out back to her vehicle. "She's past the worst of it, but it will be a couple of days before she's back on her feet. Ah, here we go." She popped the trunk to reveal an antique display table. "You grab one end and I'll grab the other."

"I got it," I said, sliding the table out. "Just grab the door for me."

"Gladly," she said, pulling the store door open so I could carry the table inside.

"Where do you want it?"

"Here, I'll show you." She led the way to the front corner. "Right here should do. I thought it would be nice to put a small Christmas display up."

"That will be nice," I agreed. "By the way, thanks for the dinner invitation."

"Oh, you're welcome! I can't wait." Her whole face lit up. "I haven't had a big holiday celebration like this in years. It will be so fun to have everyone. Willa's coming too, and Jackson—you've met him, right?"

"Jackson," I said, trying to place the name, even though my mind was focused entirely on the other name she had said—*Willa*. "Would that be Detective Ford?"

"Yes, exactly! I thought I remembered you meeting him when you were here before."

"Yeah, I did," I said, confirming. He had been part of our makeshift security team for Daphne and Emerson's wedding. Solid guy, if a little too cheerful for my tastes.

"Now be sure to come hungry," she said. "Between me and Fiona, we're preparing enough to feed an army!"

But I was still stuck on the only thing I really cared about. "You said Willa's coming?" I asked, making sure I had heard correctly.

She looked up at me with sudden awareness in her eyes. "Yes, she is."

"Huh. Could you help me with something?"

"Maybe." There was a bit of hesitation in her voice.

"Could you help me pick out a gift for Willa? I bought gifts for you, Daphne, and Fiona. But I didn't realize Willa would be there, and I want to give her something, too. Jackson too, of course, but that's easier. I don't have a clue what to get Willa though. I'm normally a gift card kind of guy."

Relief flooded her face. "Now that, I can do. Not here though," she said, waving her hand in dismissal. "She's around all of this stuff every day. I have the perfect idea." She went to the front cash register and pulled out a pad of paper, quickly scribbling down a name and address. "Go here. It's an adorable little antique store. Willa and I went in there last week looking for pieces for the store. They had this hair comb she kept looking at, a real hippie kind of thing, with a moon and stars on it."

"A hair comb?" I asked, feeling unsure.

"Yes. I could tell she really wanted it, and it wasn't expensive, but getting that girl to splurge on herself even a little bit is like pulling teeth. I was going to go back myself to get it for her, but you can get it if you want."

"Okay. Great idea," I said, taking the paper from her. "Thanks."

And I headed out the door to buy an inexpensive hair comb for a woman who used to wear diamonds.

Chapter Eleven

Willa

December passed in the blink of an eye, and before I knew what was happening, it was Christmas.

Christmas. The very idea of it filled me with joy.

A year ago, my celebration had been the strangest, yet happiest, of my life. I had celebrated alone in a dingy motel room with cartons of fried rice and egg rolls. My only company had been the Christmas movies playing on TV. There had been no gifts, no tree, no holiday feast.

But there had also been no parties where I might embarrass Daniel, no chance of accidentally angering him by buying him the wrong gift, and no pretending that the gifts he lavished on me made up for the countless times he had hurt me.

For the first time in a very long time, I had celebrated without having to pretend anything at all. The freedom was so beautiful I wanted to weep. It was the best gift I had ever given myself.

But this Christmas was even more exciting. Not only was I free, I had a community. Friends.

Friends who were starting to feel a lot like family.

I was bringing with me a collection of small gifts, something thoughtfully chosen or made for each of them. I had to be careful with my budget. A year of temp jobs hadn't provided very well, and I needed to conserve as much cash as possible with a future as uncertain as mine. The presents were small, but I knew it would be okay. They might not have been the ridiculously expensive gifts Daniel would have expected, but I knew that with Daphne and her family it truly was the thought that counted. They would cherish the gifts because that's the kind of people they were. And that filled my heart more than the most expensive gift I had ever been given.

Snow was falling lightly when I reached Greg and Janet's house, making it an absolute picture. Their ranch sat in the valley, framed by the mountains behind them. The home was lit up with Christmas lights and glowed like a beacon of safety and warmth on the cold, snowy evening. Overwhelming joy filled my heart. A white Christmas, surrounded by friends. It was so perfect it felt unbelievable.

The front door flew open before I even reached it.

"Come in, come in," Fiona called, a picture herself in a bright-red sweater and denim overalls, her waist-length white hair in a long side braid. She waved me toward her, a giant smile on her face. "I'm the official welcoming committee, seeing as how Janet's tied herself up in the kitchen. I sure hope you've brought your appetite!"

"I'm starved," I said, catching a whiff of the incredible aromas coming from the kitchen: cinnamon, apples, and what could only be freshly baked bread.

I *was* starving—for all of this. The love, the friendship, the normalcy —I hadn't realized how much I'd missed it all until this very moment. Tears sprang into my eyes: tears of homesickness for the life I knew before Daniel, and tears of gratitude for getting something of it back.

Fiona helped me carry my gifts to the tree, then wrapped me in a tight hug. I stiffened immediately, as that familiar discomfort with touch enveloped me.

She immediately pulled back, dropping her hands, and looked at me with eyes that seemed uncommonly perceptive for a woman of her age. "We're glad you're here, Willa. You know, you should come visit me sometime," she said, cocking her head. "I'll make you some tea and we'll talk."

I nodded, not even sure what to say. Fiona was kind and had even dropped off her special "flu remedy" tea for me when I was sick. I knew, despite the nearly fifty-year age difference, that she and Daphne were somehow the best of friends. But she was also something of an icon to my mind, the very essence of Rosemary Mountain. Everyone in town knew Fiona. As a long-time resident and midwife, she had quite literally helped birth most of the town. Being invited to tea at her house felt like a true sign of acceptance, a gesture that I wasn't quite an outsider anymore. And it made me feel as if, somehow, everything in my life was going to be okay.

"I'd love to," I said, meaning it—despite also being more than a little nervous about the whole thing.

"Willa, you made it!" Daphne came out of the kitchen, snacking on a cookie.

My eyes widened. "Daphne, you're—"

"Huge," she finished for me, laughing. "I know. I hit the six month mark this week, and the baby seems to have decided to fast track his or her growth."

"I was going to say adorable," I said. It was true. She was glowing and absolutely beautiful, with her perfectly round bump jutting out from her emerald-green sweater dress.

Fiona walked by and smacked her lightly on the arm. "Why don't you stop with that 'his or her' nonsense and just tell us what the baby is? It will be a Christmas gift to us all!"

"No." Daphne's eyes sparkled as Emerson came up behind her, wrapping his big arms around the bride he obviously adored.

"Love you," he said, kissing the side of her cheek. "And Willa's right. You're adorable."

"Love you," she answered back, her eyes shining.

"Oh, get a room," Fiona said, rolling her eyes. "I'm going to help Janet in the kitchen."

"I'll see if I can help too," I said, quickly following her. I adored

Daphne with all my heart, but my emotions felt like they were on a rollercoaster, and unwanted envy kept rising as I watched her and Emerson together. Envy made me feel like such a small person. It wasn't that I wanted to take even an ounce of happiness away from her. I just ached for some of that joy in my own future, and grieved the fact that it could never be.

"Oh, Willa, honey!" Janet beamed at me as I walked into the kitchen. "You look gorgeous, as always. Sometimes you make me wish I could pull off that Bohemian style the way you do."

"Thank you," I said, smiling.

There was a time when I would have taken her comment as a backhanded compliment, but after working with Janet, I knew she was sincere. Her own style was classic elegance, but she had a genuine appreciation for the rest of the fashion world.

"Is there anything I can help with?" I asked, glancing around the kitchen. There wasn't an empty spot on the counter. The island was covered with cookies, cakes, and pies. The other counters were already lined up with more side dishes than I could count. Yet Janet was still buzzing around the kitchen, checking on things in the oven and stirring things on the stove.

"Not a thing," she said, waving me off. "We're almost done here. Another ten minutes and we'll be ready to eat. Fiona, show her where the drinks are. Grab something to sip on, Willa, and go relax. We'll eat soon!"

"Ten minutes my ass," Fiona whispered, taking my arm and leading me into the dining room, where a drink station was set up. "That woman doesn't know when to stop."

"She likes to make things special," I said, wanting to defend her—even if I had often thought the same thing at the shop.

"That she does, Willa-girl," Fiona agreed, nodding. "Now, Janet recommends the champagne, but I recommend the punch." She leaned in, whispering. "Janet made it, but I fixed it."

"Fixed it?"

"Added whiskey to it. Can't have a Christmas punch without some good old Irish whiskey, now can we?"

"Sounds dangerous," I said, my lips twitching.

"Oh it is," she said, a dead serious expression on her face. "But it's Christmas. Live a little. Let me pour you a cup." She moved to the station and pulled out a punch cup, filling it to the brim before handing it to me.

I sipped it hesitantly. "Delicious," I said. "But I can tell it's as dangerous as I thought."

She winked. "It'll do you good. Now, come on. You're supposed to relax, and I'm still on welcoming duty."

Fiona practically dragged me back into the living room just in time to see Cole walk through the door. I still mostly disliked the man and felt a deep resentment that he kept sticking his nose into my business, threatening the very life I was building for myself here.

But Fiona's whiskey seemed to be going straight to my head, because when he walked through the doorway, I could barely keep my eyes off him. And it was only partly because he was one of the most attractive men I had ever seen. He was completely different from Daniel. Daniel was a classic American heartthrob—perfectly cut blond hair, bright-blue eyes, and a movie-star smile that hid the darkness within him.

Cole was almost scruffy. Dark hair and a beard. Calloused hands that told a story of hard work. No smile—I wasn't sure the man even knew how. Yet his pure ruggedness had an appeal I couldn't quite understand.

But like Daniel, he was dangerous. The last thing I needed in my life was another dangerous man. Still, there was something about him that called to me—something in his eyes that said he understood what it was like to be alone. And he had shown unexpected sensitivity at the self-defense class. I couldn't quite figure him out, but something in me really wanted to.

He hung his coat up and turned in our direction, meeting my gaze. I jumped, feeling guilty for being caught staring at him.

"That sure is a good-looking one," Fiona murmured in my ear. "If I was forty years younger..."

"He'd be lucky to have you even now," I whispered back.

She just cackled. "I knew I liked you. Drink up, Willa-girl. We're celebrating!"

"Cheers." I clanked my glass to hers and looked back at Cole just in time to see a ghost of a smile pass over his face before the broodiness returned.

Maybe the man knew how to smile after all.

"Cole, I hereby welcome you to the party," Fiona called out, getting louder with every sip she took. "I recommend you get some of this punch before it's all gone. Willa here will show you where it is. Come on, girl. Take pity on the poor man and get him a drink. God knows he needs to loosen up a bit, too."

I bit back a smile and looked at Cole.

"I wouldn't mind a glass of punch," he admitted.

"You heard him," Fiona said, pushing me toward the dining room. "Help the poor man out."

Daphne caught my eye and grinned before mouthing the word *sorry.*

I just laughed. "This way," I said, motioning for Cole to follow me. "Fiona's proud of having spiked Janet's punch with Irish whiskey. I think she wants us all to get a bit tipsy."

"Irish whiskey?" Janet called out, having overheard me. "She did not!"

"Oops," I said, unable to hide my smile. I was having more fun than I had had in ages.

Janet hurried into the dining room and poured a bit of punch into a cup, tasting it. Her eyes widened. "My word. She really did. I already had champagne *and* vodka in here. This is ridiculous."

"And delicious." I poured a cup for Cole and handed it to him.

He tasted it, his eyes never leaving mine. "I agree," he said. "Absolutely delicious."

The way he said it combined with the desire in his eyes made heat flood my body. It was something I hadn't felt in years.

And it was completely out of the question.

Still, I couldn't seem to look away, even as Janet started lecturing about how everyone needed to hydrate with water in between glasses of punch, and Fiona lectured her back about not being a buzzkill on Christmas, and Sheriff Morrison stepped in to play peacemaker. It all seemed to just fade away as Cole and I stared into each other's eyes.

I finally came back to earth when Fiona asked me to back her up in the argument.

"Oh. Um. The punch is delicious, but it's Janet's house and she should have final say," I said lamely. I was backing Janet up out of loyalty, but it seemed to backfire and take all the wind out of her sails.

She raised her hands helplessly. "If everyone likes the punch the way Fiona made it, then leave it. I just want to see that pitcher of water go down as quickly as the punch bowl." She wagged her finger at everyone.

"Mom, don't you wag your finger at me," Daphne said, laughing. "All I'm drinking is water anyway."

"Oh. Right."

Fiona smirked. "You know what you need, Janet? A glass of this punch."

Janet glared, but there was a smile behind it. The whole scene made me happy, because even when this group fought, they loved each other. There was no meanness, no cruel words, no threatening stares. No icy dread as the minutes on the clock ticked by, knowing that when the party was over there would be a price to pay.

They teased and poked each other, but it was all done in love. It was safe. It was real.

And I was loving every single minute of it.

Chapter Twelve

Cole

I couldn't take my eyes off Willa. I'd sought her out the minute I'd walked in the door, wanting—needing—to see how she was after the class that had obviously triggered her. To my surprise, all the fear and hesitation was gone.

All I saw was her beauty.

She was more confident than I had ever seen her, and somehow, she looked more like herself. I didn't know how to describe it exactly. But when she had walked on Daniel's arm, she always seemed like a ghost of a woman, a mere image of someone who wasn't entirely present. Perfect posture, demure personality, haunted eyes. Quiet. Too quiet. Always dressed to perfection, with never a hair out of place. Beautiful, yes. But she had always reminded me of a doll playing dress-up.

Standing in the Morrison's living room, arm-in-arm with Fiona, she barely resembled that shell of a woman. Her hair was piled up messily on top of her head, with wild waves spilling down around her face. She wore a chunky sweater over a long, colorful, ruffled skirt. Stone earrings, like the necklace she had picked out for Fiona, hung from her ears, and she had layered on multiple necklaces, all with colored stones and beads. She was vibrant, beautiful, and full of personality.

And she glowed with happiness.

As soon as I saw her laughing with Fiona, I couldn't help but smile. This was the real her, where she belonged.

And suddenly I knew, if I could do anything to make sure she stayed here, safe and happy, I would.

AT DINNER, I WAS SEATED IN BETWEEN JACKSON AND Emerson, at the opposite end of the table from Willa. I knew that had likely been a request from her, since she was clearly uncomfortable with me. Still, I kept stealing glances at her when I could, and what I saw made me happy. She lit up the room with her laughter, bonding with Fiona over their shared love of whiskey. It was entrancing, watching this version of her. She was so very different from the Wilhelmina I had witnessed in California.

It killed me that I could remember her so clearly, yet she didn't seem to have a clue we had met before.

That, or she was really good at hiding it.

"Earth to Cole," Emerson said, elbowing me.

"What?"

"I asked you to pass the potatoes. Three times."

"Oh. Sorry. I was thinking." I reached over, grabbed the massive dish of buttery creamed potatoes, and passed it to him.

"Obviously. And I see who you're watching," he added, his voice quiet.

"She's happy here," I said.

"Yeah. You're not going to do anything to ruin that, are you?"

I looked at him, surprised. "Why would you think that?"

He just shrugged. "You seemed to have a problem with her before."

"Things change," I said, studying her again.

. . .

AFTER DINNER, WE HEADED TO THE LIVING ROOM TO CRASH and open gifts. Fiona insisted on refilling all our punch cups, even though I had no intention of drinking a second. It was great punch, but a single drink was always my limit. Anything more than that dulled my senses too much. Some people enjoyed that—drank because of it, frankly. But I always felt it to be an uncomfortable sensation. I didn't want to relax and let down my guard.

That was just asking for trouble.

Willa had already had three though, and her shiny eyes and flushed cheeks told me she wasn't used to going that far, either. In some ways, it was a good sign. It meant she felt safe enough to let her guard down.

I envied her a little.

I wasn't expecting to receive any gifts, but everyone had bought me one, including Willa. Most of the gifts were standard Christmas fare—sweaters, wool socks, a bottle of bourbon from Emerson. But Willa's gift stopped me in my tracks. It was a set of antique throwing knives, probably from the same place where I had bought her hair comb. Good quality pieces, not like the mass produced crap sold in sporting goods stores. I could hardly wait to try them out.

"Thanks," I said, turning them over in my hand. I looked up at her and smiled. "I love them."

"I'm glad," she said, smiling back at me. It was the first real smile she had given me, and it felt like the best part of the gift.

"Here. This one's for you," I said, passing her the comb I had bought her, hoping she loved it just as much.

Her eyes lit up. "For me? I didn't expect you to get me anything." She tore into the packaging, then gasped when she saw the comb. "How did you know?" she asked, running her fingers over it like it was the most precious thing in the world instead of a flea market trinket.

"A little birdie told me," I said, winking.

"It means more to me than you can know." She looked up at me. This time, she wasn't smiling, but the depth of feeling in her eyes swept me away just the same.

Fiona leaned over and looked at it. "My, but that's beautiful! Matches your outfit, too. Want me to put it in your hair for you?"

"Yes, please," Willa said, handing it to her.

Fiona tucked the comb into the side of Willa's messy bun. "There," she said. "Perfect."

Willa stood and walked to the little mirror hanging on the wall by the door. "It's beautiful," she said. She turned to me and beamed this time. "Thank you, Cole."

My heart swelled in a way I hadn't known it was still capable of. I was damn proud to have been the one to put that smile on her face.

The festivities continued with board games and more of Fiona's punch. By the time things wound down, Daphne was rolling her eyes at Emerson and Fiona both.

"It's a good thing you two have me to be your designated driver," she said as she wrapped her wool scarf around her neck, pulling her long, red hair out of it. "Though I'm tempted to make you both sleep it off here, just to teach you a lesson."

"Oh, don't be a spoilsport," Fiona said, brushing her off. "Christmas comes but once a year, after all."

"Uh huh," Daphne said. "Load up, you two. The baby is tired and I need to sleep."

Willa wobbled on her feet as she reached for her coat. "Daphne, I hate to ask, but I may need a ride home too."

I stepped forward instantly. "I'll drive you home." The words came out of my mouth before I even had a chance to think about them.

Willa looked at me, surprised.

"I only had one cup of punch with dinner," I said. "Nothing since. I'm completely sober. Daphne's already exhausted, and you live in town, right? That's the opposite direction for her. I don't mind driving you."

"It's the opposite direction for you, too," she pointed out.

"But I'm not pregnant and sleepy," I said, feeling the corners of my mouth turn up in a ghost of a smile.

"I can drive her," Jackson offered. "I live in town too, and I've been water only the last two hours."

"Or you can sleep here in the guest room," Janet called out from the couch, where she was already snuggled into Greg's arms. "Sleep here and drive yourself home in the morning. You're more than welcome. It's your choice."

"Absolutely," Greg added. "I trust both Cole and Jackson to get you home safe, but we're more than happy to have you stay if that's what you prefer."

Willa shifted from one foot to the other, biting her lip as she thought it over. It was clear she was struggling with the decision.

"I think," she said, her voice tentative, "since Cole offered first, I'll take you up on it. If you really don't mind." She looked up at me with unsure eyes.

"I don't mind." Relief flooded my chest. She wasn't mine to take care of, yet I felt a sense of responsibility for her that I couldn't shake. Maybe it was because I was the only one who knew who she really was, the only one who had a connection with her that went beyond Rosemary Mountain—even if she didn't seem to realize it.

And the fact that she trusted me enough to drive her home, when it was clear trust didn't come easy for her, made me want to prove to her just how good of a man I could be.

Chapter Thirteen

Willa

What was I thinking? First, I had indulged in entirely too much punch. It was reckless and stupid. It made me vulnerable and way too relaxed. I couldn't even be sure of what all I had said tonight. Had I given away too much information? Said something that would put me in danger or make the sheriff look a little more closely at me? There was a reason I usually stuck to sipping a single glass of wine over the course of an hour, at least.

But no, I had to indulge in Fiona's punch. It hit hard and all my rules flew out the window. Now, I was relying on someone else to get me home safely. A terrible, terrible idea.

Even worse, when given three options, I had chosen the most dangerous one of all. Cole.

Why had I done that?

I knew exactly why. Something was shifting inside me when it came to him. It had started the night of the self-defense class. I had seen a different side of him, one that was sensitive and patient. It had earned a level of my trust, even though I had still disliked him.

Then he had given me that hair comb.

He couldn't know what it meant to me. Couldn't know that the moment I saw it, I wanted it. It reminded me of three things that kept me going through everything, even now—my mother, an astronomer who had driven me out into the middle of nowhere countless times as a child, to show me the night sky she loved so much. The moon and stars themselves, which had shone above me the night I ran, lighting my way and giving me strength. And Suzanna, my own bright star, who had always worn a necklace with a similar pattern on it. I loved that comb but hadn't felt comfortable spending any of my cash on it when I was spending so much of my reserves on gifts for everyone else.

The fact that he had bought it for me, and the look on his face when I thanked him for it, had swept away the last of my dislike for him in an instant.

Truth be told, with my inhibitions lowered, I had to admit how incredibly attracted to him I was. It was silly, but even though nothing could ever come of it, I found myself hoping he might feel the same.

Yes, I was being entirely too reckless and stupid.

Having him drive me home was a mistake, but when I tried to correct it, my mouth simply wouldn't cooperate. Instead of telling him I had changed my mind, I said thank you. Then I just stood there while he reached for my coat and helped me into it, with his fingers gently skimming my neck as he pulled a loose curl out from where it had gotten caught in the collar. My heart raced like wild horses at the touch, from the awareness of how close his body was to mine.

"You good?" he asked. His low voice in my ear sent shivers up my spine.

"I'm good," I answered, even though my heart was still racing.

I mentally rehearsed all the reasons this was a mistake. It was just a hair comb. It shouldn't change anything. He was trouble I didn't need. He was the biggest threat to the life I was creating for myself.

Yet when he offered me his arm, I took it, and oddly enough, I didn't feel any kind of discomfort at the touch. In fact, it felt comforting to be close to him. Safe. The feeling shocked me, but I knew it had to be just another sign that I had overindulged in Fiona's punch, dulling my senses. It didn't mean anything.

"You sure, Willa?" Daphne asked, touching me lightly before I walked out the door.

"I'll be fine."

She nodded, looking as unsure as I felt inside.

THE COLD, DARK NIGHT WAS A SHOCK TO THE SENSES AFTER the warmth and laughter inside. I shivered, leaning into Cole without even thinking, with my boots crunching in the snow as we walked to his car.

"Oh, she's a beauty," I breathed out, unable to help voicing my admiration for the sleek sports car he had already started from a distance with a push of a button. I had always loved fast cars, had always appreciated the craftsmanship and power of them. It had been a long time since I had ridden in one, and I felt a thrill at the thought.

"I'm supposed to say something cool and low-key about how she gets me from A to B," Cole said, chuckling. "But I'm not that cool. I think she's a beauty, too. I don't indulge in much. Generally my tastes run pretty simple. But cars are my weakness." He opened the passenger-side door for me and helped me in.

I closed my eyes and breathed in the smell of that fabulous leather, then ran my hands over the dash.

"You must like cars, too," he said when he walked around and got in on the driver's side. There was a bit of pleasure and surprise in his voice.

"I do," I said. "Always have."

"Plug your address into the GPS for me," he said, passing me his phone. "What do you drive?"

I laughed as I typed in my house number and handed the phone back to him. "Just that beater over there," I said, pointing to the sad little compact sitting in Greg and Janet's driveway. "That's all my budget allows for these days."

"Nothing wrong with that," he said, putting the car into gear.

I itched to be in the driver's seat, to push the pedals and feel the power underneath me. It was a pleasure I had missed more than I'd ever realized.

"Nothing wrong with it at all," I said, "but I'll admit, I hope to own something like this again someday."

"You owned a sports car before?" His tone was mild. In fact, it felt deliberately casual, like he knew I had slipped up.

I tensed, as I had never intended on giving that fact away.

Did it matter though? I felt certain he knew who I was anyway. I had been protecting those pieces of myself for so long it felt like second nature, but maybe, just this once, I could have a moment of honesty.

I exhaled and felt myself relax. "Yeah. It feels like a lifetime ago sometimes."

To my relief, he didn't ask any more questions. "When you've sobered up," he said, "I'll let you take her for a spin if you want."

"Really?"

"Sure." He looked over at me and smiled—a genuine, honest-to-goodness smile.

I smiled back, unable to help myself. "You're not as mean as you look," I said before I realized what I was saying.

He instantly frowned. "Do I look mean?"

I tensed up again, an automatic reaction from knowing what Daniel's response would have been to a comment like that. Criticism had not been allowed. Ever. "Not exactly," I said. "I don't know. You make me feel uncomfortable. And I've had way too much to drink, because my brain is telling me to shut up but my mouth keeps talking."

He looked my way. "You don't have to be uncomfortable with me, Willa," he said, his voice gentle. "I would never hurt you."

"Then why do you keep digging into my past?" *Shut up, Willa. Just stop talking.*

He stayed silent for so long, staring at the dark road ahead of us as he drove toward town, that I was starting to think he hadn't heard me. Finally, he spoke. "A couple of years ago, I met someone who looked a lot like you. I was at a military ball. Lots of bigwigs there, military and government both. There was a woman there. A senator's wife. Most beautiful woman I've ever seen."

I went still as fear crept up my spine.

"The thing about my job," he continued, "is that I've seen a lot of fear. I see people when everything has gone wrong and they're afraid for their lives. Brave people. Fierce people. But the fear is still there, in their eyes. You get so familiar with it you recognize it in an instant. And that night, I saw it in hers."

I swallowed hard. "What happened to her?" I asked in a whisper.

He glanced my way. "Last I heard, she died. Had a cute little sports car like this and liked to drive it fast. Drove right over the edge of a cliff, so I was told. Real tragedy."

"Yes. A tragedy." My heart pounded so hard I thought it might explode.

"I would never hurt you," he repeated, looking at me again. He pulled up into my driveway and put the car into park, sitting silent for a moment before continuing. "When I met that woman, I felt helpless. I could see the fear in her eyes, but there wasn't a damn thing I could do to rescue her. I wasn't even sure at the time what she was scared of. I had some ideas. Possibilities. But I think now I know."

"What do you think you know?" I asked.

"I think she was someone in need of rescue and that I failed her. After all, rescuing people is my job. It's practically built into my DNA. So leaving her behind there, even if I didn't have the full picture then... It left a mark on me. I never forgot her. And if I ever saw her again? I'd never do anything that would put her in jeopardy."

I sat there, stunned.

"Sometimes I wonder," he said slowly, "if she would have remembered me the way I remembered her."

I turned my head away, unable to meet his eyes as I answered. "No, I don't think she would have," I said. "Not because you aren't a memorable person. You are. But because she was probably trained to not look at anyone else. Maybe if her husband ever thought she was noticing someone, she paid for it."

"That would make sense," he said. He continued sitting there, silent, making no move to get out of the car.

After a long minute, I put my hand on the door handle, but he stopped me.

"Can I tell you another story?" he asked.

"Okay," I said. I swallowed hard, wondering where he was going with this one.

"Has Daphne told you much about what my old job was?"

"No," I said, turning back to him. The change of subject helped me relax, if only slightly. "Believe it or not, we don't have sleepovers where we stay up giggling over you." My lips twitched as I teased him. The alcohol was still running strong through my system, allowing me to say things I wouldn't normally say.

Cole just grinned. I found myself wishing he smiled more. Some of his fierceness faded when he smiled, giving me a glimpse of the man underneath.

"Fair enough," he said. "I was a PJ."

"You'll have to forgive my ignorance. I don't know what that is."

He shrugged. "No worries. Everyone knows about the SEALs and the Green Berets. Not as many people have heard about us."

"So, special forces?"

"Yeah. In a nutshell, my job was saving people. We're trained in personnel recovery—diving, parachuting, medical aid. We do whatever it takes to recover military personnel in worst-case scenarios. When something goes wrong, they call us."

"That's impressive," I said, still not knowing where he was going with this.

He ignored the compliment. "So back to my story. Our primary job is taking care of military forces, but occasionally, we get called to rescue civilians. Usually that's in the case of national disasters or something similar, but sometimes we rescue individuals, depending on the circumstances."

"Okay..."

He turned in his seat so he was looking me in the eye. "I already told you about how I once met a senator and his wife at a ball. Never forgot her. I couldn't. Those eyes haunted me. She was someone I couldn't save—couldn't even try to save." His eyes pierced my soul.

"Right," I said, my voice shaky.

He held the pause for a minute, those eyes never leaving mine, then spoke again. "About a year after that, I was back in the area for a water ops training trip. We had just finished up a grueling week and were heading back when our CRO—combat rescue officer—told us Senator Cavendish's wife had just gone over the side of a cliff in her car. We were on site less than fifteen minutes after that car went over the edge. My teammate and I were the first ones in the water to search for her."

My heart stopped.

"Wilhelmina Cavendish," he said, looking at me pointedly. "The woman with the haunted eyes. This time, I had a chance to save her. A slim chance, but a chance nonetheless."

"What happened?"

He stared at me for a minute. "We located the car quickly. She wasn't in it. Our dive search team spread out, looking for remains. Topside, teams were looking for her on the shore. But we couldn't find her body."

I didn't speak. I couldn't.

He paused for a moment, then continued. "It was a failed mission. When I got back topside, Senator Cavendish was still on site, wailing in a way that was barely human. He vowed he would never stop looking for her. Would never stop hoping she was alive somewhere, waiting for him to find her and bring her home."

I was scared to say anything. Scared to deny it. More scared to confirm it. He knew who I was; there was no doubt about that now. He seemed sincere when he said he wouldn't do anything to jeopardize me.

But Daniel had to have pulled strings to get a special operations team out looking for me. Had he offered them money to keep looking? Had he suspected I was alive? Was that the reason Cole was in Rosemary Mountain? To find me?

The panic was back before I could stop it.

CHAPTER FOURTEEN

Cole

"Whoa," I said, watching Willa's face change. "Take a deep breath. I've got you."

Instead, her breathing sped up.

"Can I hold your hands?" I asked. I didn't want to touch her without permission, didn't want to send her further into panic. But she was at risk of hyperventilating and I needed to calm her down.

The question made her eyes widen and she shook her head. It was a tiny movement, but it was clear.

"Okay," I said, reassuring her with my hands up. "But I need you to breathe, okay? You're safe."

She watched my every movement with those wide eyes.

I nodded slowly, trying to reassure her. "Just breathe."

When her breathing finally started to slow, she spoke. "Are you going to tell him? Are you going to tell Daniel I'm alive?" Her voice was frantic and her teeth chattered like she was freezing despite the heat blasting through the vents in the car.

"No," I said. "Of course not."

"He'd pay you," she said, still shaking. Still frantic. "He'd pay anything to get me back. You know that. Not just money. He has power too."

"Do you want to go back?"

Her face paled even more and she shook her head quickly.

"Then of course not. Willa, I don't want anything to happen to you."

"Why did you tell me?"

That was a good question. I ran my hands through my hair and faced the front of the car, trying to figure out how to explain it, even to myself. Truth was, I was still trying to figure out my own reaction to Willa and why I couldn't seem to just leave things alone.

I took a breath and let it out. "I failed you twice. When I walked into Janet's shop and saw you, it was the biggest shock of my life. At first, I thought I had to be mistaken, that I was imagining the whole thing, just looking for a chance to make something right. I think that's why I kept digging, trying to find out if it was really you or not. It's still hard for me to believe it really is. I mean, what are the odds that our paths would cross like this?"

"Three times," she said, her voice soft. "That makes three times our paths have crossed. That's crazy. Especially here."

"Yeah. It is crazy. I guess that's why it feels like ... like fate." I turned and looked at her again. "Willa, I couldn't save you those first two times. But I'll be damned if I fail you again."

"What are you saying?"

I chose my words carefully, not wanting to scare her. "You've changed your look. But you've got a recognizable face, and you were practically a celebrity. It's only a matter of time before someone mentions you look like the senator's late wife. Maybe someone even decides to contact him about it for the reward money, and he decides to take a look, see if it's you."

All the color drained from her face. "Reward money?"

I cocked my head. "You didn't know? It was all over the news after you disappeared. When a week went by with no sign of you or your body, he offered a reward."

She shook her head. "I was too scared to watch the news after the first couple of days. I needed to at first. Needed to make sure they were reporting me as deceased. But after that? I just kept running and avoided it all. Maybe that wasn't the smartest move, but even the sight of him on a screen was enough to cause a panic attack back then. I couldn't draw that kind of attention. It was easier to avoid it all."

"I get that." Understood it more than she could know. My heart broke for her, even as anger built inside me toward the man who had made her afraid.

"How much?" she asked. "How much did he offer for my life?" Her voice was full of bitterness.

"Fifty thousand dollars for information that leads to the recovery of your body." I snorted, unable to help myself. "Not sure why he even bothered with that one. We're the best in the world. If we didn't find you, who'd he think would?"

A faint smile appeared on her face as she let out an exhale. "Well, at least he still believes I'm dead."

I shifted in my seat. "There's also a five hundred thousand dollar reward for information that leads to your safe return, in the event that you survived but for whatever reason are unable to contact him or make your way home. One of the big stations did a story about real-life post-trauma amnesia scenarios, including an interview with a man who hit his head and lost over forty years of memories. At the end of the special, Senator Cavendish spoke, sharing his hope that you might still be found, and announced the reward."

She closed her eyes and leaned her head back. "Half a million dollars."

"Yeah."

"I'm never going to be safe." It came out in a sob, twisted with fear.

The sound broke me. I reached over and took her hand in mine without even thinking. As soon as I did it, I regretted it, remembering that when she was panicking she hadn't wanted to be touched. But she gripped my hand tight instead of pulling away.

"You are safe," I said, trying to reassure her. "I think that's why I'm here. I can't explain it logically, but I think fate brought us together again so I can protect you this time. My gut says trouble will be here sooner rather than later. Whether you stay here or run again, I'd like to help you."

She turned her head and studied me. "Why would you do that for me? We're not even friends. You could just turn me in and collect the reward."

It stung that she would even think I was capable of that now that I believed Daniel had abused her. But she didn't know me. Not really. I shrugged and kept my voice light. "I'm not interested in money, especially if it comes at the expense of someone's safety. Plus…"

"What?" she asked.

"I don't like loose ends and you're a big one for me." I caught her gaze and held it. "Maybe I'm selfishly looking for some closure."

She shook her head again. "From what I've heard tonight, I don't think there's a selfish bone in your body, Cole."

I laughed again, trying to lighten the mood. "Tell that to my siblings. I guarantee my brothers would disagree with you."

This time, I got a real smile from her. But it faded quickly. "It's getting late, and I'm a little overwhelmed by all of this. I think I need to go in. But thanks for the ride home," she said, putting a hand on the door.

"Uh, yeah, no problem," I said, switching gears. "I'll walk you to your door."

"No need," she said. She opened the door and climbed out quickly, looking back at me with a troubled face.

"What is it?" I asked.

"Nothing." She shook her head. "Good night, Cole."

"Good night," I said.

I stayed there watching until she made it safely through the door.

Chapter Fifteen

Willa

New Year's Eve. My second as Willa Monroe. An entire calendar year had passed in which Daniel hadn't touched me, and it felt remarkable.

But the joy of it all was stained with fear. I had barely slept since Cole had told me about the reward money. It added a new level of fear to my situation. Should someone realize I looked like the late Wilhelmina Cavendish, there was even more incentive for them to take the information to Daniel. His name and position had been enough reason to worry me before. Half a million dollars was a game changer in the worst kind of way.

It spoke volumes that Cole knew who I was, knew of the reward, even had a personal connection to Daniel, and yet hadn't turned me in. Trust was a hard gift for me to give, but he kept earning it. So had Janet and Daphne, for that matter. Greg and Janet seemed to be fairly well off, for Rosemary Mountain anyway, but Daphne and Emerson lived a modest life in a small cottage. They also had a baby on the way. Half a million dollars would be life changing for them, yet Daphne and Janet seemed determined to protect me.

After living in Daniel's world, where money was king and the players all snakes, it was still hard for me to trust that any of this was real, that people could really be so genuine, kind, and good. But there were people like that in the world. People like Suzanna, who had helped me escape even though it put her at risk and she gained nothing from it. People like Greg and Janet, Daphne and Emerson. Even Cole, though his goodness was different somehow. Hidden. He still came across as someone dangerous, broody, and dark. But the more I learned about him, the more I knew that couldn't be true.

LIKE CHRISTMAS, MY NEW YEAR'S EVE WAS SPENT celebrating at Greg and Janet's house, with the family in which I was suddenly included. Champagne flowed freely as jazz played on an antique record player. Fiona had brought whiskey—again—to spike her apparently famous mulled cider, and Janet had pulled out a collection of party games that had everyone rolling. The night felt like a blur of laughter and fun, but this time, I held myself apart, staying on the sidelines. I was so very grateful for this year and these friends. But I couldn't shake the fear that it was all going to fall apart.

Shortly before midnight, I excused myself from the group, slipping outside onto Greg and Janet's back deck. The black night sky was lit up with a million stars, tiny pinpricks of light piercing the darkness. It felt like the right place for me to welcome in the new year, alone under the same stars that had hung in the sky the night I'd run. The rest of the group would count down together, sharing midnight kisses. But I needed something quieter, something more sacred. As grateful as I was for how my new friends had welcomed me into their lives, the reality was that I was on my own. It felt fitting that I welcome the new year alone too, with only the stars for company.

But before the clock struck midnight, the door opened and shut quietly. Soft footsteps came my direction. I closed my eyes and took a deep breath, fighting against the adrenaline that had immediately flooded my body. I looked back up at the stars and practiced staying calm, reminding myself that everyone here was safe. I didn't have to run; I didn't have to fight. It was a lesson in discipline to keep my eyes focused on the heavens above me instead of looking to see who was approaching.

But I knew who it was before he even reached me. Somehow, I recognized his presence, though I couldn't figure out how. Had I memorized his walk? The subtle scent of his cologne? I couldn't even be sure. I only knew that, somehow, I knew it was him.

"You seem deep in thought out here." Cole joined me where I was leaning against the railing of the deck.

I wrapped my arms around myself even tighter. "Yeah. Sorry. I just needed a minute."

"Everything okay?"

I glanced back to make sure we were alone. "I'm okay. I just felt like I needed to start off my new year out here, under the stars. It doesn't feel right to start the year surrounded by them, knowing I may leave at any time. They're a family. They'll have each other forever. But I'll probably be gone by next year."

He was quiet for a moment. "Is it okay if I stay out here with you? I'll go back in if you really want to be alone. But if you don't mind the company, we can be outsiders together. After all, I'll be gone by next year, too."

I looked over at him and realized he probably felt the same way I did. Alone in the world, an outsider welcomed into this tight family group. And in another moment of surprise—something that kept happening with Cole—I realized I didn't want to be alone out here after all. I wanted him to stay.

"I don't mind," I said, feeling suddenly shy.

"I appreciate it." His face changed as he spotted the comb in my hair and reached out to touch it. Another touch that didn't hurt or make me afraid. Another moment of surprise. "You wore the comb I gave you."

"I did," I said. "I really love it. It means something to me."

"It means something to me that you wore it." He looked at me and I got lost in his eyes. They swam with depths of feeling I didn't understand. But he broke my gaze and looked away. "Wow," he said, his tone changing as he looked up at the night sky. "Incredible."

"Isn't it? It's so beautiful out here in the country. I love seeing the stars like this."

"Yeah. It's the perfect night for it too."

"It is." I looked back up at them, feeling a newfound peace. Part of it was the stars. Part of it was having a friend who knew the truth about my past, someone I could actually be honest with. That was a gift, and one I might not have again when I ran. It made me want to open up and talk—yet another surprise. "I was just thinking about how tonight is a milestone. An entire calendar year without him in my life. I'm grateful for it, but..."

"But also afraid it won't last," he said, finishing for me.

"Exactly." I let out a sigh of frustration. "I wish I could count on a future here. But that's not realistic. I knew when I left that my life would never be 'normal' again. What I didn't expect was to find somewhere that I truly loved, somewhere I really wanted to stay. Last year, I rang in the new year at a motel in South Dakota. This year, I'm here. But where will I be next year? I can't make plans for the future. All I can count on is being underneath the same stars, wherever I am."

I looked over at him, deciding to tell him one more piece of my heart. "That's one of the reasons why I loved this comb the moment I saw it. The stars have always felt like friends to me. When I was a kid, my mom would drive me out into the country, to places just like this so we could watch them. She would tell me their names and trace the constellations in the sky. Those friends lit my way that night, when I ran. They are the only thing I know I'll always have, no matter where I am."

He leaned forward on the railing, standing so close I could feel the heat from his body. But his closeness didn't trigger alarm bells in my body. Instead, to my astonishment, it made me feel safe.

"Come to think of it," he said in that quiet voice of his, "I've rang in the new year somewhere different for the last, oh, twelve years or so. Maybe more. I'm always on the move too, just for different reasons."

"Doesn't it bother you?" I asked, glancing over at him.

"It never has," he said. "I've never been the type to stay in one place."

"Why is that?"

He chuckled. "I dunno. I've never thought about it. I guess probably because I grew up feeling trapped in a tiny town. Never went anywhere, never really traveled. My parents weren't the type. Their idea of a vacation was camping at the state park less than an hour away. Me, I always felt restless. Wanted to see the world. So I did."

"Good for you," I said, smiling. "I know what it's like to feel trapped. And how good it feels to break free of that."

"I know you do," he said, turning toward me. His face turned serious. "But you don't want to be on the move. You want to stay here, don't you?"

"I do," I said, feeling the truth of it in my heart. "What I want more than anything is to just settle down and live a quiet life here. But I know it's not possible. I'm just trying to enjoy my time here while I can, and I hope I recognize when it's time to leave."

"He's a powerful man," Cole said after a moment of contemplation.

"He is."

"I've been thinking it over, from all different angles. Trying to come up with a plan. I have some ideas, but I want to think them through more before I tell you."

I couldn't help but feel amused. "Are you thinking of killing him? Because that's the only way I'm ever going to be free."

He looked at me with a sudden frown on his face. "Are you asking me to?"

Shock rippled through me. "Of course not. It was a joke. I don't believe in murder. Not even for him."

"Neither do I," he said as the frown was replaced with a grin. "For a minute there, I was worried I was going to have to turn you in to the sheriff for suggesting it."

I relaxed, suddenly liking him even more. His intensity convinced me he was more than capable of lethality, but I liked knowing that his moral compass stopped him from considering it.

"So, murder is out. What's your idea?" I asked.

He shook his head. "Give me some more time. Then we'll talk. I'm still gathering information and thinking right now. But if I can come up with a way, I would like to help you."

"Thank you." I turned toward him, wrapping my shawl tightly around my shoulders.

"You're cold," he said, frowning.

"A little. But it's okay." I glanced at my watch. "Thirty seconds to go. I want to ring in the new year out here."

He reached out tentatively, rubbing my arms with his hands. Warmth spread throughout my body, and I found myself wanting to lean into him. Wanting his arms wrapped around me. Wanting to feel my body pressed up against his. The desire was unexpected and shocking. It seemed Cole was constantly making me rethink everything.

"Willa," he said, "you're freezing. You need to go inside."

"Not until midnight."

"Okay. Then we'll stay out here together."

Twenty seconds. My heart pounded as I realized I wanted something else, something I was almost afraid to ask for.

"Cole?" I swallowed hard, as nerves rippled through my body.

"Yeah?"

"I know this is silly. But I may never have another chance at a midnight kiss on New Year's Eve. Would you..."

His eyes widened in surprise. "You want me to kiss you?"

I nodded, still nervous—but sure. "At midnight. For good luck. It's tradition."

He studied me, then nodded.

Ten. Nine. Eight.

The group inside started counting down, loud enough for us to hear. Cole's hands stayed on my arms, slowly rubbing them for warmth. I took another step toward him.

What was I thinking? This was silly, inappropriate even. Technically speaking, I was still married. Sure, Daniel had broken his vows long ago —he hadn't even waited until our honeymoon was over to break his vow of fidelity. But still. I had been entirely faithful, even after leaving him. Now, I was asking a man to kiss me? I shouldn't.

Seven. Six. Five.

"I'm sorry," I said, shaking my head. "I shouldn't have asked you, I shouldn't—"

"Willa," he stopped me, his voice quiet.

Three. Two.

One.

He pulled me to him and brushed his lips against mine. It was soft, tender, and unbearably slow. I felt myself melting into him, asking for more, even as he pulled away.

"For luck. A kiss under your lucky stars. Happy New Year," he whispered, running his thumb over my cheek.

"Happy—" I was cut off as he put his lips on mine again, firmer this time. His hand slipped to the back of my head, pulling me closer, as he took the kiss deeper, teasing, tasting. I wrapped my arms around his waist, wanting to get lost in him.

But he pulled back again, looking shocked by himself. "I'm sorry. Maybe we should go inside," he said, his voice coming out strained. "We need to get you warmed up."

I nodded, even though it was the last thing I wanted. "Yes. Yes, you're right." The truth was I felt perfectly warm now, in his arms, with the heat of our kiss running through me.

He dropped his arms and turned, walking toward the door. I followed him in, feeling shock and confusion as I realized I wanted more than to stay in Rosemary Mountain.

I wanted Cole Hawkins.

Chapter Sixteen

Cole

My fist slammed into the punching bag so hard it nearly knocked Emerson off his feet.

"Whoa," he said, laughing as he repositioned himself. "Last time I took it out on the bag that hard, it was because I was torn up over a certain redheaded woman. You having woman trouble, Cole?"

"I don't have a woman," I retorted, pounding my fist into the bag again.

But that was the problem, wasn't it? Ever since that kiss, I hadn't been able to get Willa out of my mind. I dreamed of her at night, thought of her every day. Made up stupid excuses to stop by Janet's store to check on her.

But I hadn't worked up the courage to ask her out on a date.

It wasn't even the fact that she was technically married. I was an old-fashioned guy all the way when it came to that, but I was well aware that Senator Cavendish had broken his marriage vows in multiple ways. I also had a strong feeling that had divorce been an option, Willa would have simply taken that route. A woman didn't throw away her entire life and what would have been a hefty amount of financial assets and spousal support to live in a run-down rental on barely more than minimum wage unless going the legal route wasn't an option for her. The way I saw it, a legal document didn't make a marriage. Commitment, loyalty, fidelity, and love made a marriage. Senator Cavendish had failed on all fronts.

But I didn't know how Willa saw things or if my asking her out would scare her off. We were starting to develop a bit of a friendship. She no longer looked like she was bracing herself for trouble every time I stepped foot into the store. She had started relaxing around me, even acting like she looked forward to my visits.

Asking her on an honest-to-goodness date might change all of that. But not asking her was driving me nuts.

"Wanna talk about it?" Emerson asked after I hit the bag a few more times.

"Nope," I said, grabbing a towel to dry off.

"Okay. Well, I know you're in a mood, but we need to talk about the next training exercise."

"What about it?"

"The chief's ready to kick it up a notch. Wants you to teach some rock climbing skills to those on the crew who haven't done it. Get them working in teams, teach them to belay properly. Word on the street is we're going to get an influx of climbers this summer. You and I know they probably know what they're doing, but Chief's picturing all the worst-case scenarios of needing to air evac someone from a climb where the chopper can't land."

"Alright," I said before taking a swig of my water bottle. "I'll handle it."

"I told him you would. Also, Daphne told me to invite you to dinner tonight. And before you tell me you're busy, even though we both know you aren't, you might be interested to know she invited Willa too." He shot me an amused look.

That caught my interest. "Well, as it turns out, I wasn't going to say I'm busy." *At least not after you mentioned Willa.* "What time do you want me to come over?"

"She said six."

"Okay." I hesitated a moment, wondering how to ask the question delicately. "Who's cooking, you or her?"

He cracked up. "Neither. She's picking up clam chowder from the market and bread from the bakery. You're safe."

"Sounds good."

"Listen, man," he said, parking himself next to me on the bench where I was cooling off. "I know you don't want to talk about it, but I saw you kissing Willa on New Year's Eve."

I groaned, running a hand over my face. *Great.* That's just what I needed. "Did everyone see?"

"Nah. Just me and Fiona, I think. I haven't said anything to Daphne, although honestly, she probably knows. I think she invited you both over to play matchmaker."

"Huh. Interesting."

"So, what gives?" he asked. "You were all negative and weird about Willa. Now you're kissing her and my wife is trying to set the two of you up? I feel like both of you have seriously left me out of the loop here."

I tossed the towel into my bag. "Didn't know you were so big on romantic gossip, Emerson."

He grinned. "I'm not. But if my wife's invested, so am I. And I wouldn't mind seeing you happy. So, what's the deal?"

"I dunno." I took another swig of water, wondering how to explain it. "I like her."

"Obviously."

"She's a brave woman," I said after a pause. "I like that. Life hasn't always been easy for her—isn't easy for her now. But somehow, she's still bright and cheery. Optimistic. Happy."

"Unlike your moody self," he said, punching me lightly on the shoulder.

"Point taken."

"Speaking of which," Emerson said, clearing his throat. He drummed his fingers on the bench, obviously reluctant to say whatever was on his mind.

"What now?" I asked, sighing.

"Well. I don't really know how to ask this. But why exactly are you so down these days? We haven't talked about it, but you've changed. You were a lot happier back in the day."

I cracked a little grin. "You mean back when we were both fresh to service, still bright-eyed and bushy-tailed? Back when we were idealistic and thought everything was black and white and that we were going to make the world a better place?"

He shifted. "Yeah. I guess that's what I mean."

I leaned forward, running a hand over my face. "I guess I just grew up. You know as well as I do that war is an ugly thing. Shit happens. Life-or-death decisions get made based on political or financial outcomes, barely taking the human lives involved into consideration." I let out another sigh, as my mood darkened just thinking about it all. "Emerson, I didn't join because I wanted to see people die. I know you didn't, either. We both wanted to help. But you can't always do that. There were people I couldn't save." *Including Willa.* "People I couldn't even try to save. Or people who died while I was saving someone else, often because someone behind a desk got to choose whose life was more important. After a while, I guess it just got to me."

"You did a lot of good in the world," he said. "I don't have to know all the details of your operations to know that. But people talk, and I heard some of it. What you did mattered. You have to know that."

I swallowed hard. "I know. I do know that. But it never felt like enough, you know? You can save ninety-nine out of a hundred, and it's still that one you lost that hits the hardest. That's the one that keeps you up at night."

He clapped me on the shoulder. "And yet you're here, doing the same thing. Working with us to save lives. We don't win them all here, either, you know. We try our best for every patient, but we lose some sometimes. That's life."

"I know," I said, nodding. "But it's different here and you know it. It's not as complicated. Fewer politics. No war. Working here in the life flight program, has saving someone ever meant killing another?"

He shook his head. "No."

"Exactly. You may lose people sometimes, and that's bad enough. But you never have to take a life in order to save one."

He was quiet for a moment. "You weren't around for all the trouble last year. But three times, Daphne's life was in danger. You think I wouldn't have killed to save her life?"

"But you didn't have to," I pointed out.

"No." He shook his head. "I didn't." He was quiet again. "Daphne says Willa may be in some trouble. You know anything about that?"

"I might." I trusted Emerson as much as any man could trust another. I would trust him with my life in a heartbeat. But Willa's secrets weren't mine to tell, and I wasn't going to break her trust.

"And if Willa was in trouble? What would you do to save her?"

I didn't answer, but I knew he didn't expect me to. We both knew the answer already.

If Willa was in trouble, I wouldn't hesitate to do whatever it took to save her life.

It was stupid to go by Janet's store on my way home. After all, I would be seeing Willa that night at Daphne and Emerson's.

I stopped in anyway, unwilling to wait even three hours to see her again. I shook my head, imagining what my mom would say if she saw me. "You're smitten," she'd say, wagging her finger at me. "Positively smitten with that girl."

She would have been right. It had been a long time since I had been unable to stay away from a woman. But Willa was special. And it wasn't just because of our past connection and "loose ends," like I had described it to her.

I liked her. Admired her. Thought she might just be the bravest, spunkiest woman I had ever met—and that was saying a lot, considering the nature of my own sisters. Yes, I liked Willa—the *real* Willa—and I didn't want to wait another three hours to see her.

But when I opened the door, she wasn't behind the counter where she should be. The store was unlocked, but it was empty, with no sign of Willa or Janet anywhere.

"Hello?" I called out, all my senses immediately on alert. No one answered. I moved across the store, toward the break room in the back.

I froze when I turned the corner. Willa was sitting on the couch, as white as a ghost, staring into space like she didn't even hear me.

"Willa?"

Nothing.

She just sat there, unmoving.

I crossed the room and knelt down on the floor in front of her, taking her hands in mine. They were freezing cold. She looked at me, finally, but still barely seemed to see me. Shock was written all over her.

"Willa," I repeated, keeping my voice low and calm as I rubbed her hands, trying to warm them. "What happened? Are you hurt?"

She started shaking all over at the question.

"Who hurt you?" I growled, unable to keep my voice mild.

She shook her head. "No. No. I'm not hurt. I just…"

"What?"

"You were right. Someone recognized me."

Everything within me turned cold. Even though I had known it would happen eventually, I hadn't expected it this soon. Not now, not when I hadn't had a chance to put any plans into place.

"What happened?" I asked, needing to know how bad it was. Her words had snapped me into mission mode.

She started shaking again, pulling me back to the real world. The mission could wait. She was scared, and I couldn't stop myself. I sat beside her on the couch and put my arms around her, holding her tight, wanting to soothe and comfort. Wanting to protect her from any threat, no matter what it was.

And when she melted into my arms, clinging to me like she was drowning, I never wanted to let go.

"A group came in," she said when she could finally talk. "A club of retired women from Asheville, doing some tourist scavenger hunt or something. I don't know." She shook her head like she still couldn't believe it. "One of them kept staring at me. Then she started whispering to her friend. They approached me. Told me I looked so much like that poor girl who died, the senator's wife, and asked if I was related to her. I tried to just play it off, told them no, but that I've heard I resemble her in the past. The one woman said it was uncanny. She just kept watching me."

"It's probably nothing," I said, still holding her since she hadn't pulled away. I ran my hand up and down her arm, holding back from kissing her hair the way I wanted to. "I'm sure you did great."

"No," she said, shaking her head. "Those two kept whispering about it and staring at me. I have a terrible feeling about the whole thing."

"We're talking about two retired women from Asheville," I said, trying to reassure her. "They probably like to play detective. They may talk about it for days, but I'm sure they'll move on to something else without doing anything about it."

"But what if..." She started shaking again.

"I'm here," I said. "You're not alone. You want to run again? I'll help you." I meant it. I'd drop everything and run with her if that's what it took. The certainty came over me in an instant.

"I don't want to run," she said, her voice breaking. She glanced around the room as if finally seeing it instead of the horrors of her past. "I don't want to leave this. I'll never get to build something like this for myself again if I run."

"Then you stay."

"And if he comes?"

"We fight."

Chapter Seventeen

Willa

My hands shook as I buttoned up my coat. It was silly. Even if that woman had left the store and immediately called Daniel on a direct line, he couldn't possibly have made it to Rosemary Mountain yet. I was safe.

For now.

Cole was probably right though. After all, it was two elderly women who were likely bored and enjoyed making their outings more interesting with drama and gossip. I probably wasn't their first conspiracy theory.

Maybe just the first one they'd gotten right.

But for now, I was safe. After I had calmed down, I had insisted that Cole go about the rest of his day like normal, even though he had offered to stay with me. I had been more tempted than I wanted to admit to take him up on his offer. When he held me, I felt so safe. So protected. For the first time in years, I hadn't wanted to pull out of someone's embrace. I wanted to sink into it.

Cole was making me feel things I thought I would never feel again. Making me want things I never expected to want again.

But I couldn't rely on him to protect me even if I wanted to. After all, he had already told me he wasn't the type of guy to hang around in one place for too long.

Still, I took comfort in the fact that I would feel safe for the evening with him and Emerson around. I had a feeling both of them could handle themselves quite well. And maybe after a few hours had passed and I had gotten some distance from the event, I would realize it was nothing and feel safe again. If I couldn't have Cole, all I wanted was to feel safe enough to stay in Rosemary Mountain.

Before he left, Cole had also offered to give me private fighting lessons—as if I could ever possibly defend myself against Daniel alone. I knew better than that. I had said yes anyway, trying to convince myself it was because I wanted to learn, not just because I wanted to spend more time with him.

LATER THAT EVENING, I PULLED MY CAR INTO DAPHNE AND Emerson's driveway, feeling a pang of disappointment that Cole's car wasn't there yet. The disappointment was replaced by instant guilt. Daphne was my best friend here. She should have top loyalty over a guy I didn't even know that well.

But when she opened the door and I saw Cole standing by the fireplace, drink in hand and chatting with Emerson, my heart gave an unexpected leap.

"Hey, girl," Daphne said, giving me a knowing smile before hugging me tight. "Come on in. Want a drink? The boys are having bourbon, but there's wine if you want it."

"Actually, bourbon sounds great," I said.

She raised her eyebrows in a look of approval. "Bourbon it is. Emerson, will you get Willa a glass?" she asked, turning to him.

"Sure thing."

"I'm just going to pop into the kitchen to check on dinner. Actually, come help me. Willa, you don't mind waiting a few minutes on that drink, do you?" she asked with a wink. She grabbed Emerson's arm and dragged him to the kitchen with her, leaving me alone with Cole in the living room.

"Hey," Cole said, the corner of his lips turning up into a small smile.

"Hey," I said, feeling suddenly shy. I walked to where he was, pretending it was so I could warm my hands in front of the crackling fire in the stone fireplace. Just two hours ago, I had fallen apart in his arms, and I found myself craving that intimacy. But he wasn't mine to touch. Despite the intensity of our New Year's Eve kiss, he hadn't even asked me out. Not that I blamed him. My life was a complicated mess, and so was I.

"You okay?" he asked quietly. The ice cube in his bourbon rattled against the glass as he raised it to his lips.

"Yeah." I hesitated, then made a decision. "Daphne knows who I am. I don't think she's told Emerson, and we've only talked about it once, briefly. I don't want to make tonight about me. But later, I may bring up what happened. Bring Emerson into the loop. Do you think that's a good idea or a mistake?"

"If you're asking whether I trust Emerson, the answer is yes. Completely."

"Okay." I nodded, then took a deep breath. "It's scary for the circle of people who know to grow bigger."

He reached out and ran his hand up my arm. Delicious shivers went through me. "Not if it's a circle of people who all want to protect you. Then, the bigger the circle the better."

I took comfort in the thought. "You're right. I hadn't thought of it that way. Hey, change of subject, but where's that fancy sports car of yours tonight? It wasn't out front, so I didn't realize you were here yet."

He grinned. "Hate to disappoint you, but I walked here."

"Of course you did." I smiled, picturing it. He wasn't the type to drive a car if the destination was a short hike away. Not like Daniel, who only walked if it was a photo opportunity.

"You guys ready to eat?" Daphne asked, poking her head into the living room. "The baby's hungry."

"The baby is always hungry. Morning, noon, and night," Emerson said, grinning.

Daphne elbowed him. "Watch it or I'm going to eat your helping of dessert."

"You can have my dessert anytime, babe," he said before planting a sweet kiss on her lips.

She melted into him, and they both seemed to forget we were even there.

My heart gave a little tug. I loved watching them together, even if it reminded me of how lonely I was. Lonely was okay—it was infinitely better than being with someone who took pleasure in cruelty. But their obvious affection and easy-going relationship painted a picture of what life could have been, had I simply chosen better. They could tease each other without the other one getting angry or storming off. There was no unspoken tension, no threat hiding right below the surface. Just two people who adored each other and were genuinely happy to be together.

It was beautiful.

"We should probably head to the table so they stop kissing," Cole whispered, nudging me. But there was only humor in his voice.

"Probably," I agreed.

He cleared his throat loudly enough to get their attention. Daphne jumped away, blushing, but Emerson just grinned.

"It's my house, man," Emerson said. "I can kiss my wife if I want."

She swatted him. "Sorry, guys. Pregnancy hormones. Dinner's ready. Come on."

"After you," Cole said.

I walked ahead and felt his hand go to my back, which made me catch my breath. He instantly removed it, and I realized he had probably misinterpreted my little gasp. But it wasn't fear or discomfort I felt with his hand on me. It was pure pleasure. But there was no way to smoothly correct his assumption and let him know how very much I wanted his hands on me again.

Dinner was full of laughter, teasing, and fun. It was another one of those incredible slices of normal that I had been missing for so long—ever since I had met Daniel, honestly. He had swooped into my life and taken every bit of normal away, initially replacing it with excitement, then with horror. Every time I got a piece of normal back, it felt like I was winning. But it also made it harder to know I could lose them all again.

Despite telling Cole I would talk to Daphne and Emerson about the situation, the pure normalcy of the night made me not want to. I didn't want to ruin even one moment of the evening with talk of Daniel or the past.

It would wait for another day.

After dinner and board games, where Cole once again surprised me by how funny he could be when he relaxed, I decided to be bold.

"It's getting late," I said. "I should probably drive home. Janet needs me to open the store for her tomorrow. Cole, I know you walked here. Would you like a ride home?"

"Yes. Thanks," he said.

Our eyes met, with so much unsaid between them. It felt like I was offering more than a ride home. But I wasn't exactly sure what. I only knew I wasn't ready to say goodnight to him.

Daphne and Emerson exchanged looks, both appearing to be trying to hide back smiles. Cole and I both ignored it, despite how obvious they were being. And instead of drawing out slow goodbyes, as was the typical custom here in Rosemary Mountain, Daphne practically pushed us out the door. I wasn't sure if she was deliberately playing matchmaker or if those pregnancy hormones she mentioned meant she was in a hurry to have Emerson to herself. Either way, it made me smile.

"You live pretty close, right?" I asked as we loaded up into my car. I knew that Cole was renting Emerson's old cabin and that it was on the mountain too. I just wasn't sure where.

"Yeah," he said. "It's the log cabin about halfway down the road."

"Oh, okay. Not far at all then."

"No. No, it's not."

In fact, we pulled into his driveway way more quickly than I would have liked.

"I guess we're even now," I joked. "You brought me home on New Year's Eve. Now I've returned the favor."

He looked at me, so serious, like he was heavily debating what to say next. "Would you like to come inside?" he finally asked.

"Yeah," I said, feeling suddenly shy again. "Yeah, I'll come in. For a bit."

Relief flashed across his face. I suddenly laughed.

"What?" he asked.

I just shook my head, laughing again. "Us. Cole, what's happening between us? I feel like we're both completely awkward and dancing around this, like two high school kids who don't even know how to talk to each other."

He grinned. "Yeah, that sounds about right."

"So can we skip that and just talk about it?"

He nodded. "Absolutely. Let's start with this. I'd like for you to come inside. I'd like to talk and get to know each other better. But I didn't know if you would feel comfortable with that. I don't even know if you feel comfortable with *me*. I also don't know anything about what you went through with Daniel, so I'm always scared to make a misstep. I don't want to push too hard or scare you."

"I'm not scared when I'm with you," I said softly. "Not anymore. In fact, I feel safer with you than I've felt with anyone in a long time. The main reason I was uncomfortable in the beginning was because you recognized me, and that was a threat. And you're intense. But I know now that you have a good heart, no matter how broody and grumpy you come across."

He frowned. "Am I really that broody and grumpy?"

"Yes." I laughed out loud again. "Didn't you know?"

He shook his head. "I guess I'll have to work on that."

I bit my lip. "So, going back to what you said ... I'd like to come in. I'd like to talk and get to know you better, too."

He reached over and took my hand in his, running his thumb over my wrist. "That sounds like a good place to start."

· · ·

I followed Cole up to his front door, where he let me into the small cabin. It was rustic, charming, and entirely masculine. No decorations at all, just furniture, though I supposed that made sense. Emerson had probably taken all of his personal items to Daphne's when they'd gotten married and moved in together. And Cole was just here temporarily—no need to decorate.

A pang of sadness hit at that thought, but I brushed it off. Tonight wasn't a night for that.

"Here, let me take your coat," Cole said, helping me out of it.

"Thanks," I said, relishing the feel of his hands as they slid down my arms. "Your cabin is nice."

"Yeah." He glanced around as if noticing it for the first time. "It works. For now."

I turned to face him. "I feel like the awkwardness is coming back."

He grinned. "Me too."

"I haven't been on a date in a very long time." My face turned hot as I realized what I was saying. "Not that I'm assuming this is a date."

A look of contemplation crossed his face. "What if I said I want it to be a date?"

"Do you?"

He looked me dead in the eyes. "Willa, I've wanted to take you on a date since the minute I laid eyes on you."

Heat swept through my body. "At Janet's store?"

He shook his head. "No. At the ball where I first met you. From the very first moment you spoke to me. You captivated me even then. I never forgot you."

"We've really met before?"

He nodded.

I shook my head in disbelief. "I know you mentioned having met us at a ball, but I guess I thought you meant you met Daniel, and I was just in attendance. I wish I could remember when we met. I wish I could remember *you*."

He took my hand and led me over to the couch. "It was October the year before you disappeared, at a military ball held at some fancy hotel. I forget the name of it now. Didn't seem important at the time. You were wearing this gorgeous dark-blue gown, an off-the-shoulder thing with crystals on it. I remember looking at you and thinking your beauty shined like a star in the midnight sky. But you were the saddest star I had ever seen. Eyes fighting back tears, and fear written all over you, no matter how hard you tried to be brave. I couldn't keep my eyes off you. Then, imagine my surprise when I found myself alone with you. I tried to talk to you, but you ran away, just like Cinderella at the ball."

I knew the exact dress he was talking about. At the mention of it, the memories of that night came roaring back.

Daniel placed a hand lightly on my back. I tensed immediately, but when I looked up at him, his face was calm—cheerful, even.

"I think we've had enough of this party, don't you?" he whispered, toying with the zipper of my dress. It was one of his favorite games, reminding me that he had total control of me, even in public. That he could humiliate me at will, and I couldn't do a thing about it.

"It's been a lovely party, but I'm happy to leave whenever you want to." I chose my words carefully, knowing that his comment could be a trap. If he was enjoying himself but I indicated that I wasn't, he would blame me for ruining his fun. If he wanted to leave but sensed I wanted to stay, he would start stewing in anger. The only right answer was to be happy and compliant and to have zero opinions of my own. It burned like acid.

"Go upstairs to our room," he whispered, tugging the zipper down another inch, despite the fact that we were surrounded by people.

I blushed in humiliation, mortified as one of the older women saw what he was doing and sent me a knowing smile. All she saw was a man who appeared desperately in love with his bride, unable to keep his hands off her.

She had no idea how right—and wrong—she was.

"Okay," I replied, forcing a tiny smile. At least here, in a public hotel, he wasn't likely to hurt me. He only wanted sex. I could endure that, despite how much I despised his every touch. Hated that he owned me and that no was never an option.

"I'll be up later. I expect you to be on your knees, waiting for me." He tugged the zipper down another inch, loosening my top dangerously.

I swallowed back bile, forcing myself to breathe and not respond with any of the retorts I was thinking, knowing I would pay for it if I did. I just nodded, turned, and walked wordlessly to the elevators, fighting back the tears. The minute I got out of his sight, I reached toward my back and tugged up the zipper to the dress. If he followed me and saw it, I would pay for that. But I couldn't bear to be seen with it unzipped. It was humiliating, being his toy.

When I got into the elevator, a man in military dress uniform was inside. I didn't make eye contact—Daniel had trained me not to. I kept my head down and pushed the button for our floor, trying not to weep.

"Are you okay, ma'am?" The low voice startled me.

I looked up at him, unable to help it, but my eyes swam with tears and I barely saw him. "I'm fine. I'm always fine. I have to be."

He stepped forward. "You don't seem fine. Do you need help?"

The elevator doors opened and I left the man inside without saying another word.

I looked at Cole, my mouth open in shock. "You were the man in the elevator."

He nodded. "Yeah, I was. I should have gone after you."

I immediately shook my head. "No. Daniel came up right after. He would have killed us both if he had seen you follow me to my hotel room."

Anger flared in his eyes. "I'd like to see him try."

"You don't know what he's like."

He shook his head. "No, I don't. Not like you do. But I've known plenty of dangerous men, Willa. I'm not scared of them. And I'm not scared of him."

The look in his eyes told me he meant every word. He wasn't scared of Daniel.

But I still was.

Chapter Eighteen

Cole

Willa left soon after the mention of Daniel. I cursed myself for even bringing that night up, no matter how much I wanted her to remember. Our first "date" should have been about us, not about him. It was a mistake to bring the past into it.

But I was bound and determined to get a second chance.

Second chances would have to wait temporarily though. If those two women were going to cause issues for Willa, we needed to prepare, and we might not have a lot of time. I'd happily play bodyguard and stick with her all the time, but she hadn't asked for that, and I wanted to be careful about how far I pushed. I still didn't know what all she had experienced while being married to Daniel, but I was certain he had controlled every aspect of her life. I sure as hell wasn't going to do the same thing, no matter how much I wanted to keep her safe. Freedom mattered. I, of all people, knew that.

· · ·

The next evening, I let myself into the training room at the sheriff's station, grateful Greg had loaned me the use of it. Willa wouldn't be returning to any of our public classes after her reaction at the first. But she had agreed to take some private self-defense lessons from me, despite her obvious skepticism that it would do her any good.

I hoped she never needed any of the skills, but the pessimist in me said she would. Even if her sorry excuse for an ex never came after her, the world was a dangerous place for women. Rosemary Mountain felt like a pretty safe place in general, but shit still happened. And as cautious as Willa was about certain things, like that backpack she took everywhere she went—clearly a go bag in case she needed to run—she took a hell of a lot of chances in other ways. Closing the store alone, walking to and from work instead of driving her car, living in the worst neighborhood in town. I knew it was likely all she could afford, but still. I didn't like it.

I didn't like how much I was worrying about her, either. It felt like I was crossing some sort of line, thinking of her as mine to protect when she wasn't. But I couldn't deny how I felt about her. The more time I spent with her, the more I liked her. She was funny, smart, interesting— and braver than anyone else would ever know. Watching her blossom and build something for herself here in Rosemary Mountain was incredible. *She* was incredible.

But she looked incredibly tentative when she opened the door to the training room and stepped inside.

"Hi," she said, watching me from across the room.

"Hi." I stuck my hands inside my pockets and wondered how it was possible that just the sight of someone could make me immediately feel better.

She didn't seem to have the same reaction to me though—at least not tonight. It was clear she was terrified of even coming into the room.

"Willa," I said, clearing my throat. "It's normal to be nervous. Especially after last time. We'll take it slow, okay? Nothing scary tonight."

"What are we going to start with?" She remained frozen in the doorway.

"How about we start by working on your punches? You can hit me, and I promise not to hit back. As we go, I'll start blocking some of them, but I'll do it gently."

"I don't want to hurt you," she said, shaking her head.

I grinned, trying not to laugh. "I promise, you're not going to hurt me. But if it will make you feel better, we'll start with a punching bag. Think of it as taking out some aggression. You can even print out a picture of his face and tape it on there if you want."

That at least got a smile and two steps forward.

"Okay," she agreed. "I'll hit the punching bag. No photographs though. I'm not ready to even imagine hitting him."

"Deal," I said, knowing I had won another small victory. The first was getting her here again; the second was getting her to relax and agree to hit the damn bag.

It would be more therapeutic than she probably realized. The woman had taken amazing steps toward empowering herself in other ways, but she seemed to have a real block as far as protecting herself went. It made sense. But I wanted to help her work on that block if I could.

"Alright," I said when she finally made it over to the bag. "First things first. Start by making a fist."

She did, doing exactly what I had been afraid she would.

"We've gotta fix this," I said, reaching over to adjust her thumb. I glanced at her, making sure she was okay with the contact. It seemed she was getting more comfortable with that, but I worried that here, where she had panicked before, the rules might be different.

She didn't react though, so I breathed a little sigh of relief.

"Don't tuck your thumb in like that. It could break, and then you're in more trouble than before. Hold it here. Keep these knuckles lined up. You're going to want to strike primarily with this surface right here." I tapped her top two knuckles. "Keep your wrist straight. Give it a try."

She gave the bag a halfhearted punch that barely moved it.

"You can do better than that," I said. "Come on. It's just a bag. You aren't hurting anyone, and it sure isn't going to hurt you. Give it a real punch. Use your whole body, not just your arm. The force comes from your core. Like this." I demonstrated on the bag, then held it in place for her.

She blew out a breath, then put a look of determination on her face and tried again, with significantly better success.

"Excellent," I said, grinning. "You're improving already. Now do it again."

AFTER AN HOUR OF WORKING ON THE BAG, TEACHING HER different strikes and kicks, I decided to call it good for the night. Her mood had shifted in a positive way, and I didn't want to try anything that might put a damper on it. Not yet. That would come in time. For now, I just wanted her to stay in the empowerment zone and get comfortable hitting things.

Next time, I'd get her comfortable with hitting me.

But for now, I was happy with her progress and told her so as she downed a bottle of water.

"Thanks," she said, flushing happily. "That was actually kind of fun."

"It is," I agreed.

"I was nervous about coming," she admitted.

"I know. I threw you in too fast in the group class. I'm sorry for that."

"It's not your fault," she said, waving it off. "You didn't know."

"I knew it was a possibility though," I said, the guilt still eating at me. "It was an error in judgment. I want you to learn these skills and feel empowered to protect yourself. Wanted it so much I thought I could just throw you into the deep end in a group class and it would be fine. That was a mistake."

She plopped down on the mat. I lowered myself to the floor beside her, happy she wasn't running for the door. If she wanted to talk, I'd sit here and talk to her all night long. Happily.

"You were special forces," she said, fiddling with the top of her water bottle. "Your group of friends probably wouldn't freak out over something so minor, no matter what they had been through. Right? So you couldn't have seen it coming, even if you knew there might have been an issue like that in my past. I'm just a weaker person than you're used to working with."

I shook my head. "No. You're wrong about that, Willa. You're not weak at all. You're one of the strongest people I've ever known."

She laughed. "I assure you, I'm not."

I looked at this woman, wondering how on earth she couldn't see what I saw. "You got out of a bad situation," I said, "and you're building a life for yourself on your own. That's no little thing."

She blew out a breath. "No, I guess it's not," she agreed. "Thank you for seeing that." Her voice was soft as she looked at me, like my approval really meant something to her. It made my heart swell a bit, knowing I was the one to put that look of happiness on her face.

"And trust me," I said, wanting to reassure her, "even in special forces, trauma is trauma. You think we never have issues with any of it? You would be dead wrong about that."

"Really?" she asked, cocking her head. "Have you ever…" She trailed off like she wasn't quite sure how to finish the sentence. Or was afraid to.

"Of course I have," I said. As hard as it was for me to talk to people about my own experiences, I wanted to talk to her, if only to let her know she was totally, completely normal. That she wasn't weak at all. "Willa, you can't see the worst of humanity without it changing you. Changing the way you see the world. The only people who never feel fear are the people who don't realize there are very real things to be afraid of."

She stared at me for a long minute, but it didn't make me uncomfortable. It was like she was trying to see if I was being honest with her.

"So how did you deal with it?" she finally asked, her voice quiet. "You don't seem to be afraid all the time."

"I'm not afraid for myself," I answered. It was the most honest answer I could give. "Our experiences were different, and our response to them is different. I haven't lived through what you lived through. Even without knowing the details, I know that's true. So my fears and reactions are going to be different than yours. We have different monsters in our closets. But as far as how we deal with them? Therapy is a good start."

Her expression changed to one of surprise. "You go to therapy?"

"Damn right I do."

"Daniel always said therapy was for losers who wanted to blame their problems on everyone else."

I snorted. "And look how healthy he is."

She threw her head back and laughed out loud. "You have a point there."

"Have you ever been able to talk to someone about it all?" I asked.

"A therapist, you mean?"

"Yeah."

She shook her head. "Of course not. I could never have done anything like that when I was with him. And it would still be too dangerous now. I might let something slip, or they might start putting pieces together and realize who I am."

"If you could talk to someone safely, would you?"

She stared at me again, thinking a long minute before answering. "I don't know."

"No pressure. But if you ever want to, I know someone. A friend. Former military turned therapist. I trust him with my life, and he's completely discreet."

She laughed. "And probably expensive."

This time, I was the one shaking my head. "Nah. He wouldn't charge you. He owes me a favor. A big one."

"I have a feeling a lot of people owe you favors," she said, grinning.

"You're not wrong," I admitted.

She shook her head and tossed a towel at me. "I'll think about talking to your friend. No promises. But I'll think about it. And I'll come back for another lesson. I *don't* have to think about that one. But that means I owe you a big favor too, so I guess you can keep adding to that stack of people who owe you."

"No," I said firmly. "Willa, you don't owe me anything."

"Okay," she said, suddenly looking away like she couldn't quite meet my eyes. "But maybe, if you're up for it, I could buy you dessert tonight? As a thank-you? Unless you're busy."

I reached out and put my hand over hers until she looked at me again. "I mean it," I said. "You don't owe me anything. But I'd love to go grab some dessert. On one condition."

"What's that?" she asked, suddenly guarded.

I grinned. "I'm buying."

Chapter Nineteen

Willa

"Separate cars, or would you like to ride with me?" Cole asked, brushing his hand lightly against my back as he held the door open for me.

I laughed. "I'll never turn down an opportunity to ride in your car."

"Perfect. My car it is." He flashed me a grin and I began to wonder why I had thought he was always so serious.

"Do you have a preference on dessert?" I asked, sliding into his passenger seat. Once again, I had to fight back a groan of pleasure as I sank into the leather. Oh, how I loved to dream of owning a car like this again someday. It wasn't realistic. Even if I managed to save up enough for one, there was no point. I'd just have to leave it behind at some point, like everything else in my life.

But it sure was fun to dream.

Cole got into the driver's seat and started the engine. "No prefer-ence at all," he said. "I'm here mostly for the company."

I flushed at the compliment. "There's an old-fashioned soda shop in the town square. They have the best ice cream and milk shakes. Might be fun."

"Ice cream it is," he said, putting the car into reverse.

The drive to the town square was way too short, but we made the most of it, chatting about music preferences and favorite movies—light conversation for us, considering our history, but it made it all the more fun. It was one more little slice of normal, and I cherished every one of them.

When we parked, he came around to my side and took my hand like it was the most natural thing in the world. I bit my lip to keep from smiling. It was just dessert. But he made it seem like a real date, and I was loving every minute of it.

"You look beautiful," he said, glancing over at me as we walked to the door of the little shop.

I laughed. "I'm in sweats."

"So what? You're beautiful all the time." He let go of my hand to reach for the door, opening it for me.

"Thanks," I said, flushing again.

He let the door fall closed behind us, then took my hand back in his. "So, what's good here?" he asked, studying the menu.

But the question sent a wave of anxiety through me. Somehow, he must have felt it, because he turned toward me, his face serious.

"What is it, Willa?" he asked, squeezing my hand.

"Nothing," I said, shaking my head. "Um. Everything's good here, so I've heard."

"Willa." His voice was quiet. "What's happening? Talk to me."

I took a deep breath in, glancing at the kid behind the register.

Cole looked over at him and frowned, then tugged me toward a booth in the very back. When I was tucked safely in, he asked, "Is it the kid? Is he a problem?"

"No," I said, shaking my head, offering an embarrassed smile before covering my face with my hands. "No, it's not him. I just... Oh gosh. I'm sorry. Cole, I have a lot of baggage from the past. I guess it just popped up tonight, when I wasn't expecting it. I'm sorry."

"You don't have to apologize," he said, "but I wish you would explain it."

"Explaining it would be humiliating," I said, forcing a smile. "Don't worry about it. Why don't you go order for us? I'll take whatever you're having."

But he sat there frowning, not making a move.

"Listen," I said, leaning forward. "It was nothing. A memory popped up that I had forgotten. That's all."

"Tell me," he said.

I let out a sigh, feeling so embarrassed. "He and I were on our honeymoon, walking the boardwalk by the beach. There was a little ice cream shop I wanted to stop at. He told me no, that I was already fifteen pounds overweight and needed to begin rectifying that immediately. He said some cruel, humiliating things—I won't repeat them tonight. I learned quickly that he was in control of what I ate and to never, ever express interest in dessert. To be honest, I thought I had moved past all of that. But for some reason, when you asked me what was good, I just felt panicky—like it was a trap. Anytime he ever asked my opinion, that's what it was. A trap, just him looking for another reason to correct me. I learned to stop giving them. I'm sorry."

His face was an odd mixture of sorrow and anger. He closed his eyes and took a deep breath.

"Cole," I said, reaching across the table to squeeze his hand. "I'm a mess. We both know it. And now I've screwed up two dates by bringing him into them. Maybe this just isn't going to work. I'm really sorry for dragging you into my drama."

"We all have baggage, Willa," he said, taking my hand in both of his and bringing it to his lips for a kiss. "I'm not upset at you. I'm upset at *him*. Fifteen pounds overweight? He told you that? On your *honeymoon?* Good lord. I saw the wedding pictures in the tabloids—everybody did. You were beautiful."

"Anything over a size two was unacceptable to him, apparently," I said, rolling my eyes. "Like I said, I thought I was over it. But you're the first person I've had any sort of, well, romantic thing with since him. And I guess some of that old stuff keeps popping up. I really am sorry."

"Don't be. You didn't do anything wrong. And for what it's worth? I think you look a hell of a lot better now than you did then."

I could see by the look on his face that he meant it, and it made me smile. "Well, I sure feel a lot better. Nobody enjoys being hungry all the time."

He shook his head. "Damn right. But what did I do that triggered you? I don't want to do it again."

"Oh, Cole," I said, shaking my head. "It wasn't you. You just asked me what was good here. That's a completely normal thing for a person to ask. But if he had asked it, it would have been a way to get information he could use against me. He was always playing games like that. You can't avoid ever asking me anything. I think it will just take some time for me to get over it all. And, Cole? I understand completely if this is too much for you. If you just want to be friends, that's okay. I really do understand. I know I'm a mess."

He looked at me with that odd expression again, the mix of sadness and frustration. But this time, there was heat behind it. "Willa. Don't ever again apologize to me for something he did. Okay? We're done with that."

"Okay," I said, nodding.

"And I'm way past just wanting to be friends with you. If that's all *you* want, I'll respect it one hundred percent. But that's not what I want at all. I'm not going to push you. But I want you to know where I stand."

"Okay," I said again, my heart speeding up at the heat in his eyes.

"So you get to decide. Are we here as two friends grabbing ice cream? Or is this a date? It's up to you. But you should know, if this is a date, I have every intention of trying to kiss you goodnight. Ice cream is good and all, but all I've been dreaming about is tasting your mouth again every night since New Year's Eve."

I flushed again, feeling heat pool in my center. "If I'm not too much for you then ... then I guess this is a date."

"Oh, Willa," he said, shaking his head. "You're not too much for me. But you might find out I'm too much for you." He winked, shooting me a cocky grin. "Now, I'm going to order us some ice cream.

No more of this 'whatever you want' crap. Tell me what your favorite is so I can order it."

"The Smoky Turtle," I said when I had recovered enough to speak.

"Two Smoky Turtles, coming up," he said, sliding out of the booth, then walking over to me. Before he went up to order, he planted a long, smoldering kiss on my lips.

All I could think when he walked away was that the Smoky Turtle wasn't half as delicious as him.

CHAPTER TWENTY

Cole

I ORDERED TWO SMOKY TURTLES—DELICIOUS-LOOKING
concoctions made of chocolate ice cream, hot fudge, caramel, candied
pecans, whipped cream, and a cherry on top—and brought them back
to the booth where Willa was sitting, still looking half stunned.

Had to admit, it gave me a swell of pride to know that my kiss had
knocked her off her feet.

"Nice choice on the dessert," I said, passing hers to her. I slid in
beside her in the booth, rather than across from her where I had been
before. This was an official date—that had been decided. Might as well
enjoy sitting close to her.

"I have a rule," she said quickly.

"Okay. What's your rule?"

"No more talking about him tonight." She looked at me with a bit
of hesitation on her face, like she wasn't sure I would agree. "Even if
something happens and I get a little panicky. Let's just let it go and move
past it. I don't want him intruding on this anymore."

"I think that sounds fair," I said, "if it's what you want. Willa, I am always here if you want to talk. Always. But if it feels right to kick him out of your thoughts and your life? That's fine too. All I ask is that you're honest with me. If I do something that bothers you? Tell me. If you need to go slower? Tell me. Have an opinion? Tell me. I don't ever want for you to just go along with things to avoid any kind of negativity, okay? Not with me."

She relaxed, smiling. "Deal."

I took a bite of the ice cream, almost groaning in delight. "Damn. You know how to order."

She took the tiniest bite of hers. "It's good, right? My favorite since I moved here."

"It is good." I slid my arm around her in the booth, noticing she snuggled in instead of pulling away.

"It's strange how comfortable I feel with you," she said. "After all, I barely know you."

"What do you want to know?"

She twisted up, looking at me as she took another small bite of her ice cream. I nearly came undone watching her slowly pull the spoon from those plump lips.

"Tell me about your family," she said. "Do you have brothers or sisters?"

I nodded. "Six of them."

"Six?" Her eyes widened. "Really?"

"Yep. Four brothers, two sisters. Seven of us altogether."

"What was it like growing up in such a big family?" she asked, cocking her head.

"Cramped," I answered with a snort. "Loud. But fun. My sisters are great. You'd love them and they'd love you. Mary Beth's a total girlie girl. Obsessed with Jane Austen and Louisa May Alcott. Wants to be a writer someday. Mary Claire's the exact opposite. Total tomboy, lives for adrenaline and adventure. We got into lots of trouble together."

"Why are they both named Mary?" Willa asked, a curious expression on her face.

"Isn't it obvious? Mom's a devout Catholic. Seven kids, remember?

If more had been girls, they probably would have been named Mary too."

Willa giggled. "What about your brothers?"

"Travis is the oldest, and he's kind of a stick in the mud. Good guy though. Just needs to loosen up a bit. Finn's actually Mary Beth's twin, and he's a lot like her. All into books and that kind of thing. Rhett's kind of a wild child—which works out well for me. Mom doesn't like my life choices, but compared to Rhett, I look pretty good." I shrugged. "Jonathan's the baby of the family. Still trying to figure out who he is."

"I can't even imagine growing up with that many siblings," Willa said, shaking her head. "You're so lucky."

I snorted again. "You must not have siblings."

"You're right," she said.

"I was joking. But really? None at all?" No matter how much I joked about my brothers and sisters, the truth was I'd die for any of them. I couldn't imagine growing up alone.

She shook her head. "No. Just me. I always wanted a brother."

"What about your parents?" I asked.

She turned her eyes away and sighed. "No more talking about the past," she said. "It makes me sad. Let's talk about the future instead."

"Okay. Here's an idea for the future," I said, knowing it would make her smile again. "How about sometime we come split a milkshake? Two straws and all that. I've heard it's romantic."

It worked. She turned back to me and laughed. "Trying to be more romantic, are you?"

"It doesn't come naturally to me," I said, being honest. "Not like it does to Finn. All that Jane Austen stuff makes him a total babe magnet."

"Oh, come on," she said, gently shoving me. "You're a national hero. You served in the special forces. You're telling me you don't have a long line of ex-girlfriends with broken hearts, all desperately hoping you'll return home?" she asked, teasing.

I shook my head. "Nope. Not me. I tried the girlfriend thing a couple of times, but it didn't stick."

"Why not?"

I grinned, and gestured at the ice cream in front of us. "Probably because working out at the gym, then grabbing ice cream is basically my idea of a perfect date. The only one that might top it is going backpacking together, but let's be honest. Most of the girls I've met have exactly zero interest in tramping miles through the wilderness to camp at a primitive campsite without another human being—or bathroom—in sight. I've only met three girls that are into that kind of thing. The first is my sister, Mary Claire. That's a no go, obviously. The second was married. Got snatched up real fast by a guy in my unit, no surprise. The third, well... Let's just say she let me know she'd rather go camping with my sister than me."

Willa laughed. "Gotcha. Well, I've never tried backpacking before, but so far, I'd say the workout plus dessert feels like a pretty great date to me, too."

"Oh yeah?"

"Yeah." She smiled up at me.

"Well, how about we repeat it tomorrow night? Another workout, then we'll come here and split one of those milkshakes."

"Are you asking me on another date, Cole?" She bit her lip and gave me a playful grin. It was as sexy as hell.

"Hell yeah I am."

"Okay. Tomorrow night."

"Tomorrow night."

Chapter Twenty-One

Willa

My workouts with Cole were quickly becoming my favorite part of the week. Every time, I felt a little stronger. A little more empowered. A little more me.

But I still hadn't gone beyond the bag. I was happy to take all my emotions and pour them into the punching bag, and Cole was delighted by the progress I was making with the techniques he had shown me. But whenever he suggested we move to my hitting him, I would shut down.

I knew that Cole was safe and he only wanted to help me. But I couldn't shake this completely irrational fear that if I hit him, he would change—that he would turn into someone like Daniel, someone full of rage and hatred and a desire to hurt me back. It hadn't taken me long to realize that the best way to survive Daniel's abuse was to simply take it. Resistance only prolonged and worsened it tenfold.

Cole wasn't Daniel. But the fear of fighting back gripped me so strongly I didn't think we would ever break past it.

So, for a while, the routine was the same. I would practice what he showed me on the bag. He would suggest I start sparring with him. I would immediately shut down. We would end the workout and grab a snack or a drink, talking about anything except the past, pretending like none of it existed and I wasn't refusing to go any further with training. To his credit, he didn't push.

Until he did.

On our seventh training session, we went through the usual paces more quickly than normal. Half an hour into the workout, he gave me a nod of approval. "You're doing great," he said. "But it's time to move on. I want you to spar with me tonight."

I immediately shook my head, preparing my excuses, but he reached out and put his hands on my shoulders. It still amazed me that I never recoiled from his touch, that I absolutely loved his hands on me. In fact, I found myself wishing he would touch me more. But so far, he had kept everything on exactly the same level as our first night training together. Small touches here or there. Holding my hand while we went in for our post-workout snack. An intense kiss when he dropped me off back at my house, leaving me breathless and surprised every time he said good night and walked away.

I loved every moment of it, but I was aching for more.

"Willa," he said, looking me straight in the eyes. "There's no point in even doing this if you're never going to get comfortable fighting back against an actual human. I promise you, you're never going to be attacked by a punching bag." His eyes twinkled, despite his serious face.

"You don't understand," I said, shaking my head.

"Try me."

I looked into his eyes, trying to figure out how to say it without feeling embarrassed or breaking down into tears, which would have been even worse. "I just can't," I finally said.

"Willa." He kept his hands on my shoulders, gently stopping me from turning away. "Talk to me. We've been avoiding it all week. But we've got to move forward."

I shook my head at first, but he still didn't move. He just waited, with that deliberate patience of his.

Finally, I bit my lip and whispered the truth. "Punching bags don't hit back, Cole."

"I already told you I won't hit you," he said. "That's a promise. I'm not even going to block in a way that might hurt you. We'll eventually get to the point where you can handle mutual sparring. You need to train in situations that mimic real-world problems. In real life, an attacker *will* hit you. But I know we aren't there yet. Not even close. And that's okay. But it's time for you to get comfortable hitting something with a face on it."

I dropped my head, ashamed of my fears. "You're not exactly the first man to promise not to hit me. I've heard that a thousand times, Cole. It was never true. And I know you aren't him. But..."

"Willa. Do you still not trust me?"

I looked up at him, brokenhearted at the disappointment on his face. "I do, Cole. I trust you. But no matter what I know to be true, it doesn't stop the fear. Even just thinking about fighting back makes me start to panic. That night, at the group class? It wasn't your hand on my neck that made me panic. It was that I fought you off. Remember? I can't begin to explain how terrifying that was. I can't even tell you the things he made me endure when I tried to fight back." I started shaking, unable to control it.

"Oh, baby." He pulled me to him and held me tight until the shaking stopped. "I'm so sorry you went through that. I get it. It's just fight or flight. It's a normal thing, a physiological reaction. We'll work through it."

"How? I don't see how this is ever going to get better. Cole, if he ever comes for me, I would probably just fold and let him do whatever he wants to me."

"No," he said, pulling back so he could look me in the eye. "Willa, don't you ever let that man lay a hand on you again. If he comes after you, you fight. *We* fight."

I wanted so much to promise him that I would, but I couldn't. Not when just thinking about resisting made my belly clamp with fear. Daniel was so much stronger than I was. I would never win against him. "I just don't know how to get past this."

"Hmmm." He dropped his hands and screwed up his face, thinking. "Well, I'm going to suggest therapy again. My friend probably has way better ideas than I do. I'm not going to push you, but I'd really like for you to consider it. For now though, what if you tied my hands behind my back?"

"What?" I looked up, confused.

"You tie my hands behind my back. That way, you'll know I can't hit you. It won't be possible. Maybe that will make your brain chill out a little if you can see that you're safe."

"But that's crazy," I protested. "I can't hit someone who's tied up. That's just wrong."

"You can't hit anyone at all right now," he pointed out. He flashed me an easy grin. "Look, I'm not suggesting you tie me up and beat me to a pulp. I just want to get you past the hurdle. Tie my hands behind my back and throw a few light punches. Maybe once you've gotten past it in a way that feels safe to you, we can move forward with your training."

"You're crazy," I said, laughing.

"You're not the first person to tell me that," he said, winking. "Come on. Let's move forward together."

"Cole, I don't want to hurt you," I said, shaking my head. "You have to at least be able to block my punches."

He grinned again. "Look, Willa, I'm proud of how far you've come. But you're not exactly a professional boxer yet. You think I haven't taken worse than anything you can throw at me? Trust me, I have. I know how to take a punch and I willingly signed up for far worse during training."

I hesitated.

"Come on," he said, giving me a reassuring smile. "It will be fine."

"I really don't want to hurt you," I said. And it wasn't just about the fear of being hurt back. Cole didn't deserve any pain, and I absolutely did not want to inflict any. No matter how strong he was.

"You won't," he said, shaking his head. "I'm dead serious. But even if you did? It would be worth it. It's okay, Willa. I'm offering because we both know there's a chance he'll find you someday. And if he does? I want you to kick his ass."

I grinned, despite myself. "I like the sound of that."

"Me too. So I'll take one for the team. Come on." He gestured toward his gym bag. "I've got some rope in there."

My eyebrows rose. "You always walk around with rope on you?"

"You always walk around with a backpack full of cash and clothes?"

I stopped, shocked. "How did you—"

He just chuckled. "We're more alike than you realize. Always be prepared, right?"

"Right." I relaxed and smiled, despite what we were about to do.

He walked to his bag and pulled out a short length of rope. "Here go you," he said, handing it to me, then turning around and putting his hands behind his back. "Make it tight. I want you to feel safe."

I fumbled with it, feeling more than a little awkward as I attempted to bind his wrists. As I was finally getting it, the door to the gym flew open.

"What in the world?" Sheriff Morrison's voice rang out in obvious bewilderment.

I jumped, flushing in embarrassment.

"It's not what it looks like," Cole said, laughing louder than I had ever heard him laugh.

"I'm not even sure what it looks like," the sheriff said, still confused.

Cole attempted to clarify. "She's tying me up so she can punch me."

"I don't think that makes it look any better," Sheriff Morrison said, cocking his head.

Cole looked at me and shrugged. I realized he wasn't going to explain the reason behind it because he didn't want to break my trust. It meant something to me that he was willing to live through an awkward situation rather than throw me under the bus. It was yet another way he was so very different from Daniel, and it gave me the courage to explain.

"I was nervous," I said. "Cole wants me to learn to spar, but he knew I was worried he would hurt me if I hit him. He wanted to prove he wouldn't hit back."

"Ah," Sheriff Morrison said like that explained everything. "You could have just borrowed my handcuffs. Would have been easier. Mind if I stay and watch?" he asked, his tone mild. "I always like a good sparring match. Even if one opponent is more than a little handicapped. Besides, it might give you extra reassurance. He's not likely to break his word and hit a woman in front of the sheriff, now is he?"

I glanced shyly at Cole. "I don't think he's likely to break his word ever. No matter who is or isn't watching."

The look on Cole's face made my heart swell. "Thanks," he said, his voice a little gruff.

"Well, get on with it," Sheriff Morrison said, taking a seat against the wall and putting his hands behind his head. "This should be fun. About time someone put Cole in his place."

Cole just rolled his eyes and turned around to face me. As soon as he did, the nerves came back. "It's okay," he murmured under his breath. "You aren't going to hurt me."

I nodded, even as a trickle of fear went through me. This absolutely did not feel okay. It didn't feel right to do something that might hurt Cole even a little, and it didn't feel right to hit someone who could crush me like a bug after. Cole wouldn't though. I knew that now. Even without his wrists bound and the sheriff watching, he wouldn't hit back.

Cole didn't want to hurt me. He wanted to protect me.

I took a deep breath and got into the fighting stance he had shown me. Then, feeling more than a little shaky, I lightly punched his right shoulder.

"Good job," he said, smiling in approval. "You got past the first hurdle. Now, do it again, and this time pretend I'm the punching bag and not a ceramic doll that might shatter."

I laughed in embarrassment and tried again, putting a little bit of force behind it.

"Better," he said, nodding.

"You can do better than that," Sheriff Morrison called out from the side. "Come on, Willa."

But I dropped my fists. "No," I said. "Not unless we untie your hands and you start blocking."

"Willa," Cole said, obviously going to argue.

"No," I said, interrupting him. "We did it your way. And you're right. I needed that to get past it. But I'm not going to use you as a punching bag. Besides, if I'm ever in a situation with"—I glanced at the sheriff, then back at Cole—"you know who, he's not going to stand there and take it. Like you said, there's no point in doing this if I don't train in real-life scenarios, right?"

"I don't want you to feel even a moment of fear with me," Cole said quietly enough that the sheriff couldn't hear him. Or at least pretended not to.

"I don't," I said, truly meaning it this time. "I trust you, Cole. It's okay. *I'm* okay. Look, no shaking." I held out my hand to show him.

He held my eyes for a long minute and realized I was serious. "Okay," he said. "I'll block as gently as possible."

"I know," I said.

"Willa?"

"Yeah?"

"I'm proud of you."

I smiled. "I'm proud of myself too."

Chapter Twenty-Two

Cole

Every night when I dropped Willa off at her house after our training sessions, it got harder and harder to leave. I refused to push her in our relationship while I was pushing so hard in our lessons, but I wanted so much more than cups of ice cream and goodnight kisses.

I wanted to take her on a real date. Wanted to hold her in my arms. Wanted to be invited into her house, even if it was just to curl up and watch a movie with her on the couch. Wanted to spend the night in her bed and wake up with her in my arms.

I wanted everything.

But I wouldn't push, and whether I wanted to or not, I had to put a short pause on our evenings together. Weeks ago, I had committed myself to an overnight backpacking trip with Emerson. It was a chance for us to flex some of our skills and test ourselves in the great outdoors. Emerson had always loved cold weather camping and was looking forward to going with a buddy, since Daphne wasn't up for it in her condition.

I had to admit I was looking forward to it too, even though I would miss Willa like crazy. Plus, I owed Emerson one. More than one, if I was being honest.

Even I had to admit that my time in Rosemary Mountain was changing me, and only part of it had to do with Willa. Truth was, I had felt completely lost when I came here. I had been a man with no idea what I wanted out of life anymore. I could feel that changing as a vision for my future started taking shape.

A vision that might even include staying here.

Emerson pulled up out front at 700 hours sharp the next morning. He was all grins as he climbed out of his truck. "You ready?" he called out.

I lifted my cup of coffee in answer. "Not until I finish this."

He walked up the steps of the front porch. "Got any more of that? I remember how hard you like to push it on the trail. Probably won't even let us take the time to make coffee out there."

"There's a full pot. Help yourself."

He disappeared into the cabin, leaving me alone again on the porch. It was just the kind of morning I liked. Crisp mountain air, cold enough to see your breath. Not a sound to be heard except the breeze rustling through the branches. Peace and solitude. It was the kind of morning that loosened up all the tension in my soul and made me feel like the world wasn't such a bad place after all.

When you'd seen the kind of things I'd seen, you took every bit of that you could.

Emerson returned quickly, a steaming mug of coffee in hand. He took the seat next to me and let out a long breath of his own, looking around at the land that still technically belonged to him.

"Always liked it out here in the morning," he said. "It's a great spot."

"It is. You miss it?"

He chuckled and shook his head. "Nah. Don't get me wrong. I loved this cabin. But the cottage has been in Daphne's family for years.

It's where we're supposed to be. Besides, we have this great balcony off our bedroom upstairs. Looks out over the forest with an even better view than this. And more importantly, she's there, enjoying it with me."

"You ever miss being alone? Single, I mean. Free to do what you want, when you want it? Being able to go where you want, move around, with no ties?"

"No." The answer was immediate. "Life's a hell of a lot better when you're living it with someone who cares about you. Someone willing to go the distance. Marriage? It's awesome, man. I'll have a blast backpacking with you, but at the end of it, I get to go home to my best friend. I wouldn't trade that for anything."

Looking at him, I believed it.

We sipped our coffee in companionable silence for a bit, content to listen to the breeze rustling through the branches of the trees, until I broached the subject that was on my mind.

"Listen," I said, "I was going to wait and talk to you about this later. But it seems like a good time."

"What's on your mind?"

"I think I'm going to hang around Rosemary Mountain a little longer than we originally talked about. Wanted to ask how you felt about renting this cabin to me on a long-term basis."

"It's yours as long as you need it," he replied easily. "You know that."

"I appreciate it," I said. "But I'm not really sure how long I'll be here. Might be six months, might be years. On the other hand, things might happen and I might head out in a week. That's not fair to you, and I wish I could give you a clear answer."

"Don't worry about me," he said, brushing it off. "But when you say things might happen, what are we talking about?"

"Just things," I said, keeping my gaze on the trees in front of me.

"Let me be more specific. Do you mean you might get the itch to just roll out of here in a week, or is this about Willa?"

I stayed silent, unwilling to answer.

"We both know she's in trouble," he said, still pushing. "And I'm annoyed as hell that you and my wife aren't letting me in on it. You know, I might actually be able to help. You aren't the only one with connections and certain skill sets. If you'd tell me what the hell is going on, we could face it together."

But I refused to confirm. Willa's story wasn't mine to tell, and even though I knew she was going to tell Emerson herself eventually, it was her place to do it. Not mine.

"You're as stubborn as my wife," he muttered under his breath.

I cracked a smile. "Must be why you like me so much."

He gave me a shove. "Come on. Coffee's cold. Let's get on the road."

Chapter Twenty-Three

Willa

I pulled up into Fiona's driveway feeling oddly nervous. I had never been to her house and honestly wasn't sure what to expect. She was a sweet, generous person. But truthfully, I had always avoided getting close to her. She gave me the impression that she didn't miss a trick, that those eyes saw everything—even what you were hiding.

That wasn't a safe person for me.

But I had promised her I would come visit, and I felt I owed it to her after she had saved me a trip to the doctor. Her tea had knocked my flu out when I was getting desperate enough to spend some of my cash on a doctor's visit and prescriptions. I was grateful for it and wanted to show her that.

It didn't make me any less nervous though.

Her door flew open before I even reached it, a habit she and Daphne both seemed to have. It made me smile, despite my nerves.

"Welcome, Willa!" she called out. "Get inside and warm yourself up!

It's as cold as a witch's nipple out here. And some people would tell you I should know!" She roared in laughter over a joke I didn't totally get.

"Thanks for having me," I said, stepping into her house. My nerves dissipated the moment I walked into the cozy space.

A fire roared in the fireplace, and the space felt alive somehow. Alive and welcoming. It was the exact opposite of the home I had shared with Daniel, which made me instantly like it. Fiona's house was tiny, warm, colorful, and full of texture. Botanical prints hung on the wall, and there were houseplants in every corner. Lovely throws and pillows adorned every piece of furniture, making the space feel like it was just welcoming you to sit down and snuggle up for a cozy chat. The air was scented with lavender, sage, and woodsmoke. Looking around, I felt like I could spend all day exploring every nook and cranny of the place.

"What are you standing there gaping for, Willa-girl?" Fiona asked, laughing.

"Oh, I'm sorry," I said, realizing she had caught me staring. "I absolutely adore your house. It feels exactly like a home should."

"Prettiest house on the lane, I've always said." Fiona beamed. "You spend so much of your life at home—might as well make it cozy."

"It is," I said, still taking in the details. I had always known that Fiona had style. She never dressed like you would expect from someone her age. But I hadn't realized what a truly artistic eye she had until now. I was absolutely delighted. I immediately zeroed in on a quilt she had hanging on the wall in her hallway. "May I?" I asked, pointed toward it.

"Of course," she said, beaming again.

I walked over and studied it, longing to reach out and run my fingers over the fabric. "This is magnificent," I said. "Such intricate details and beautiful hand-stitching. The designer had an incredible eye for color. So many different colors and patterns, yet the effect is perfect. It's not overwhelming or busy. It's calming." I continued studying it, trying to take all of it in. "Fiona, this is the kind of piece you see in museums. Where in the world did you get it?" I glanced back toward her. "Did you...?" If Fiona made quilts like this, then she and I were going to get along very well.

"No, not me," Fiona said. Her voice went soft as she lovingly stroked a hand down the quilt. "It's a very special one. My grandmother made it to carry with me when I came over from Ireland. It's a piece of her I've always held dear. So many memories in this quilt." She began pointing out different fabrics and explaining their origins. "This one was from my mother's wedding dress. And this, from my grandmother's. This was from the tablecloth my grandmother used to use on our birthdays. This here is from the dress my sister and I wore for our christenings. And this one..." Her voice trailed off as she stroked the lovely cream fabric. "Well, there's a lot of history there. That's all. Many memories held within this quilt. Plenty of love there, too."

I turned to study the woman beside me, truly seeing her for the first time. "You moved here from Ireland?"

"Aye," she said, her voice still soft and dreamy as she stared at the quilt.

"I didn't realize. Your accent..."

She laughed, returning to herself. "Oh, I'm as Southern as I can be now. I've spent most of my life here. You lose things, you know. Though Daphne'll be the first to tell you the Irish brogue starts to slip back in sometimes when I've had a bit of whiskey and get caught up telling stories from the home country."

I looked back at the quilt. "So you understand what it's like to start completely fresh. To leave and start a brand new life, somewhere different from anything you've ever known," I mused, almost without realizing I was speaking aloud.

She reached over and squeezed my hand. "I do, Willa-girl. I do."

I looked back at her, feeling my guard go back up again.

But she just shook her head, keeping a hold of my hand. "Nothing to be scared of here. I'm good at keeping secrets. Daphne will tell you that. Not that you have to tell me yours. It's plain as day you have them, but it's not my place to pry them out of you. Just know you're safe with me, whatever your reason is for being here in Rosemary Mountain. It's a good place to land. I should know."

Her eyes were filled with so much kindness that the walls inside me started breaking down. "I don't really want to talk about it. Not today. I feel like I've talked about it more the last few weeks than I have in the past year," I said with a shallow laugh. "I'm tired of thinking about the past. But I appreciate the offer, and I appreciate your kindness."

She let go of my hand and nodded, giving me an approving smile. "Sometimes, it's best to let the past stay in the past. But if there's anything I can do for you, just let me know, okay? The offer stands, even if we never mention it again."

"Thank you. Really. Everyone here is so nice," I said, following her as she turned to head into the kitchen. "I'm not sure I've ever lived somewhere so warm and welcoming."

She let out a loud laugh. "That's just because you met the best people first. It's a good place to live alright. It's where I chose to spend my life, and I've been happy enough here. But I'll be the first to tell you it's not all hearts and sunshine. Tea?"

"Tea sounds lovely."

"Sit down," she said, pointing to the rustic wooden table in her kitchen. "I'll put on the kettle. How 'bout a muffin, too? I made some good apple nut oatmeal muffins this morning."

"You're a busy lady," I said, smiling. "A muffin sounds great."

She laughed again. "Daphne can't cook worth a lick, no matter how many times Janet and I have tried to teach her. Though sometimes I wonder if she's just being stubborn. My, but the girl has a stubborn streak! Always has. That baby has to eat proper food though, not just whatever granola bars or other pre-packaged nonsense Daphne manages to pick up at the store. Someone's gotta make sure there's real food around!"

I frowned, feeling like that was a bit unfair. "I think Daphne's doing just fine. She may not be an accomplished cook, but she takes good care of herself and the baby."

Fiona looked at me and grinned. "Loyal, aren't ya? That's a good sign. I was hoping you would be."

I raised an eyebrow. "So that's what this is? You're testing me?"

She gave me a sheepish look. "Daphne's my own. Always has been. And I've liked you from the beginning, but I'll be the first to tell you. She hasn't always been the best judge of character when it comes to her friends. Gives people the benefit of the doubt when she shouldn't. I look out for her in all the ways I can."

My heart softened again. "Then we'll get along just fine. I haven't always been the best judge of character, either, to say the least. But I've learned my lesson there. Daphne's friendship means the world to me. I would never hurt her."

She shook her head. "Never said you would. And I know we agreed not to talk about the past. But if trouble comes for you, you should know, Daphne's the type to get herself in the middle of it. Can't hardly help herself."

I bit my lip, wondering. "You said Daphne's yours. I guess you know her really well?"

She nodded, peering at me. "I delivered her myself. Her mama, Eileen, was like a daughter to me. Daphne was born in the cottage where she lives now and grew up like my own grandbaby 'til her mama died and her daddy took her away from here. I was never so happy as the day she came back. She's family."

"Daphne shared some things with me about herself." I couldn't bring myself to say what on the small chance Fiona didn't know. It was highly unlikely Daphne had shared something with me that she hadn't with Fiona, but I still didn't want to say anything that would breach her trust.

"Ahhh," Fiona said, nodding. "So you know, if trouble's coming, she's apt to know it."

"Right," I said slowly. "She hasn't said anything like that yet."

Fiona let out a little breath of relief. Until that moment, I hadn't realized how nervous she was. "Well, that's a blessing, anyway."

"If it comes, I won't let it get to her," I said, wanting to reassure. "I would never put her or the baby at risk."

Fiona just shook her head and sighed. "Honey, if you think you could stop Daphne from getting involved, you don't know her half as well as you think you do."

Chapter Twenty-Four

Daniel

Daniel Cavendish smiled politely at the woman who stood practically cooing over him. He nodded, allowing his grief to visibly wash over him as she told him how glad she was that he was out socializing again. He hid his smile as the empathy crossed her face while he told her how he was trying to make the best of things. Pathetic whore, begging for attention. They all were, the women who had attempted to swoop in and win his heart after the devastating loss of his beloved wife.

Ridiculous, all of them.

Oh, he would make use of her for a night. Maybe even enjoy it. But it wasn't real. Not like his relationship with Wilhelmina.

His darling Wilhelmina. She had been so close to perfect, so willingly molded by his hands. Until she had gone mad and taken her own life, defying him and taking away his every happiness. The thought made him so angry he clenched the champagne flute in his hand, nearly breaking it until he caught himself. That wouldn't do. No need to make a scene here.

The woman in front of him—Jennifer? Jessica? They all ran together at this point—touched his hand lightly.

"You poor dear," she said, shaking her head. "You must be so lonely."

"Oh, I am," he agreed. "So very lonely. It's been such a difficult year."

It was all a game, a stupid dance that always ended the same way—with some beautiful woman in his bed, trying her hardest to prove that she could be the next love of his life, the next Mrs. Cavendish on his arm. Just another woman wanting her fifteen minutes of fame, hoping to use him to get it. Little did they realize he didn't care enough to even remember their faces after, much less their names.

Wilhelmina was the only one who had ever mattered.

Oh, how he craved her! Craved her beauty—and the way she looked on his arm in front of all the cameras. The press had adored her nearly as much as he did. He craved the feeling of power he had over her, craved the pleasure he felt while punishing her for displeasing him. The lengths she went to to please him and avoid her punishments. The fact that she never could.

A few times, he had been tempted to try recreating that relationship. He had even gone so far as to test it out on a couple of the women he had invited back for a second night—open-handed slaps, nothing that would leave a mark for long, of course. Nothing that could be proven. Neither woman had satisfied him. Both had willingly signed NDAs in exchange for money—and his tearful apologies and explanations of how he had suffered so since the death of his wife.

Ridiculous, debasing himself like that.

Once, he had done far worse to a prostitute his lawyer had procured for him. A nobody that would never be missed and would never be able to fight back in a court of law. That had been slightly more satisfying.

But it still wasn't Wilhelmina. Nothing would ever satisfy him the way his wife, his *soulmate* had.

Damn her for leaving him alone to suffer.

With the dance complete, he told the lady—he still couldn't

remember her name—to get her coat so they could leave and go back to his place. But while he was waiting, rather impatiently, an elderly lady approached him.

"Yoohoo," she called, waving her handkerchief as she walked up. "Senator. So good to see you." She leaned forward, stretching up in an attempt at kissing both of his cheeks.

"Wonderful to see you too," he said smoothly, despite not having a clue who the lady was.

"I was hoping we'd get a chance to talk tonight," she said coyly.

"Oh, yes? What can I do for you?"

She shook her head. "It's not what you can do for me. It's what I can do for you."

He smiled politely, feeling his patience wear thin. "If you'd like to make a donation to our campaign fund, I'd be happy to get you in touch with my campaign manager."

"Oh, no," she said, wagging her finger. "You misunderstand. What I have is better than that." She reached into her handbag and pulled out a photograph, holding it to her chest. Her eyes were bright with excitement. "I have a cousin who lives out in North Carolina. She was out shopping recently, and you will never believe it!"

Daniel's patience was very nearly gone. He was ready for his date to return so he could get on with his evening and not waste another minute with this insufferable old gossip. For a brief moment, he wondered what it might be like to hit *her*. Then he lectured himself internally on the importance of political allies and forced another polite smile that didn't quite reach his eyes.

"Well, you better tell me since I won't be able to guess," he said, attempting playfulness.

"Look!" She turned the photograph around and showed him.

It wasn't the best photo. It had clearly been a discreet shot taken with a cell phone at an odd angle.

But the face? That was clear enough. Daniel's heart nearly stopped.

He took the photograph from her hands and looked at it again, unable to disguise the shock rippling across his face.

"My God," he said. "Is it really her?"

"My cousin sure seems to think so," the lady said proudly. "I mean, we all know the odds of poor Mrs. Cavendish surviving that wreck are almost nothing, but what if she did? Senator, what if she has amnesia and is just waiting for you to rescue her? What a romantic story that would be! Everyone knows how in love you two were. If it's really her, it would be the story of the century!"

Daniel stared at the photograph, making quick calculations. The odds were against him, but was it possible? Could this be the answer he had been looking for? A thrill rippled through him just thinking about it. Finally reunited with his darling Wilhelmina. Finally able to reclaim the truth of who he was. It was almost too much to imagine.

He forced himself to tear his eyes away from the photograph. "I need all the details," he said. "Everything. And listen, let's keep this between us, okay? If it's not her, we don't want to get everyone's hopes up. Nor do we want to disturb the privacy of this poor lady if it's just a lookalike. But get me all the information you have, and I'll take care of it."

The lady tapped the side of her nose. "Good thinking, Senator. Always thinking of others, you are. I'll get all the details of exactly where my cousin saw her for you. And God bless you. I'll be praying it's her and you can be reunited with your love."

"Yes," Daniel said slowly, returning his gaze to the photograph. "So will I."

Chapter Twenty-Five

Cole

When Emerson and I returned, I settled into a routine working with the life flight crew three shifts a week, hosting a weekly community self-defense course, and training Willa privately three nights a week.

It was all fun, but there was no question about which part was my favorite. I found myself counting down the hours until I saw her again. She was a remarkable woman, and I was beyond proud of her progress. Her comfort level grew every single class, and she had managed to land a real punch on me. It had shocked her—she immediately dropped her fists and apologized, turning white. But when I laughed, told her I was proud of her, and scooped her up into a hug, she flushed the prettiest pink and we kept going.

Progress.

I was proud of her, but it was more than that. I had never enjoyed spending time with someone as much as I enjoyed spending time with Willa. There was never a single night she didn't gasp over how beautiful the mountain was or take the time to look at the stars in wonder. When her car broke down, she just laughed it off and said it was about time. When I got annoyed by a particularly rude waitress, Willa just put her hand over mine and said the lady was probably having a bad day, not to worry about it. Then she left a ridiculously generous tip on the table, hoping it would brighten the woman's night.

She was shockingly optimistic, a trait I typically found annoying in other people. But with Willa, it was different. I knew that her optimism didn't come from looking at the world through rose-colored glasses. No, she had seen the darkness in the world. Knew it better than most. She had just decided not to let it change her for the worse.

I admired the hell out of her for it.

I was training her, but she was also teaching me. I found myself smiling more, relaxing more—even letting my guard down more than I ever would have thought possible. It was addictive, the peace I felt when she was around.

Every session, I thought about asking her out for more than just another post-training snack. I wanted more time with her. But I didn't know how fast to push things. Just when I thought I couldn't wait anymore, she surprised me after landing her third legitimate punch of the night that I had failed to block.

"So," she said, grinning, no longer white and afraid that I was going to hit back.

"So, you nailed me again," I said, returning her grin. "You're getting good at that."

"I'm quick on my feet."

"Yes, you are. And you're a fast learner."

The beaming pride on her face made me want to wrap her up in my arms and kiss her again. Her joy was a magnet, drawing me in.

"I am. But that's not what I wanted to talk about."

"Oh yeah? What's on your mind?" I put my fists back up in a defensive posture, staying aware. After all, we were still in the ring, and I half hoped she'd try to nail me again. Distraction was a great technique, and I'd be proud of her for using it to catch me off guard. But now that she was getting the hang of things, I was going to stay on my toes and make it harder for her.

And damn, was it fun to spar with her.

"Well, we've been hanging out a lot."

"Yes," I said.

"And enjoying some incredible goodnight kisses," she said, blushing.

I grinned. "Glad to hear you think they're incredible too. It's good for my ego."

"Your ego doesn't need any help," she joked, dancing around me in the ring. "But I was just wondering where you are with everything. I mean, are we just hanging out, or—"

"Willa, do you want to be my girlfriend?"

She stopped suddenly, looking at me. "Yeah, I guess I do," she said, laughing.

I grinned at her. "Good. Because that's what I want, too. And since we got that out of the way, how about we skip the workout tomorrow night? Let me take you to dinner somewhere nice."

She bit her lip, giving me a shy smile. "I'd like that."

"It's a date then."

"It's a date." Her eyes sparkled. Then she moved in and aimed a punch right for my kidneys.

I saw it coming though and swooped out of the way, grabbing her around the waist. All of a sudden, I was holding her, staring into her eyes. The room faded away and I leaned in, unable to hold myself back.

My lips touched hers, slow and soft. Nothing in me wanted to rush. I wanted to savor every second with this woman, cherish every little touch from her.

She reached her arms around me, opening her lips, just begging me to take the kiss deeper. So I did, reveling in her taste and the feel of her body pressed up against mine. This woman was an angel, and kissing her was heaven.

I didn't think I would ever get enough.

THE NEXT NIGHT, I STUDIED MYSELF IN THE MIRROR FOR THE first time in years. I wasn't used to giving much thought about how I looked. Clothes, to my way of seeing it, were meant to be practical. If I could move without impediment and have decent pockets to stash gear, that was good enough for me. And if the women I dated felt differently, well, that was their problem. I wasn't interested in a future with someone who cared that much about what I wore.

I felt an odd desire to look nice for Willa though. After all, she was in the fashion world. It meant something to her. Even so, not once had she ever criticized my way of dressing or suggested I change to suit her. Maybe that's why I was willing to do it.

Personally, I spent even less time noticing what other men looked like than I did checking out the mirror, but I had seen enough tabloid headlines at the grocery store to know that the world thought Daniel Cavendish was one of America's sexiest men.

And Willa had been married to him. What the hell could a beauty like her possibly see in someone like me? I figured I might need to call in reinforcements.

An hour later, Daphne and I were both staring at my closet.

"Hmmm..." Daphne said, tapping her finger against her lips. "Where did you say you're taking her?"

"That place where you guys had your wedding reception," I said more gruffly than I'd meant to. "It's nice, right?"

"Very nice," she said, reassuring me. "It's perfect." She turned back to my closet. "Do you have anything that's not a cargo pant?" she asked, biting her lip.

"There's a pair of tan slacks in the tub up there," I said, pointing to the tub I had stashed in the top of the closet. The one with the clothes I never wore.

"Okay, let's look at those," she said, reaching for it.

Emerson immediately crossed to her from where he had been leaning against the doorframe, watching in amusement. "Nope," he said, stretching above her to reach it before she could. "No heavy lifting, remember?"

She rolled her eyes but gave him a kiss. "Thanks."

"No problem." He put the tub on the bed and she immediately began digging through it.

"Ahh. Yes. These are the same ones you wore to the rehearsal dinner, aren't they?" she asked, looking to me for confirmation.

"Yep."

"Those will work. They fit you well and are *very* flattering."

"Hey," Emerson protested. "Are you telling me my bride was checking out one of the groomsmen the night before our wedding? I'm hurt." He lifted his fist to his chest in mock complaint.

Daphne laughed. "Of course not, silly. But Abby sure was, and she was extremely vocal about how great Cole looked in them."

Emerson threw his head back and laughed. "Yeah, that tracks." He kissed her again, not even caring that I was standing right there.

"Back to the clothes," I said, not wanting to waste time talking about a bridesmaid I didn't care a thing about. "What shirt to go with these pants?"

Daphne turned back to the closet and sighed, wrinkling up her mouth. "Maybe Emerson could loan you a sweater," she finally said. She turned and looked at us both. "Yeah. You're about the same size. Emerson has a green sweater you could borrow. It's nice, very classic. If that doesn't work, I think we'll need to go shopping. Sorry," she said, throwing me an apologetic look. "But everything in your closet is more suited for the gym than a fancy dinner out."

"The sweater it is." The only store I enjoyed shopping in was the one where Willa worked, and they didn't sell men's clothing.

AN HOUR LATER, I WAS WEARING EMERSON'S SWEATER AND the Daphne-approved slacks, standing on Willa's doorstep with a bouquet of flowers in my hand. The nerves I felt were an odd thing for me. I had spent my life jumping wholeheartedly into the kind of things that terrified most people—rock climbing, scuba diving, parachuting, skydiving... Standing on Willa's doorstep had me feeling the kind of nerves none of those other things ever had.

Control was part of it. I knew that. The reason I didn't feel fear doing something like a deep-water night dive was because I had trained for it. After countless hours of training, I could control my body. I could control checking my equipment and ensure that it was set up properly. I knew how to read the conditions and adjust for them. Sure, accidents happened. There was always an element of luck in completing a mission safely. Still, a lot of it was under my control.

I couldn't control what Willa thought of me, and that scared the hell out of me.

But when she opened the door, her face lit up, and my fears melted away.

"For me?" she asked, obviously delighted.

"No, for your neighbor," I said. I immediately regretted it, wishing I would have said something smooth and cool instead of making a lame attempt at humor. But she just giggled and took the flowers from me.

"You can come in while I put these in water," she said, suddenly turning shy.

She held the door open, a gesture that meant the world to me. Willa had lived through hell, but she trusted me enough to let me in her home. I didn't take that for granted.

"Thanks," I said, following her inside.

"You can sit down if you want," she said, gesturing to her couch. "I'll just be a few minutes." She disappeared into the kitchen, leaving me alone in her living room.

Her house surprised me, though I realized it shouldn't have. It was a total reflection of her—all color, texture, and beauty. Her walls were white, but nothing else was. The couch was covered in colorful fabric with about a million different colored pillows on it, all greens, golds, and dark reds. She had a green velvet armchair with a colorful little footstool. Candles, blankets, and artwork seemed to be everywhere. It was a world apart from my austere cabin, and oddly enough, I liked it.

"I like your place," I said when she returned with the flowers—not in a clear glass vase like I had expected, but in some oddly shaped piece of pottery.

"Thanks," she said, beaming. "I can't paint here since it's a rental, so I had to find a way to bring in some color and life. It's all repurposed thrift store finds and craft projects, but I think it came together nicely. It was a fun way to keep me busy before I had much else to do here, and it makes me happy."

"It feels warm," I said. "Welcoming."

She perched on the little footstool and smiled at me. "That's so funny. I thought the same exact thing when I visited Fiona's house this week. So I'll take that as a wonderful compliment."

"I mean it as one." I looked at her, maybe with too much intensity, because she quickly stood up.

"Are you ready to go?" she asked, looking a bit flustered.

"Yeah," I said, standing. "Wanna drive?" I tossed her my keys.

She caught them easily then looked at me with wide eyes. "Really?"

"I told you I'd let you drive my car. If you promise not to drive off any cliffs, that is." I winked at her to let her know I was teasing.

She blushed anyway. "I should say no, but ... I don't want to. I'm dying to drive it. I'll be really careful, I promise."

"I know you will. Let's go then."

She picked up the brown backpack she always carried and grinned. "Let's do it."

Chapter Twenty-Six

Willa

Sliding into the driver's seat of Cole's magnificent car just felt right. I practically groaned in pleasure as I ran my hands over the steering wheel.

"You really do like cars," he said, chuckling.

"I do," I said, unable to hold back my grin. "I always have. This is really fun. Thank you."

"You're welcome. You know how to drive a stick, right?"

"Right," I said, laughing. "I haven't done it in a long time, but I think it will come back to me."

He nodded. "We're heading to Mountain View Bistro if that's okay with you. I made reservations."

"It's perfect. I've only been there once, but I loved it."

He grinned. "You know, our reservation isn't until seven. We can drive around for a while if you want."

"Oh, I want," I said, putting the car into reverse. I let out another sigh of satisfaction when I pulled out, heading immediately for a road where I could drive with a little speed. Pleasure and contentment hummed through me. This felt even better than I remembered—and I wasn't just talking about the car.

"You look nice," I said, glancing in Cole's direction. It was an understatement. The soft green sweater he wore combined with the intoxicating fragrance of his spicy cologne made me want to slide right across the car into his lap.

Which was really saying something, considering how much I was enjoying being in the driver's seat.

"Thanks," he said, looking my way. Our eyes met for a moment before he turned his back to the road. "You look gorgeous. But that's nothing new."

I looked down at my outfit. "It's a pretty skirt, isn't it?"

"It is," he said, his voice level. He glanced back over at me with heat in his eyes. "But you could show up in sweats and I'd still think you're gorgeous. It isn't about what you wear. It's just who you are."

I flushed under the compliment. "Thank you." I looked back down at the skirt. "But I made the skirt, so it's okay if you think it's extra pretty."

He laughed out loud, catching me off guard. "It's a very pretty skirt, Willa."

I laughed too, feeling silly all of a sudden. "It's fun, you know."

"What's fun?"

"Dressing however I want." I let out a contented sigh. My life suddenly felt more full than I had ever imagined it would again.

He glanced over again. "You do dress differently than you did back then. You look different, too. Better. Don't get me wrong. You've always been beautiful. But you glow now."

I flushed again. "I don't always want to bring up the past. But I love clothes. Fashion. I always have. This kind of style though," I said, gesturing at my chunky boots and layered sweaters, my long necklaces and textures, "is me. The real me. I wasn't allowed to be me when I was with him." I grew quiet for a moment, remembering. "My look was the first thing he changed. When I think back to it now, I know that should have been a warning sign that something was horribly wrong. I didn't see it though. I just accepted it when he said I needed to look the part of a senator's wife. I was so stupid."

"Innocent maybe, but not stupid. I get it," said Cole. "Even in the military, we have uniforms. Certain standards for how we cut our hair. It makes sense that politicians have their own kind of uniform. I don't think it's stupid at all that you didn't see it as a red flag."

My heart warmed, knowing he understood. The truth was, it had been a confusing time. And Daniel had been right. The other wives didn't wear hand-crocheted sweaters or feather earrings. I, of all people, understood that fashion told a story about who you were as a person. It had felt so reasonable that he wanted me to present myself as the type of woman who should be on his arm.

"So," I said, turning my attention back to Cole. "Why did you change your uniform tonight?"

He looked over at me, the side of his mouth turning up in a grin. "You noticed?"

"Noticed that you aren't in a t-shirt and combat boots?" I laughed. "Yes, Cole, I noticed."

"I wanted to look nice for you," he admitted.

"You don't have to change for me," I said. "I like you the way you are."

He looked back over at me before taking my hand in his and bringing it to his lips for a kiss. "I like you the way you are too, Willa Monroe."

We could have driven around holding hands all night and I would have considered it a perfect date. But when seven rolled around and we finally parked, Cole took my hand and led me into the restaurant. It felt like a new phase for us. We weren't just hanging out with a group or grabbing a snack after a workout. I was his girlfriend, and we were on a real date. In public. It was something I never expected to have again, and sharing it with Cole made it absolutely wonderful.

We talked non-stop at dinner, about everything and nothing. He told me more about his childhood, and I told him about mine, for once not having to hide the details of my past for safety. With him, I could be honest. It was a beautiful gift.

"I'M NOT READY FOR TONIGHT TO END," HE SAID AS WE slowly walked through the parking lot back to his car after dinner.

"Me either," I admitted.

He ran his thumb absently over my hand. "Want to go somewhere and keep talking?"

"Yes." I didn't even have to think about it.

"I think I know the perfect place," he said, glancing over at me. "Are you dressed warm enough to be outside for a little while?"

I ran my hand over my thick wool coat, smiling. This coat had been purchased specifically to keep me warm if I ended up on the run again. It felt like a sweet twist of fate that instead it would keep me warm while I lingered late into the evening with Cole.

"I'm set," I said, squeezing his hand.

"Perfect."

MOONLIGHT SHIMMERED ON THE SURFACE OF THE LAKE, illuminating the reflection of the soft mountain slopes beyond. The park was empty other than us, and it was so quiet I could hear our footsteps on the dirt path leading down to the water. It felt magical being out here at night, with the place to ourselves.

"It's beautiful," I breathed, entranced as Cole led me to a concrete picnic table at the water's edge.

He lifted me up like I weighed nothing and placed me on top before climbing up beside me. Even through my thick coat, I could feel the cold of the concrete, but I didn't mind as long as he was by my side. I just didn't want the night to end.

"Not as beautiful as you," he said, reaching for my hand.

I just laughed, even as my heart swelled. For someone who thought he wasn't a romantic, he seemed to always know exactly what to say.

"Can I ask you a question?" he asked.

"Anything."

"You talked a lot about your family tonight," he said, nudging me with his shoulder. "But all the stories were from your childhood. Have you been able to talk to your parents since you went on the run? Do they know you're okay?"

I sighed, suddenly feeling heavy with grief. "No. My mom was wonderful. But she died just a few weeks after Daniel and I married. It was completely unexpected. I miss her so much, but in some ways it was a gift. She died thinking I had a fairytale marriage, that I would be happy and taken care of for life. I'm glad she never had to see what I went through."

Cole was silent for a moment. "And your dad?"

It stung my heart, even after all this time. "My dad... Well, he's less wonderful. He's political. Ridiculously so. And Daniel happens to be on his side of the political coin. It was easy for Daniel to convince him that I was the problem, that I was some wild child who just couldn't fall in line."

Cole stilled beside me. "Willa, maybe I've misunderstood or assumed more than I should. We've avoided talking about it for the most part. But with everything we have talked about, I assumed that Daniel physically abused you." He said it as a statement, but there was a question beneath it.

"He did," I said softly.

Cole clenched his fists beside me. "You're saying your husband physically abused you and your dad sided with him?" He couldn't hide the anger in his voice. "Did he know? Did you tell your dad what Daniel was doing?"

I swallowed back the hurt I had never been able to fully release. "In the beginning, yeah. I actually tried to leave Daniel and move in with my dad. I told him Daniel had hit me. But I didn't have any marks on me at that point. Not any that I could show my dad anyway. Daniel was very, very good at hurting me in ways he could hide, in the beginning at least. And then Daniel came over and smoothed the whole thing over with him, calling me dramatic and saying I was just having a hard time adjusting. Dad bought the whole thing, hook, line, and sinker. Kicked me out. Told me to go home to my husband to make things right. Called my cousins, aunts, and uncles and told them all not to give me a place to stay, that I was being immature and needed to grow up."

Cole's anger was so palpable I could feel it radiating off him. "That makes me want to punch something," he finally said before glancing at me with mortification all over his face. "Sorry. That's probably the worst thing I could say right now."

I laughed. "Nah. It made me want to punch something too. The difference is, we want to punch some*thing*. Not some*one*. There's a difference."

"How long did it go on?"

I didn't answer right away.

"I'm sorry," he said, "I'm asking questions that are way too personal."

"No," I said, shaking my head. "It's not that. Believe it or not, it's actually a relief to have someone I can be honest with about it all. But I'm ashamed of the answer to that question."

"How long?" he asked again.

"Three years," I finally answered. The shame of it made me want to throw up.

"Three years," he repeated. But there was no judgment in his voice. Just sadness. "Three years is a long time to live through that."

"Yes, it is. To be honest, it's surprising to me that it was *only* three years. It felt like a lifetime."

"Why did you stay as long as you did?" Again, there was no judgment in his voice. Just curiosity. It made it easier to talk about somehow.

I sighed, stretching out my legs and leaning back against the hard table. "It's hard to explain. Until you're in that situation, you don't understand how you really will blame yourself. Before Daniel, I would have laughed at the very idea of my staying with someone who hit me even one time." I shook my head, wishing I knew how to make sense of it all. "And obviously, I tried to leave in the very beginning. I tried more than once, actually. I went to my dad first. Went to the police the next time. Neither worked, obviously. But then, somehow, Daniel changed my reality. He would beat me, and when I was cleaning myself up after, I would feel so much shame. Somehow, he made me believe it was my fault."

"How on earth could you have thought it was your fault?"

I looked up at the stars twinkling in the black sky, trying to find words to make a senseless situation make sense. "Because I knew how he was. I knew how hard it was for him to control himself, yet obviously I had done something to set him off again. Afterward, I would rehearse everything leading up to it, seeing so clearly how I had made a mistake— how I had missed the signs, how I had let things escalate instead of soothing him. How I hadn't predicted what he would want or need in any given situation. How I hadn't had enough self-control to be what he needed me to be. Every time he hurt me, it was because I had said the wrong thing or done the wrong thing. Broken a rule or failed to keep things the way he liked them. It was always my fault."

"Like hell it was. It wasn't your damn fault. Not one bit of it," Cole spit out, his face pure fury.

I flinched, a reaction I still couldn't help when faced with rage, no matter how much I trusted the man in front of me. Anger still terrified me.

"I know that. Theoretically, at least." I forced a small laugh. "In the beginning, I knew that clearly. Like I said, when going to my dad failed, I tried going to the police. But I paid dearly for that, and it changed things. Cole, I was trapped. And after living that way for a while, my perception changed. I stopped seeing clearly. All I could see was where I went wrong. How easily I could have avoided it had I just been more vigilant, more careful, more—"

"Perfect?"

"Yeah." I swallowed hard. "I tried so hard to be perfect."

"Dammit, Willa. It didn't matter what you did or didn't do. The man had no right to hit you."

"I know that. I see it clearly again now that I'm out of it. I can't explain what it feels like when you're living it though. You become someone you don't even recognize. You believe things you would never have believed before."

"There's nothing that can ever excuse what he did." Cole's voice was firm. "A man who hurts a woman like that isn't worth the dirt he's standing on. I don't understand how you could have thought it was your fault."

I looked at him and squeezed his hand. "Haven't you ever blamed yourself for something that wasn't actually your fault?"

He grew quiet, letting go of my hand to pick up a stick that had fallen onto the table. Silence surrounded us, but I didn't mind. Not with him. With Cole, the silence wasn't threatening. It felt safe. Peaceful.

"Maybe," he finally said, snapping the stick in half.

"Maybe what?" In the silence, I had nearly forgotten what we were talking about.

"Maybe I can understand blaming yourself for something that wasn't your fault."

"Oh yeah?"

He tossed the sticks into the water in front of us. "My job was rescue, and I was good at it. But sometimes you lose. War always has a body count."

"I'm sorry," I said. I could feel the heaviness in his voice and wished I knew how to take all of it away from him.

"Yeah," he said, still quiet. "Saving someone feels amazing. Like you have a real purpose. You know what you're doing matters—to them and their families. Bringing someone home so he can be there to watch his kids grow up? It's awesome. But as amazing as the highs are, the lows when you lose someone are just as bad. Maybe even worse. It haunts you, knowing someone didn't make it home safe to his family."

"You can't save everyone," I said.

"I know. But still. I would beat myself up over it, wondering if there was anything I could have done differently. I'd go over every detail of the operation a thousand times in my mind, trying to figure out where I went wrong, if there was something I missed or something I could have done better. Even if the situation was hopeless from the start. And sometimes they were. You'd go in knowing there was a ninety-nine percent chance you were just retrieving a body. But still. There was that one percent chance you could save them. That hope you'd hold on to. And it broke me everytime."

"So you do understand," I said, rubbing his shoulder.

"It's not quite the same."

"No. But you understand what it's like to blame yourself for something that isn't your fault."

"Yeah." He sighed.

"My turn to ask you a question," I said.

"Uh oh." His face twitched. "I guess I have that coming."

"Why didn't you go home for Christmas?" I asked. I was genuinely curious. He had only spoken about his family with love, so it surprised me he hadn't traveled back home.

A shadow crossed his face. "It's complicated."

"If you don't want to tell me—"

"No," he said, twisting his body to face me. "It's not that. It's just hard to talk about. I don't know, Willa. You know, they all stayed there, in that small town where we were born. Every one of them, except me and Rhett—the two black sheep. And the rest of them are all still this picture-perfect family, you know? They believe life is simple and easy."

"And you know it's not," I said softly.

"Exactly," he said, nodding. "I left, and I changed. I'm not the kid I was when I grew up there. I don't see the world the same. I know what happens in the darkest corners on earth. I've seen what human beings can do to each other." He turned back to look at the water, deep sadness etched on his face. "The last few times I went home, it just felt awkward. Like I didn't fit. Like they all wanted me to still be that kid, you know? And when I wasn't, it just made them sad and disappointed. I don't like making people feel that way. Seems easier to stay away."

It was my turn to frown. "Why would they be sad?"

He grinned, but it didn't reach his eyes. "You're the one who said I'm moody and grumpy."

"Yes," I said, reaching up to stroke his face. "You're moody and grumpy. But you're also good. So good. You're strong and brave, and I suspect you would give the shirt off your back just to make someone else warm. You've seen the worst of the world, and yet you keep trying to make it better. They should be so proud of you. I sure am."

He pulled me closer to him, running his hands through my hair. I leaned in, hoping he would kiss me.

"Willa, you're shivering," he said, frowning suddenly. "We've been out here too long."

"I think you've said that to me before," I said, smiling.

He looked deep into my eyes. "On New Year's Eve. You always want to talk more outside in the cold. Time gets away from us."

"I like it under the stars," I said, touching my cold nose to his. "Even if it's cold. And I don't want to leave yet."

"Maybe I can warm you up," he said slowly.

"Maybe you could," I answered.

He stood up and pulled me close, wrapping both arms around me and holding me tight to him. I slipped my arms around his waist, inside his jacket, and let out a little sigh of satisfaction as I rested my head on his shoulder.

"Careful," he said, chuckling. "You make the same sounds with me that you make when you touch my car and it will go straight to my ego."

I giggled and planted a light kiss on his neck. "Cole, I like you even better than your car."

"Damn. I'm a lucky man."

I looked up at him. "Or maybe I just have lucky stars."

CHAPTER TWENTY-SEVEN

Cole

THE WOMAN SNUGGLED UP TO ME WAS SO BEAUTIFUL I really did want to thank my lucky stars. The whole thing was unbelievable. Who would have thought that, years later, I would have my arms around the woman with the haunted eyes or that she would be looking at me with that look in her eyes? No more fear. No, the look she was giving me was pure trust and contentment.

It was incredible.

I pulled her closer and lowered my lips to hers. Funny. No matter how many times I kissed her, it was as exciting as the first time.

The taste of her mouth was intoxicating. The scent of her perfume —hints of jasmine and orchids, wild and exotic, like her—was dizzying. And when she slid a hand underneath my shirt, tracing my bare chest with her fingers, I nearly came undone.

I drank her in like a man dying of thirst.

When she pulled away, I thought my heart might stop.

"I should ... I should probably go home," she panted, breathless.

I ran my hand through her hair, massaging the back of her neck. "Do you have to?"

She nodded slowly. "Yes, I think I better."

"Okay." I took a deep breath and got myself together, reluctantly letting go.

She slipped her hand into mine, exactly where it belonged. "Thanks," she said, looking up at me as we walked back to the car.

"For what?"

"For not pushing."

"I'll never push you, Willa." I looked at her, needing her to see me— to see who I was. "I'll never push you and I'll never hurt you. I'm not him."

"I know," she said. "I know you aren't. I just need more time."

I squeezed her hand. "Then we take all the time you need."

I woke up the next day with renewed purpose. Gone were the thoughts of running with Willa or of just hanging out until I felt she was safe. The dust had cleared and I could see. My future was here, with her. Permanently.

And I would wait as long as I had to.

In fact, I decided to make it official. First thing that morning, I drove straight to the air evac base and asked Chief if I could talk to him.

"What's up, Cole?" he asked, gesturing for me to take the seat across from his desk.

"Well, sir, I wondered if that permanent position you mentioned was still available."

Chief looked surprised but pleased. "Absolutely. Have you decided to hang around here with us after all?"

I interlaced my fingers in my lap, tapping my thumbs together. "Yeah. Yeah, I have."

"Excellent. I'll get a contract worked up for you to look over by the end of the day. Despite your qualifications, there are still some certifications you'll need to obtain. I'll help arrange those, and we'll cover the cost of them. Once those are complete, as an official part of the crew, you'll work three twenty-four hour shifts a week. I'll keep you on Emerson's rotation if you'd like. We'll work in additional training duties for you monthly to continue the work you've been doing with the crew. It's a two-year minimum commitment. Sound good?"

"Sounds great." I was surprised to find I actually meant it, and again, not just because of Willa. I liked the work. The team was great, and it was fun to be part of it.

I felt like a new man here in Rosemary Mountain. Like I had finally found where I fit in the world again. It was a good feeling.

We talked salary and shook hands on it. Then I left so he could get back to his paperwork. Emerson was in the main room when I walked through and pulled me aside.

"What's up, man? I didn't know you were doing anything out here today."

I grinned. "Well, as a matter of fact, Chief and I just shook hands on a job. Looks like I'll officially be assigned to your team soon, which means you'll technically be my new boss."

Emerson laughed. "It's about time I outranked you somewhere."

"Don't let it go to your head," I said, smirking.

He punched my shoulder. "Hey, I get off at six, and Daphne's got her book club tonight. I'll call Greg. We can grab a drink at the pub and celebrate your news."

I shook my head. "Can I get a raincheck? There's someone else I want to tell first, before I do any celebrating with anyone else."

Emerson grinned. "Of course, man. Any chance we're going to be gathering for another wedding soon?"

I just snorted. "Dude. One thing at a time."

"Uh huh. Have fun." He stood there grinning like a proud dad, making me roll my eyes as I walked away.

"Hey, Cole," Willa called, lighting up the minute I walked in the door to the shop. "I just need to finish closing out the register. Then I can go."

"No hurry," I said, walking to her and pulling her into my arms. I wasn't in a rush to leave, but I sure as hell was in a rush to get my hands on her again.

"Hi." She giggled before kissing me, long and slow.

"Hi yourself." I kissed her again, taking my time, stroking my hands up and down her back.

She sighed contentedly. "Five minutes," she said.

"Take all the time you need," I said, pushing her up against the counter and moving my kisses to her neck.

She giggled again. "You have to let go of me if I'm going to finish up my work."

"Work's overrated, you know."

This time, she threw her head back and laughed out loud before pushing me away. "Neither of us really feels that way, do we? You love your job, and I love mine. I'm more grateful for it every single day. But I'll admit you've been a fun distraction lately." She winked at me before turning back to the cash register.

I leaned up against the counter and trailed a finger up her arm. "Distraction, huh? Is that all I am to you?"

She looked up at me from where she was counting bills. Her eyes were soft. "You're a lot of things to me, Cole Hawkins."

"You're a lot of things to me, too, Willa Monroe."

She held my gaze for a long minute, then smiled and turned back to the bills, tuning me out so she could focus. I didn't mind. I was happy just to stand and watch her.

"Done," she said a few minutes later as she zipped the day's take into a bag. "Now, where are we going for this celebratory dinner, and what are we celebrating?"

"The what is a secret," I said, still not ready to give it away. "I'll tell you later tonight. As far as the where, anywhere you want. The choice is yours."

"Hmmm..." Her face turned thoughtful. "Anywhere I want?"

"Anywhere you want."

She looked a little tentative before speaking. "Then how about we go back to my place and I cook you dinner?"

"Really?" I cocked my head, surprised that's what she would suggest.

She immediately backtracked. "I mean, only if you want. It's probably a stupid idea. We're celebrating. You probably want to go somewhere nice. I shouldn't—"

I put my hand over hers. "Willa," I said, getting her attention.

"Yes?"

I could feel her pulse pounding under my fingers. She was spiraling into panic, and I knew it didn't have anything to do with dinner.

"Willa, you're okay," I said.

"I'm sorry," she stammered. "It was a stupid idea."

"It was a wonderful idea," I said, correcting her. "And I'm honored that you would go to the effort to cook for me."

"Really?"

"Really."

She closed her eyes and took a deep breath. "I'm sorry. Sometimes I think I'm over it all. Then something little will happen, something absolutely stupid like this, and it rushes back."

"I get it," I said. "It's okay. *We're* okay."

She nodded, then bit her lip. "I don't want to bring him up if you don't want to hear it."

I squeezed her hand. "You can tell me anything. I know it helps to talk, and I like listening to you."

Relief flashed on her face. "I like cooking for people. Always have. It's fun. But one year, I cooked for Daniel on his birthday. I thought it would be nice, but he was offended. He took it as an insult that I would give him homemade food on his special day instead of making plans at an expensive restaurant."

Anger flared within me. "He was angry because you went to the trouble to make him a home-cooked meal?"

She gave a small laugh. "Angry is an understatement."

I pulled her to me, wishing I could make it all go away. "I'm sorry he hurt you," I said, running my hand through her hair. "I wish I could do something to make it better."

"You do," she said, wrapping her arms around me. She sighed, burying her face in my jacket. "You really do, Cole. You make me believe in happiness again."

.   .   .

We swung by the liquor store to pick up a bottle of champagne on the way to Willa's house to make it a real celebration. *I* was celebrating, anyway. I wasn't entirely sure how Willa would take my news. She was the kind of person who would be excited for me no matter what, but it was also kind of weird to tell a relatively new girlfriend you had decided to permanently put down stakes just to be close to her. That was big, and I still worried about pushing too hard, too fast. I never wanted to make Willa feel controlled or boxed in.

But for the first time in my life, I really wanted a future with someone. I was determined to figure out the right balance of moving forward without pushing. So yeah, I was nervous about what Willa might think, but I hoped she would be excited, and not just for the job.

I hoped she would be excited for us.

I perched on a barstool in Willa's kitchen, while she started heating spices in a pan. As the aroma hit my nose, a whole set of sensory memories kicked in. "Well, that smell sure takes me back," I said.

"Back to what?" she asked, shooting me a curious look.

"Time overseas," I said simply. There wasn't any reason to go into detail, and frankly, there were things about my time in service I couldn't answer questions about anyway.

"That would make sense," she said, gesturing to the book on her shelf, a cookbook of recipes from around the world. "I haven't looked at this one in a while, but I think it's Lebanese. Does it bother you?" she asked, hesitant. "I can change recipes if it brings back bad memories."

"Nah," I said. "Some of those memories are good. I enjoyed seeing the world. Met a lot of great people. Ate a lot of delicious food. Have you traveled much?"

She leaned her head back and laughed. "Yes and no. Yes, I've been on a lot of vacations, but not a lot of variety, to be honest. I've seen a lot of resorts in the Bahamas and the Caribbean. And, of course, some of the higher-end spots here, too—the Hamptons, Bar Harbor, Jackson Hole, Vail, places like that."

"Touristy spots."

"Exactly. And after I left, I did a lot of driving around the United

States, exploring parts of it I hadn't seen. That was fun." She smiled as her eyes drifted off like she was remembering happy times. "I enjoyed that a lot, actually. But I haven't been to the sort of places I really want to go. I'd love to travel the world like you did, honestly. Who knows? Maybe I will someday."

"I thought you wanted to stay in Rosemary Mountain?" I asked, suddenly feeling uncomfortable about my announcement.

"Oh, I do." She turned to me, sincerity in her eyes. "You need a solid home base, you know? Traveling is fun, but I want a real home. I have one here. When I say I want to travel the world, I don't mean I want to live everywhere. I'd just like to explore it a bit on vacation. See real culture instead of resorts, you know? Walk the streets where the locals walk, eat where they eat. I love seeing how other people live."

"I gotcha." I felt a touch of relief, realizing she still wanted to live here and wasn't contemplating moving away the same day I signed a two-year contract. "I've been lucky to do a lot of that. But you're right. I think you need a home base. Makes it more meaningful. And with that," I said, clearing my throat. "I guess it's the perfect time to tell you. Tonight, we're celebrating my new job. I accepted a permanent position here."

Her whole face lit up. "Cole, that's wonderful! You've decided to stay?"

I nodded. "I'm staying."

"I thought you weren't the kind of guy to settle down somewhere," she teased.

I was dead serious when I answered. "I think maybe I met someone who changed all that. Truth is, Willa, I can't imagine losing you again. You're settled here. So this is where I want to be."

Chapter Twenty-Eight

Willa

I turned back to cooking, overwhelmed by Cole's words. Was he really staying in Rosemary Mountain for me? And if so, was it because he felt an obligation to protect me, or... Or was it because he actually wanted a real future with me?

I didn't want to ruin anything by bringing up the past. But I wanted to know.

"Cole," I said, turning around again.

"What is it?" he asked, wrinkling his brow. "You look upset."

I shook my head. "I'm not upset. But I just have to know. Are you doing this because you feel some sort of obligation to protect me from Daniel? Because if so, I—"

He rose off the stool and walked toward me, cupping my face in his hands. "Willa. Do I want to protect you from Daniel? Hell yeah I do. I don't want that man to ever lay a hand on you again. But if you're asking if I'm staying here out of some sense of duty, some *obligation,* then you don't understand at all. Willa, I love you. I know it's too soon to say that, but it's true."

He ran his hands through my hair, then slid them down my back, pulling me to him. "I love everything about you. All I think about is you, how I want to see you every day. Hold you. Kiss you. Be with you. I've tried not to tell you that because I don't want to ruin this by pushing. And the truth is, I'm staying for a lot of reasons, some of which don't have to do with you at all."

"Really?" Hope began to grow—hope for our future, and hope that Cole had fallen in love with this place the way I had.

"Really. I like my work here. I like my friends. The mountain is starting to feel like home. But I'm also staying because I can't imagine my world without you in it, and that has nothing to do with some 'obligation.' You've changed everything for me."

I wrapped my arms around his neck, sinking into him as I listened to his words. I could see the truth of them in his eyes. They weren't hollow words, thrown out meaninglessly in an effort to manipulate me. His eyes were full of love, trust, and honesty.

And in that moment, I realized I loved him, too. It was more than just a fun distraction, more than enjoying my newfound freedom. More than attraction or romance, though there were both of those in spades. Cole held a place in my heart no one ever had, and all I could think was how grateful I was that he was staying.

"I love you, too," I whispered back, leaning my forehead on his chin.

He pulled back, looking me in the eyes. "Really?"

I giggled at the surprise on his face. "Yes, really. Why do you look so shocked?"

He chuckled. "Honestly, I never thought someone like you could love someone like me. I mean, I'm moody and awkward, and I always think the worst. You're sunshine and light, and despite everything you've been through, you always see the good in the world." He ran his hands through my hair again, kissed me softly, then pulled me tight against him. "But you make me want to be a good man."

I put my hands on his chest, shaking my head. "Cole, you sell yourself short. You're the best man I've ever known. I love you in a way I never thought was even possible. And you telling me you're staying here in Rosemary Mountain? It's the best news ever."

He ran his fingers up and down my back, sending beautiful shivers up my spine. "I think so too. And, Willa?"

"Yes?"

"I never want you to think I'm here out of obligation. But if Daniel ever does find out about you and decides to come for you, well, I'd like for him to have to come through me first."

"I see," I said, biting my lip. "So you just want to be my knight in shining armor?"

"Baby," he said before kissing me again. "I want to be your everything."

WE ATE DINNER TOGETHER IN MY LIVING ROOM, AND I marveled over how surreal it felt. On one hand, it was just as comfortable as our post-workout snacks. It felt normal. Routine. Safe.

But it also felt like something entirely new. Every step forward with Cole felt like freedom, and the sheer beauty of it made me want to laugh, cry, and write poetry all at once.

A year ago, I still hadn't even found my way to Rosemary Mountain. I had been living a transient life, completely alone in the world, never totally sure where I would lay my head each night.

To have gone from that to this—this love, this new stability, this *life* —was absolutely unbelievable.

And when we finished dinner, I realized that I might actually be ready to take one more step.

"Cole," I said with just the slightest bit of hesitation as I gathered up our plates to carry them to the kitchen.

"Yeah, babe?"

I looked him in the eye and bit my lip. "Do you want to spend the night?"

"Yes," he said, looking up at me with no hesitation of his own. "Of course I will. But I want to be totally sure about what you're asking. Do you want me to stay and sleep on the couch because it will make you feel more safe? Or are you asking me to stay because you want me in your bed? To be clear"—he grinned—"my answer is yes either way. I just don't want to assume anything."

I suddenly felt shy. "I'm asking because I want you in my bed."

Heat flared in his eyes. "Are you sure, babe? There's no rush. We've got the rest of our lives, and I'm a patient man."

I walked to him, putting the dishes back down on the coffee table before kneeling in front of him. He ran his fingers through my hair, looking at me with so much love in his eyes. "I don't know how far I'll want to go," I confessed. "I've never once been triggered by you touching me or kissing me. I feel safer with you than I ever have with anyone else. But..." I trailed off, not wanting to bring any ghosts from the past into our future.

"I understand," he said, running his hand up and down my arm. "I've told you before. I never want you to feel even a moment of fear with me. We only do what you want to do. We stop when you want to stop. Like I said. I'm a patient man."

I took a deep breath and smiled, feeling relieved. "Then stay with me tonight. But maybe we just cuddle. I don't know. Can we just see how it goes?"

He grinned. "I'd be honored to cuddle you, Willa. Of course we can just see how things go. No rush, remember?"

"No rush," I repeated, stretching up to plant an easy kiss on his lips.

Although the truth was I didn't want to wait at all. I ached to be held and loved by Cole. But there were things he didn't know—things he would learn when we finally crossed that bridge.

And that thought terrified me more than anything else.

Cole helped me tidy up the kitchen, and we fell into an easy rhythm as we worked together. Afterwards, we cuddled up on the couch to watch a movie on his laptop. I had never invested the money in a TV, thinking it was too frivolous a purchase for someone on my budget. But it was so fun watching a movie with him that I promised myself I would rethink that logic. If I was staying in Rosemary Mountain, maybe a TV would be worth the investment.

After all, curling up in his arms for two hours was well worth the chunk it would take from my paycheck.

He never pushed, but his hands never seemed to tire of exploring and teasing me—slipping just underneath my sweater, tracing little circles on my waist, pulling me closer to him. Every touch drove me crazy, distracting me completely from the movie he seemed immersed in. Before it was over, I flipped over, facing him on the couch.

"You're driving me crazy," I breathed, slipping a hand of my own up his shirt, tracing those firm muscles that always looked so good during our workouts.

"Oh yeah?" he asked, looking both pleased and amused as he pulled me tight against him. "You're driving me crazy too, you know," he said before nipping my neck lightly with his teeth.

"I want..."

"What do you want, Willa? Tell me." He nipped me again and slid his hand farther up, sending new thrills through my body.

I couldn't take it anymore. "I want you," I whispered as he groaned into my ear.

In an instant, he was standing, holding me in his arms. "Where's the bedroom?"

"Down the hall. Last door on the right."

He carried me the whole way, those hands still somehow managing to explore even as he held me in his arms. I was practically vibrating with anticipation, wanting everything he could give me.

But when he put me gently on my bed, he stepped away, back to the doorway—and flipped on the light.

Immediately, my guard came back up. I trembled as he walked toward me. He saw it and instantly stopped.

"It's okay," he said. "We don't have to. No rush, remember?"

"No," I said, trying to make him understand. "It's just that I-I have scars."

"I know. We all do, baby," he said, looking at me with empathy in his eyes.

"I'm not being figurative." I swallowed hard, lowering my head in shame. "He...he put scars me. Where I could still wear evening gowns and nobody would see. But if we... When we... I mean, you're about to see and... Cole, I'm not beautiful." I couldn't say anything else. The nausea was overwhelming as I thought of Cole seeing how Daniel had ruined me. How he had marked me as his, putting a literal brand on my skin. It was bad enough that I had to live with it. Cole seeing it was a million times worse.

"He scarred you," Cole repeated, rage flashing in his eyes. But I wasn't scared of him. Not anymore. I knew Cole would never hurt me.

I nodded. "Yes," I whispered. "I'm sorry. I wish—I wish..."

Cole just stared at me for a long moment. Then he stripped his shirt off and turned around, baring his back to me. "Scars," he said. "We've all got them."

My eyes filled with tears as I saw the long mark across his back. I slid off the bed and walked toward him, running my hands across the marred skin.

"What happened?"

"Training accident," he said. "An ugly scar for a stupid accident on some sharp rocks." He turned to face me again, this time stripping off his pants. "See this one?" He pointed at his thigh, marked with an angry-looking scar. "Knife wound. Not even a war wound, believe it or not. Got that one in high school. Saw the local bully beating up a younger kid on a playground. I pulled him off. Little monster had a knife in his pocket and sliced my thigh open. I was too scared to show my mom, so I washed it out and superglued it closed myself. Should have gotten stitches. It would have been prettier."

"Cole," I said, touching the scar on his leg. "You really are the best man I've known."

"And you're the bravest woman I've ever known. Now. I showed you mine," he said, gently touching my face. "Your turn."

My head dropped as the tears began to fall.

"Willa," he said, lifting my chin with his hand. "Listen to me. This doesn't have to happen tonight if you aren't ready. I understand this might be hard for you, for a million reasons. I'll wait as long as you want to. But if the only reason you're holding back is because you're afraid of what I'll think, you don't have to worry about that. You're beautiful, and I love you. And that's not going to change, no matter what scars he left on you."

I nodded and took a deep breath. I wanted to be brave for him. My only worry was that he would be as disgusted with the scars as I was, that he would look at them and never be able to see me as more than the woman Daniel had ruined.

I slowly pulled my shirt over my head, feeling more vulnerable than I ever had standing there in my skirt and bra.

"Oh, baby," he said, running a finger over the angry, red scar on my ribs where Daniel had burned me. "What did he do to you?"

"Fireplace poker," I said quietly. "That was the second time." I slowly slid my skirt off, revealing the one I hated most of all. "This was the first. He did this after I went to the police, to mark me as his. And to prove that even with marks on me—clear marks that would never go away—he still had the power to get away with it. That there was literally nothing I could do to be free of him. He would never be held accountable for what he did."

Cole's eyes filled with tears as he lowered to his knees. He stared at the spot on my lower waist where Daniel had burned his initials into my skin.

"I'm sorry," I repeated.

He looked up at me with fury on his face. "Don't you ever say that to me again about something he did. You don't have a damn thing to be sorry about, Willa. You did nothing except survive." He held my hips and gently placed his lips on the scar, kissing it like he could somehow make it better. "I hate him for doing this to you. But only because it hurt you." He rose to his feet and looked deep into my eyes. "You're so beautiful."

I didn't say anything at first. I couldn't. I just wrapped my arms around his neck and sobbed on his shoulder. Until this moment, I hadn't realized how difficult it would be for me to ever be this vulnerable with someone again.

When I could finally speak, I had to ask. "How can you think I'm beautiful when I'm scarred like this?"

He ran his thumb along my cheek and frowned. "Do my scars bother you?"

"No, of course not." I shook my head. "But you got your scars doing what you do. Saving people, or training for it. They just prove who you are: a hero."

"And yours prove who you are: a survivor. Someone who survived something that never should have happened. Something that could have broken you, forever changed you, and turned you into someone bitter or angry." His eyes were focused on mine with such intensity. "You faced darkness, but it didn't break you. It didn't change you. You're still pure light and love. You survived him, and you broke free. How could I not love that part of you? Willa, I admire the hell out of you. Your scars just add to that."

I saw the truth in his eyes and wanted to hope. "But I'll always have another man's initials on my body," I said, swallowing back the tears. No matter what he said, he couldn't change that. And I hated it.

He looked down, studying the scar with a thoughtful look on his face. "Who says they're his initials? Maybe DC stands for dangerously clever. Or devastatingly cute. Both things that describe my girl perfectly."

He looked at me and grinned, and suddenly everything in my heart loosened.

I giggled, something I once would have thought impossible while standing nearly naked in front of a man. "Or disastrously clumsy," I laughed.

"No," he said, shaking his head. He pulled me back into his arms and nuzzled my ear. "I've got it. Daring and courageous. Two perfect words that describe you."

I wasn't laughing anymore as he ran his hands down my back, warming me in ways I hadn't experienced in so long. "Or maybe," I whispered in his ear, "it stands for my Darling Cole."

His hands stopped suddenly and he pulled back again, his face serious ."I don't need my name branded on your body, Willa. I love you. My heart is yours. But you belong to yourself. I'm not the kind of man who wants to own you."

"I know," I said simply. "That's why I kind of like the idea of being yours."

He ran his thumb along my cheek again, then kissed me, teasing me with his tongue before whispering in my ear. "In that case, I might as well tell you the truth. My first name is Dennis."

I giggled until I realized he wasn't joking. "Wait, are you serious?"

"Dead serious. You can look at my driver's license."

"Why do you go by Cole, then?"

"A few years of being called Dennis the menace and you'd switch to your middle name too," he said, grinning before he kissed me again.

"Dennis Cole," I whispered before closing my eyes and losing myself in him. "It really was fate, wasn't it?"

"Hell yeah it was."

Chapter Twenty-Nine

Daniel

Daniel Cavendish parked his rental car at the town square, slipped on a pair of sunglasses, and began his exploration of Rosemary Mountain. He had seen it in pictures, of course, having done his research online before flying in. Briefly, he had considered sending a private investigator instead. But he had soon realized that would be pointless. No matter what an investigator said, he would have to see it for himself. He wouldn't rest until he knew that this whole thing was a ridiculous error, that Wilhelmina hadn't dared defy him in this way.

So, despite how important his time was, this was something he simply couldn't entrust to someone else. Hopefully it wouldn't take too long, he thought, sneering as he surveyed the little mountain town. Nobody in their right mind would want to spend any longer than necessary in this podunk place.

It didn't take long to spot the little boutique where his contact claimed the Wilhelmina lookalike worked. Originally, his plan had simply been to walk into the place and see for himself. But as he walked toward it, he realized that might be an error in judgment.

If this really was Wilhelmina, he wouldn't want to make his presence known. Not right away.

He paused, clenching his fists at the rage that passed through his body as he imagined Wilhelmina—*his* Wilhelmina—living here. Working here. Going on with her life without him, having *tricked* him.

It was unfathomable.

But, he reminded himself, it likely wasn't her. Once the initial shock had passed after seeing the photograph, he had to admit that it was unlikely. This girl was a bit heavier than his Wilhelmina had been, and her hair was completely different. Besides, thanks to his connections, the best rescue crew in the world had been in the water searching just minutes after her car had gone over the edge. Had she survived, they would certainly have found her.

No, Wilhelmina was dead. She had to be.

But a tiny sliver of doubt was enough to make him want to avoid a face-to-face confrontation until he knew for sure.

So he changed course and headed for the coffee shop on the square to grab a well-deserved cup of coffee—no matter how bad it would likely be, coming from this town—and to think.

An hour later, he remained seated there, in a window spot he had chosen specifically because of the view of the boutique. It had given him plenty of time to brood over the situation. He was still fairly certain the woman wouldn't be Wilhelmina. But the resemblance was uncanny. It would be even stronger if she lost fifteen pounds and did something with that mess of hair.

Finding a lookalike presented an interesting opportunity to fulfill the cravings he had been suffering ever since Wilhelmina's disappearance.

It also presented the possibility for what could be some incredibly good press. The old lady at the party was right. It would be the story of the century if he "found" Wilhelmina, suffering from amnesia, and brought her home. The press had grown tired of him shortly after Wilhelmina's disappearance. They had always been more interested in her than in him, even though *he* was the one who mattered. Anger flared again at the thought.

Still, a fresh love story would get him back in the press. And it would almost certainly boost his numbers in the polls if he was presented as the devoted husband who never gave up believing his wife would one day be found. It was a good angle, he mused as he flagged the lady behind the counter to warm up his coffee.

He would have to figure out the right tack to take with the girl to get her to play along. Money, perhaps. Everyone had their price. Money would make things simple—unless she decided she wanted more and threatened to expose his plan to the press. It was always dangerous, giving someone leverage like that.

Romancing her would be cheaper, and it would give him greater influence over her. He could pretend to be shocked to find someone who looked so much like his late wife, play the part of the grieving widower, and romance her. Convince her that, because of his position and the optics associated with it, it would be better for her to pretend to *be* Wilhelmina than for him to be seen as having a new romance. If anyone could pull off something like that, it would be him.

On the other hand, while it might have fewer complications in the long run, it would be infinitely more time consuming. And frankly, romancing someone was a drag. Romancing a woman meant making everything about *her,* and that was intolerable for more than brief periods.

Of course, he could simply take her. A thrill of pleasure hummed through his body at the thought. That would be a bold move, even for him. But if she was to be his future wife, she'd have to learn what he expected of the woman in that role. He took a sip of his coffee, contemplating the idea. Perhaps that was where he had gone wrong with Wilhelmina. Perhaps he had been too soft with her from the beginning, had spent too much time romancing her and convincing her to marry him.

The spoiled brat had expected him to continue on with the romance after the contract was signed. It had been utterly annoying. Though, to be fair, the irritation of it all had made it that much more satisfying the first time he had finally shown her her place.

But starting out with clear expectations from the beginning could be a better move.

Besides, it would allow him to take care of these cravings and exercise his rights all the faster if he skipped the romance and simply took what he deserved from the beginning.

Yes, he decided. He would simply take her. After all, he was Daniel Cavendish. It was his right.

Another hour passed with no sign of his future bride, so he decided to move on for a while. He didn't want to draw attention by spending too much time in the coffee shop, staring out the window. These backwoods folks likely had no clue who he was, which worked to his benefit. Still, it wouldn't do to draw attention. Not yet anyway.

Once he had control of the narrative, it would be fine for someone to recognize him. Endearing, even, for the local shop owner to give an interview about how the senator himself sat in her shop, just waiting and hoping to have found his bride again. Daniel chuckled, picturing it. Yes, this whole thing would be a good move for him. He was sure of it.

As he stood up, a sports car pulled up in front of the boutique, catching Daniel's eye. Impressive, he thought. He hadn't expected anyone in a town like this to own a car like that. Had to be a tourist. He smirked.

But when the man got out of the car, he seemed vaguely familiar. In fact, as Daniel watched him, he became more and more sure he had seen that man before. Met him, even.

He was trying to put his finger on it when the man walked into the shop. All the warning bells in Daniel's body went off. This was too much of a coincidence. A man he had met before, here in Rosemary Mountain, going to the boutique where a Wilhelmina lookalike worked?

This couldn't be a coincidence.

Daniel sat back down at the table, deciding to wait until the man left. He didn't have to wait long. Moments later, the man emerged from the store with Wilhelmina herself on his arm. He walked her to the passenger side and opened the door for her. Wilhelmina—for Daniel knew now it had to be the *real* Wilhelmina, not some cheap lookalike—stretched onto her tiptoes and wrapped her arms around the man's neck, kissing him right there on the sidewalk in broad daylight, before getting into the car.

Rage boiled within Daniel as he watched his *wife*, the spoiled *whore*, kissing another man for the whole world to see. The bitch had tricked him after all. She was alive, dammit. Alive with a lover, mocking him.

She would pay. By God, that woman would pay for making a fool of him. She would suffer as he had suffered this past year with her gone. She would pay for every single moment of this mockery. And Daniel would enjoy every last minute of it.

His mind raced as he began to calculate a plan. It would take some time. A few weeks at least. After all, someone like him couldn't simply skip his obligations at the drop of a hat, and he was due back in California tomorrow. Besides, he would need time to think everything through. It wouldn't do to rush things and make a mistake. This was a game of chess, and he was the master. So he would take the time required to put the pieces in place and make sure every base was covered before he made his move.

Because when he did, she would never see it coming—and nothing would stand in the way of his plans for her.

Wilhelmina wasn't the only one with a trick up her sleeve.

CHAPTER THIRTY

Willa

"Sorry I'm late," I said, unwrapping my scarf and sliding into the booth across from Daphne, excited to catch up with her. Cole and I had practically cocooned ourselves for the past few weeks. "I got held up at work." I couldn't quite hide the blush that accompanied my lie.

"Right," Daphne said with a knowing smirk on her face as she pushed the already half-empty basket of hushpuppies my way. "Work. How's that going anyway?"

"Oh, it's great! Your mom has been wonderful to work for," I said as I popped one of the hushpuppies into my mouth. "And I'm designing a new line of linen wear for the summer tourist crowd. They're fairly easy pieces that I can put together quickly. Janet asked for beach vibes. An odd choice for a mountain town, but she's convinced they'll be hot sellers, especially if they're marketed as handmade and local."

Daphne sipped her water, nodding as I continued to talk. When I finally stopped to breathe, she gave me an amused look. "Well, that's wonderful, but that's not the 'work' I was asking about. I was more curious about the 'work' that has your shirt on inside out." She dipped her chin as she bit back a laugh and gestured toward my top.

I glanced down and felt my cheeks go red. "Oh. Well. You know, I do have to try on the products…"

"Oh stop. Spill it. I want details." She grinned at me.

I grinned back, unable to hide it anymore. "I was wrong about him."

"I know. Me too," she said. "I didn't know if I could trust him at first, but I do now. And it's clear how happy he makes you."

"He does make me happy. Very happy." I shook my head, still in disbelief. "Honestly, Daphne, when I left you-know-who, I never expected to find love again. I never even really imagined my future. All I could see was the next step. The next town, the next job. Even signing the lease on my house was a huge deal. Then your mom offered me a job. Job isn't even the right word. She offered me a chance, and even that was more than I hoped for. It felt like a dream come true. Then I met Cole." I shook my head again, knowing I was barely making sense. I was so giddy I could hardly put two sentences together. "I just never thought I would be this happy again."

"I'm so glad for you, Willa," she said. "And for him. He's changed since he first came here. You've lifted that dark cloud off of him."

I bit my lip. "Daphne, can I be honest?"

"I hope you always will be."

I leaned my head back and sighed. "I'm happy. But I also feel so guilty."

"Guilty?" She cocked her head and looked at me, puzzled. "Why do you feel guilty?"

I glanced around the room, making sure no one was close enough to hear. "Because," I said, lowering my voice to a whisper. "Legally, I'm married."

She shook her head. "No. Wilhelmina Cavendish was married. Willa Monroe is not."

"I wish it were that simple."

"Maybe it is." She shrugged. "I don't know. I don't know the first thing about the legal ins and outs of it all, but personally? I don't think you should feel an ounce of guilt about finding happiness with someone who loves you and treats you well. You-know-who cheated on you and abused you. Brutally. He was no husband to you, and he doesn't deserve your guilt. *You* don't deserve your guilt. And Cole doesn't deserve it, either."

I looked down. "And yet it remains and seems to come back at the most inopportune times." I let out a breath, then looked up, meeting her gaze. "Daphne, I need you to know I would have ended things legally if it had been an option. I tried. I really tried to do the right thing." My eyes filled with tears I couldn't quite blink away. "I paid dearly for it," I finally said over the lump in my throat. "No need for details. Had I tried again, he would have killed me for real. Doing what I did, leaving the way I did... It was my only option."

Daphne leaned across the table and squeezed my hand. "Willa, the only one judging you here is you," she said gently. "You don't owe me any explanations."

"Thank you," I said as my heart swelled with gratitude. This, too, felt like a miracle—having a true friend who genuinely wanted me to be happy. Rosemary Mountain had brought miracle after miracle into my life.

"So, back to the inside-out-shirt thing," Daphne said, lightening the mood. "Are you going to give me details or what?"

I just laughed as a weight lifted off of my chest. "I never kiss and tell."

Cole picked me up after work that day, like he insisted on doing every day he wasn't on shift. It had become routine in the very best way. Some people despised the ordinary, everyday things. Me? I reveled in them. They had been missing from my life for so long that I was absolutely delighted by every single one of them.

When Cole put an empty milk carton back into the fridge instead of tossing it, I actually smiled.

We weren't officially living together, but we might as well have been. We spent every night he wasn't working together, either at his place or mine, and we were both beginning to have quite a collection of clothes at the other's place. He had made it clear that whenever I was ready, we would make it official and move into either home—my choice. He had even talked to Emerson about buying the cabin if I chose that one. Emerson had been delighted and agreed we could make it happen whenever the time was right.

I hadn't told Cole yet, but I was almost ready. He had never once pushed. He had even acknowledged that my rental house was a symbol of independence and I might not want to give it up. It was one of the things I loved most about him. He didn't treat me like I was broken or weak. He told me I was strong. But he also understood that, because of my past, I might need certain things or might need to go slow.

It was a breath of fresh air to be with someone who didn't belittle me, play mind games with me, or deliberately hurt me. When I had first met Cole, I had compared him to Daniel, thinking they were both dangerous men. But the truth was they were complete opposites.

"What sounds good for dinner?" Cole asked, looking over at me from the driver's seat.

"Want to pick up a pizza?" I asked. "I have a surprise for you at the house, and pizza would go perfectly with it."

He shot me a look, eyebrows raised. "A surprise, huh?" His eyes raked over my body as he gave me a devilish look. "One of the fun surprises?"

"Yes," I giggled. "But probably not the kind you're thinking."

"Damn. Got my hopes up for a second. But pizza it is." He turned left, heading toward Rosemary Mountain's only remaining pizza place. "Ham and pineapple?"

"You know it," I said, smiling. I loved that we both liked the same kind of pizza. It was a silly thing, but it was just one more reason to feel like we were meant to be together. I loved that I could be myself with him, that I never had to hide my preferences for his. If we wanted different things, we got them, no problem—like when we ordered Chinese food and had complete aversion to each other's favorites. It was no big deal at all to order a carton of his and a carton of mine. No drama. No arguing. But with pizza, we were a perfect match.

Everything was easy with him and I loved it.

I waited in the car while he grabbed the pizza, smiling over the surprise I had waiting for him. When he returned, he slid into the car and kissed me before putting the pizza box in my lap.

"I love you," he said simply.

"I love you too." My heart soared. Every day with him seemed to get better and better.

"Home?"

"Home," I said, smiling over the word.

I UNLOCKED THE DOOR, SO EXCITED TO SEE COLE'S FACE. When we walked inside, his sharp eyes immediately honed in on what was different.

"A TV?" he asked, surprised.

"Yeah," I said with butterflies circling in my stomach. "I thought it would be great for us to watch movies together. And in a few weeks, when I move in for good, I thought we could move it to the cabin."

He turned and looked at me. "What are you saying, Willa?"

I handed him a key to my house. "I'm saying my rental is up in six more weeks. Until then, I want you to think of this place as ours. But after that, I think we should make an offer on Emerson's cabin. Together. And we'll move the TV there."

"This is a big step for you," he said, pulling me to him.

"It is," I agreed, nodding. "And yet it doesn't feel scary at all. Not with you."

"Man, I love you," he said, shaking his head. "I never thought in a million years I could be this happy."

"Me either," I whispered.

He leaned his forehead to mine and just held me.

CHAPTER THIRTY-ONE

Cole

THE BUDDING LEAVES AND BIRDS CHIRPING IN THE TREES declared that spring had arrived early. I wasn't the poet my brother was, but even I had to smile as I looked around the land that was officially ours—mine and Willa's. It felt poetic in the best way that we were making a fresh start of things just as the world was waking up from winter and coming to life again.

"Just two more boxes," I called out to Willa as Emerson and I headed back out to his truck to get the last of her things.

"Thanks, babe!" she called back from the kitchen, where she and Daphne were unpacking the dishes she had collected since moving to Rosemary Mountain. The cabin would never look like a bachelor's pad again.

And I couldn't be happier about it.

"Thanks, man," I told Emerson as I pulled the last box from his truck. "For helping today, and for everything else."

"Man, I'm happy for you. You know, we weren't really in touch when I first moved here. But I'll tell you, I was in rough shape. Almost as moody as you were when you got to town."

I rolled my eyes. "Yeah, yeah. I get it. I was miserable to be around."

"Nah. But *you* were miserable. I get it though. I was too. Everything changed for me when I met Daphne. And it looks like everything changed for you when you met her," he said, nodding toward the house. "I'm happy for all of us. And we're tickled pink to have you guys as our permanent neighbors. I know Daphne's thrilled to have one of her best friends living on the mountain."

"It's more than I ever hoped for," I confessed, propping the box back on Emerson's tailgate and leaning on it. "I thought I was going to live the life of a nomad forever. My mom's thrilled," I said, chuckling. "I actually talked her and Dad into flying out here next week to meet Willa."

Emerson's face lit up. "That's great. They'll love her."

I nodded. "I know they will. They already do, just because she's the woman who makes me call them every week. She's helping me find my way back to a relationship there, and they've let me know they adore her for it. But once they meet her? They'll love her like I do. Well." I smirked, raising an eyebrow. "Not exactly like I do."

Emerson just rolled his eyes and laughed.

"Hey, there's something else I want to talk to you about," I said.

"What's that?"

"I might be starting something new, and there's a spot for you if you want it. No worries if you don't. I know you already work long hours with the air evac team. But if you want a part-time gig to earn some extra money..."

"Oh yeah? What kind of gig are we talking about?" Emerson asked, putting his box down to settle in for a chat.

"Training gig. Maybe a little security work. There's a private security firm in Asheville that contacted me about doing some training simulations for them, similar to what I did here. More security focused than rescue, but a good mix of both. Hinted that there might be some potential private security gigs too, for big money."

"Hmmm," Emerson said, mulling it over. "I'm not as qualified for that as you."

"Doesn't matter. We work well as a team, and you have skills I don't. Plus, I trust you with my life. So there's that."

"Look at you getting all sentimental and mushy on me," Emerson said, grinning.

"Been spending too much time with you I guess," I said, smirking.

"Yeah, yeah. Marriage made me a softy. Come on. The women will be wondering why we're slacking off if we take too much longer out here."

At that very moment, Daphne stuck her head out the door. "Where are you guys? We need one of those boxes."

"Coming, dear," he called, winking at me.

By late afternoon, Willa and Daphne had everything unpacked and settled. Willa didn't own much, but it completely transformed the cabin anyway. It turned it into a home—a real one.

"It's beautiful, baby," I said, pulling Willa to me and planting a kiss on the side of her head.

"Not too girly?" she asked, chewing on a thumbnail as she looked around. "We can tone it down if you want."

"Not at all," I said. "It's you. Your personality is everywhere, and I absolutely love that. Besides, the barn is my man cave."

"Yep," Emerson said, laughing. "You know, we men may give you women a hard time about all your throw pillows and decorations, but I think we secretly like being domesticated."

Daphne threw a pillow at him. "Go pick us up some dinner. We're starving."

"Yes, ma'am," he said before planting a kiss of his own on her. "Come on, Cole. Let's go get some food for these lovely ladies who have been working *so* hard today. You know, it's exhausting to fluff pillows and arrange photographs."

He winked and ducked as Daphne chucked another pillow at his head.

I shook my head and followed him toward the door. "Lock up behind me, babe," I said to Willa. "We'll be back soon."

"I will," she said. "We'll be fine."

She followed me to the door, knowing I would wait there until I heard her lock the deadbolt. Even now, I wasn't entirely ready to let down my guard. But every day, it felt less and less likely that Daniel was ever going to give us any problems.

Every day, I was getting a little closer to relaxing and allowing myself to just be happy.

My phone buzzed while Emerson and I were in line waiting for a pizza. I must have had a strange expression on my face when I checked the message, because Emerson immediately asked if everything was okay.

"I'm not sure," I said slowly as my mind raced a million miles an hour.

"What is it?"

I stared at the message for a good minute before answering, willing it to give me more information than was actually there. When I finally looked up, Emerson was studying me with a frown on his face.

I shook my head and sighed. "It's about a buddy of mine. I just got word he died in a car accident."

"Oh, man, I'm sorry to hear that. Close friend of yours?"

I shook my head again. "No. Not exactly."

Emerson frowned. "Cole, what's going on? There's more to this story, isn't there?"

I hesitated, knowing that Willa still hadn't told him her full story. "When I first met Willa, I thought I recognized her," I said, deciding to tell him anyway—I'd just leave out Daniel's name. "Long story short, I knew her ex-husband. He's a powerful man with a reputation for corruption. I asked this friend of mine to do a little digging into things, see if he was facing any legal problems or anything like that."

"Okay," Emerson said, drawing the word out. He was obviously tracking the same place I was. "That's quite a coincidence. It may have been an accident though. What does the message say?"

"Not much," I answered. "It's from a mutual friend of ours. I guess it happened several weeks ago, which may explain why I hadn't heard back from him. But it's weird, isn't it?"

"Exactly how powerful is Willa's ex?" Emerson asked.

"Very," I said, setting my lips in a thin line. "He has a lot of connections and even more money."

"Worst-case scenario. If it wasn't an accident and it was because this guy was looking into him, what are the odds it will trace back to you here?"

I stuck my hands into my pockets and let out a long breath. "Very low, I'd say. This friend is—was—discreet to the max. The very definition of the word 'ghost.' Honestly, it's hard for me to believe they caught onto him at all. But on the other hand, Willa's ex probably has the best working for him too."

"Better stay on your guard," Emerson commented before walking up to grab the pizza boxes that had just been slid onto the bar.

I sighed again. So much for relaxing and just being happy.

CHAPTER THIRTY-TWO

Willa

WORK SEEMED TO GO BY IN A BLUR. I DID MY BEST TO STAY focused, but the truth was I was completely distracted by everything that was happening between me and Cole. I had never felt so happy in my entire life, not even when everything had seemed golden and beautiful between me and Daniel. Even then, when he had swept me off my feet in a romance that made tabloid headlines, I hadn't felt this kind of deep, soul-satisfying happiness.

Everything was different with Cole.

After I messed up two different orders, Janet laughed good-naturedly and told me to go home early, that she would take care of things.

"I'm so sorry," I said, blushing. "I don't know what's wrong with me today."

"I do," she said, giving me a knowing smile. "And nothing's wrong at all. You're happy and in love, and I couldn't be happier for you. Take the rest of the afternoon for yourself. We're slow anyway. Besides, I'm sure you wouldn't mind an extra couple of hours with Cole, now would you?" She winked at me.

"I'd love it, but that's not even an option," I said, unable to hide my proud smile. "He drove into Asheville today. I guess word is spreading about the training he's been doing with the team here, and a private security firm in Asheville wants to talk to him about doing some contract work for them."

Janet leaned up against the counter and cocked her head sideways. "He's really making a place for himself here, isn't he?"

"He is."

"You are too," she said, pointing out the obvious.

"I am." I couldn't hold back my smile.

Janet wasn't smiling though. Her face had turned serious. "I know your situation will always be a little up in the air. I hope with all my heart you're able to stay. But I understand there may come a day when you have to run. I'm glad you have someone in your life who will run with you. Someone you can count on."

"Me too." It was such a gift, knowing I had someone in my corner. Someone who was so used to moving all the time that he wouldn't even bat an eye if we needed to pick up and leave. At the same time, I hated that it had to be that way. As much as I loved Rosemary Mountain, I could tell Cole had fallen in love with it too. And he was making a true career for himself here, something far more important than making clothes.

I didn't want to be the one to take him away from all of that.

"Well," Janet said, interrupting my thoughts. "The offer still stands. We're as slow as molasses today. You're welcome to head home if you want."

"How about you head home instead?" I offered. "I don't have anything important to do with Cole out of town. He won't be back until late. You can go surprise Greg. If either of us is going to leave early, it should be the one who has someone to spend the extra time with."

Janet's face lit up. "Oh, that would be lovely. Are you sure you don't mind? You've pulled more than your fair share lately."

"I don't mind at all," I said, waving her off. "Go, have fun. The work will make the time pass more quickly for me." My face lit up in an unexpected grin. It was such a new feeling, having something to look forward to. It had been such a long time since I had needed to make the time pass by in order to get to something so wonderful. Last year, this job was the best thing in my life. But now, Cole had far surpassed it, which made me feel all the richer. I would never take it for granted.

"Well, if you're sure," Janet said, but it was just to be polite. She had already made a beeline for the back room.

"I'm sure," I said, laughing. I went back to tidying up one of the displays, humming as I worked with what had to be a ridiculous smile on my face.

"See you tomorrow," Janet called out as she headed out the back door.

"Tomorrow," I echoed in answer.

An hour later, my phone buzzed. I slipped it out of my pocket, expecting to see a text from Cole. Instead, the message was from Daphne.

> ***Daphne: Where are you? Where's Cole?***

> ***Willa: I'm at the store, getting ready to close up. Cole's in Asheville for a meeting. Why? Is everything okay?***

> ***Daphne: I don't know. I was napping and had a terrible nightmare that Daniel came after you. I'm worried it might be more than just a dream.***

My belly clamped with fear at the message. But I took a deep breath, fighting off the anxiety. I was safe. I was at the store. Daniel wasn't here.

> ***Willa: I'm sorry. That had to have been terrible. I'm safe and okay though.***

> ***Daphne: I still have a bad feeling. Don't walk home alone, okay? I'm calling Greg to pick you up and give you a ride.***

I frowned at the message. Not that I minded the ride, but if Daphne was this worried, did I need to be? I believed her when she said she had "the sight," but I didn't know what that meant. Not really. Was this just a nightmare or a warning? And if so, how much time did I have?

I stared at the phone for a minute, wondering how to ask my questions without sounding crazy myself. In the end, I just sent her a message thanking her, telling her I would stay put until Greg arrived. Then I immediately tried to call Cole, but it went straight to voicemail.

"Hey, Cole," I said, leaving him a message. "I hope your meeting is going well! Sorry for bothering you. Just wanted to check in. Or maybe I just wanted to hear your voice. Call me when you can."

I hung up the phone when I heard the little bells on the door ring. "Oh, Sheriff," I said, turning around to say hello to Greg.

But the man standing in the doorway was the one person I never wanted to see again.

"Hello, Wilhelmina, my darling. I've missed you more than I can possibly say."

I couldn't force myself to move. I was frozen as I stared at the man from my nightmares. It felt like all the color had suddenly drained from the world, taking all the warmth with it, leaving the room ice cold and gray.

This couldn't be happening; it couldn't be real. Not now.

"Wilhelmina," Daniel said, frowning. "Aren't you even going to give your husband a proper greeting? After all, it's been a very long time."

I just continued standing there in shock. I couldn't speak, even if I had wanted to.

His eyes glittered cold and mean across the room. He strode toward me, putting a firm hand on my elbow. "Now, Wilhelmina. Let me tell you exactly how things are going to go. We're going to walk out that door. Do you understand? The press is waiting outside to snap their photographs of the reunion of the century. The story I've told them is that you were injured in your accident and that you suffered from a very serious case of amnesia. That I never gave up hope I would find you again. *That,* at least, is true."

His eyes narrowed, making my belly clamp with fear. "I told them one of my best men found you a few weeks ago, and I've been communicating with you from a distance, with the assistance of a physician who specializes in these issues to help you remember your old life. I've told them you aren't yourself and still don't have a full recovery of your memory yet, but that we've made enough progress for me to bring you home to continue your rehabilitation. See, I need for them to realize you might not be quite the same. Though I am hoping you'll remember your place and put on a good show for the cameras. The loving-wife act, gazing at me with adoration like you used to. You know the drill."

I opened my mouth to speak, but nothing came out.

He shook his head. "No need to say anything now. You'll have a chance to offer me your explanations and apologies later. This is not the time for it. Right now, you simply need to shut up and come with me to the car that's outside waiting for us."

I finally found the strength to speak. "I'm not going anywhere with you," I said, choking out the words.

His eyes glinted like steel. "Oh, I think you will."

I shook my head. "Never."

"If you ever want to see your boyfriend alive again, you'll do as you're told." His face was perfectly calm, sympathetic even. I knew this face. It was a stage face, one he chose in case someone shot a photograph through the window. But his eyes revealed the truth. He was angry. And he meant every word of what he was saying.

"What did you do to Cole?" My lips quivered even as I said the words.

"Arranged a meeting for him." Daniel's eyebrows rose as his face betrayed the slightest hint of a smirk. "That meeting didn't go anything like he was expecting, by the way. And now, his future is in your hands. Whether he lives or dies, and how much pain he'll suffer either way—it's all in your hands, Wilhelmina. I do hope you'll make the right choice. But I'll enjoy myself either way." He reached his hand up, stroking my face. To anyone watching, it would look like an act of affection. To me, it felt like the promise of pain and humiliation.

Bile rose in my throat, out of hatred for this man and fear for what Cole was enduring. "Please don't hurt him," I said. "Please." The word came out as a sob.

"That's entirely up to you," Daniel said coldly. "You can walk out with me right now, putting on a good show for the cameras. Return to your real life as my wife. Or you can refuse and his blood will be on your hands. And I mean that quite literally, Wilhelmina. Refuse me now and I will ensure that you get an up-close, personal view of everything he will suffer because of it. You will watch as he dies, and I promise it won't be quick. You will beg for my mercy. I will not give it. Do you understand?"

I wanted to collapse under the weight of it all. There wasn't a choice—not really. There never had been. I had been given a beautiful year of respite, a year for which I would always be grateful. But I had never truly escaped Daniel's grasp. He had told me I never would, and he was right.

"Don't hurt him," I repeated softly this time. Broken. He had beaten me again, and I despised him for it.

I saw the flash of triumph in his eyes.

"Are you ready for your return to the big leagues?" he asked, offering me false charm along with his arm.

I closed my eyes and prayed for strength before slipping my arm in his. It felt like I was sticking my head into a noose.

"That's the version of you I like to see," he said approvingly, patting my hand with his. "Submissive. Broken. As much as I hate the fact that you stole this past year from us—a year you will pay for, I assure you—perhaps it had to be this way. Perhaps this is what you needed to finally learn your lesson. You are mine, Wilhelmina. Mine to do with as I please. Now, it's okay to look a little frightened. After all, this is a big change for you, no longer being used to the press. But do try to look grateful and loving as well. And above all, keep your mouth shut. Remember, Cole's life depends on it."

I nodded in misery. He took a breath and moved to the door, opening it to the flash of a thousand cameras, all eager to get a glimpse of the newly found Wilhelmina Cavendish.

CHAPTER THIRTY-THREE

Cole

The road felt good underneath me as I sped down the highway toward Asheville for my meeting. The only thing that would have made it better was if Willa had been sitting in my passenger seat, keeping me company on the drive. That thought made me crack a grin. Things sure had changed since I had first driven into Rosemary Mountain a few months back. Then, all I'd wanted was to be alone. Now, I felt incomplete without her beside me.

I had found the kind of thing that I didn't think was in the cards for someone like me, and it had changed everything. In fact, the more I thought about it, the more I wondered if I should maybe stop at a jeweler while I was in Asheville. It was probably too soon to ask her for forever. After all, she was enjoying her freedom. Hell, after what she had been through, she might not ever want to get married again.

That thought made me frown more than I'd expected. Was marriage really that big of a deal to me, of all people? It was something I had never considered before. Never imagined I'd want to settle down and promise a lifetime to someone else. But the more I thought about it, the more I knew I wanted that with Willa.

Apparently she had changed me more than I had even realized.

Truthfully, I wasn't sure a legal marriage was possible for her. She had told me about her fake documents, but I wasn't sure how good they were or if they would work for a marriage certificate. Wilhelmina Cavendish was technically still married to Daniel. Marrying me would just add another felony to her list.

If she got caught.

I made a mental note to ask one of my contacts to quietly look into that. If she even wanted to marry me, I reminded myself.

If she didn't, well, there was still nothing stopping me from offering her a ring, was there? Or from making my own promises, regardless of hers.

That settled it. I would stop at a jewelry store before heading back to Rosemary Mountain. When I did get around to giving it to her, I'd let her know there was no pressure. That I understood marriage had been awful for her, and I wasn't going anywhere even if she couldn't give that to me. That I just wanted her to know how I felt about her and I was committing to her. To us.

To a future together, whatever that looked like.

With those thoughts in mind, I pulled into the parking lot of the building where my meeting was scheduled. Even as I did, unease trickled up my spine. Nothing definite, just a feeling—a feeling that something was off.

I backed into a parking space, where I could scope out the building before going in—and where I could pull out quickly if this feeling got stronger.

Something was definitely off. There weren't nearly enough cars in the parking lot for an office building of this size, just two sedans and a van parked on the side. The sign with the company name looked brand new. That in and of itself didn't mean anything. On the phone, they had mentioned being a start-up.

But still.

A man in a suit came out the front office door, giving me a friendly wave and making a beeline for my car. Also a red flag. No executive I knew ever met a potential employee in the parking lot. They usually wanted their potential hires to come inside and be impressed by the setup. An executive would keep himself in a power position behind his desk.

I put a smile on my face but discreetly reached for my pistol, slipping it into my jacket where it was hidden but I could grab it in an instant.

The man was all smiles when he reached my window, but it didn't matter. I knew an operative when I saw him. He positioned himself where it would be difficult for me to drive away and scanned the inside of my car with his eyes, clearly looking for weapons. Then, as he approached my window, I saw the quick signal he made with his fingers —and the sound of the van's engine as the driver turned it on.

It was a trap. But unfortunately for them, I wasn't going to walk into it.

I threw the car into gear and peeled out, not caring that I ran over the man's feet as I did. A glance in the rearview mirror told me I was right in my assessment—his gun was drawn and pointed toward my car, even as a team of three jumped out of the van and ran after me.

Idiots.

They would never chase down this car on foot.

Two shots rang out, making me wince. My pretty car would never be the same.

Within seconds, the van was in my rearview mirror, giving chase. It just made me grin. Tactical driving was one of my favorite games to play. Granted, I'd never had an actual criminal trying to chase me down and kill me, and I'd only done this on a closed training course where the stakes were low. But the rush of adrenaline was the same, and God, I loved adrenaline.

They had picked the wrong guy to mess with.

It took less than five minutes to lose the van and get back on the interstate. I'd need to keep a watch out for backup, but with the initial threat over, I had more important things to think about—namely, Willa.

There was only one person I could think of who would send a team after me: Daniel Cavendish.

. . .

I grabbed my cell and called Emerson, barking out orders before he even had a chance to say hello. "I need you to get to Willa!" I shouted. "I think she's in trouble. Her ex sent a team after me. He's probably going after her, too. Call Greg. Call whoever. Just get there and get her somewhere safe. I'm on my way."

But instead of jumping to action, Emerson was silent.

"Did you not hear me?" I barked. "This is serious. Please, Emerson."

"Cole," he said, his tone strained. "I don't know how to tell you this."

"Tell me what?" My heart sank as all the color and warmth seemed to fade out of the world.

"Cole. I'm sorry. She's gone."

Chapter Thirty-Four

Willa

Daniel ushered me inside the town car, looking every bit the protective, loving husband. The mask dropped the moment the car doors locked, with us hidden inside behind the dark tinted windows.

The look he gave me then was pure hatred.

"Privacy," he snapped to the driver, who instantly put up the barrier between us and him.

I sat silent, with my hands in my lap.

Daniel loosened his tie, glaring at me. All the control he had held when the cameras could see him was gone. His face was now pure rage.

"Well?" he said as if expecting something from me.

"Well, what?" I answered. I felt hopeless, defeated, and alone.

His hand lashed out, slapping me hard across the face. "How dare you speak to me in that tone," he said. "I'm waiting for you to apologize, you filthy whore. This is when you should be down on your knees, begging me for forgiveness."

I wanted to smart off, wanted to tell him exactly what I thought. But I couldn't. Not when he held Cole's life in his hands.

"I'm sorry," I said hollowly.

A measure of his control returned. "You're not," he stated. "Not yet. But you will be."

A frisson of fear passed through me, breaking through the numbness I had felt from the moment I'd realized this was hopeless. My heart raced when I felt the car stop. "What's happening?" I asked, feeling a sudden sense of alarm. "We can't be at the airport yet."

He looked at me, clearly amused by my fear. It was practically entertainment for him. "Of course not. A little game of switcheroo," he said, motioning for me to get out of the car. "You remember it, I'm sure."

I did indeed. It was a way of losing the press. A second town car would have already taken our place on the driving route, leading the press behind them. The car we had been in would disappear, hiding out somewhere until the coast was clear. Meanwhile, we would be in a different car altogether, headed somewhere else.

Alone.

Daniel motioned toward the getaway car. Everything in my body urged me to run, to fight, to do anything except get inside.

But as long as he held Cole, he was in control. So I overrode my body and climbed into the passenger seat of the nondescript vehicle—something the press would never associate with the wealthy Daniel Cavendish.

And as he pulled out onto the road, going the opposite direction from the airport, I wept.

"Where are we going?" I finally asked.

Daniel had surprised me by heading toward the mountain where Cole and I now lived. My fear grew. Had he found our home? Invaded it? It was almost too much to think about. Our little cabin in the woods was a safe haven, a place Daniel had never touched. It would break my heart to see him anywhere near it.

"A cabin I rented," he said, barely glancing my way. "Or, rather, that my security team rented. I promised you would pay for the year you stole from us. And for giving your body to another man. I intend to punish you so that you'll never dream of doing such a thing again. When I'm satisfied you understand your place, we will return home. The press will understand we needed privacy to reconnect as a couple."

"Privacy, right." Despite my fear, I couldn't bite back my sarcasm. "You'll paint a romantic story of reconnection for them when all you really want is to hide somewhere for a few weeks where you can beat me and nobody will be around to photograph my bruises."

He chuckled. "You always were a smart one."

"I want reassurances," I said.

"You're hardly in a position to ask for anything."

"I could still jump out of the car," I pointed out. "Make a run for it. Tell my story to the press. If you want me to keep playing along, I want to know Cole's safe. I want him released, and I want proof. Now."

He looked at me, amused. "As I said, you're not in a position to ask for anything."

I put my hand on the door to make my point, but he didn't react.

"Go ahead. Try," he said, shrugging.

I tried the door, but it wouldn't open—nor would the window roll down.

"Told you," he said, chuckling again. "Wilhelmina, you know me. Do you really think I wouldn't have thought through everything? I've been planning this for weeks. As I said. You're in no position to negotiate. This will all be done my way."

He put his hand on my upper thigh, squeezing hard enough to leave a bruise. Letting me know he owned me.

I just put my head on the window and wept again.

As Daniel pulled the car up to the isolated cabin, I scanned the surrounding area. This might be my only chance to escape. Though truth be told, I wasn't sure I should. An internal battle was waging within me, trying to decide if I should go willingly with Daniel in order to protect Cole or if I should try to run and go for help.

I couldn't stand the thought of Cole suffering for my sake.

And there were practical things to consider, too. We were in the middle of nowhere. If I ran, could I even get to safety before Daniel found me? If not, that would just be one more infraction to add to his list. More punishment to suffer. Maybe even more for Cole to suffer, too, in order to teach me a lesson.

If I was successful at escaping, would he kill Cole just to keep us apart?

Or worse, had he already killed Cole? That seemed like a Daniel move. Take out the threat immediately so there wasn't even a chance Cole could come for me. But keep the truth from me so I would comply.

Killing Cole right away was the smartest move, as much as I hated admitting it. Hated even thinking of it.

As I closed my eyes, I could almost hear Cole's voice whispering in my ear. *Don't be afraid. You're the strongest person I've ever met. Do what you need to do. Promise me you won't go down without a fight.*

I couldn't stop the tears, no matter how much I hated for Daniel to see me cry. Hated him knowing he had that power over me.

He was clearly amused by my emotion. "Starting to have regrets, darling? I can't tell you how happy I am to see that. I admit, I was worried your newfound defiance might hold out, despite my best attempts at correcting you. I would hate to have to kill you, truly."

"Yes, that would be difficult to explain to the press, wouldn't it?"

"Not that difficult, no. Easy enough to blame it on your new lover." Daniel's tone was matter of fact. "A fit of rage over you leaving him once you learned your real identity. I, of course, would shoot him in self defense—not until it's too late for you, sadly, but nevertheless. I'll be a hero anyway and all the more sympathetic for having been twice widowed by the same woman."

"Your ability to spin things will run out someday," I said. "People will start looking more closely."

"Doubtful." He moved his hand farther up my thigh, squeezing again so hard it brought tears to my eyes. "Wilhelmina, darling, it is *so* nice to have my hands on you again. I've missed you more than I can say."

"I can't say the same in return."

"I'd watch that sharp mouth of yours if I were you," he said with a clear warning in his voice.

It was a warning I heeded. It was one thing to test the limits when he was calm and amused. It was another altogether when he was starting to get irritated. I clamped my mouth shut and continued watching carefully as we drove, looking for anything that might help me when I had a chance to escape.

Chapter Thirty-Five

Cole

I stared in disbelief at the TV screen, watching the news footage of Willa being "reunited" with her husband. It was sold as the most romantic story of the year. The saintly husband who had never given up on his wife. The beautiful woman with amnesia, who had forgotten her entire life but was being swept away into a fairy tale.

It was bullshit, and I couldn't believe that the world was buying it.

"She's terrified," I said, my heart breaking as I rewound the footage to watch it again. "You can see it in her eyes."

Those beautiful, broken eyes. The same eyes that had haunted me once were haunting me again. She was terrified and sad, and I would literally rip my heart out if it meant protecting her from all of it. I wanted to explode with frustration over the whole thing.

"I know," Greg said, putting his hand on my shoulder. "I see it too. Obviously, I believe your story that she didn't go with him willingly. I saw the same thing you did the night of your self-defense class. It was clear she had been abused, and the Willa we're seeing on the screen isn't at all the Willa we know. Even I can see that."

"She left him," I said, my words coming out ragged. "He hurt her. Bad. Then trapped her so she couldn't leave. She tried. She tried to get help, but he bought off the police. And now he has her again. So help me..."

Greg squeezed my shoulder. "Believe it or not, I know what you're going through. I know what it's like for the love of your life to be in danger and to feel like you can't do a damn thing about it. But I promise you I'll do anything I can to get her back safe."

I shut the TV off, despite wanting to watch it again—wanting to cling to that last piece of Willa like it would somehow bring her back. But every minute mattered, and it was time for action.

"What do we have on her location?" I asked, detaching from my feelings and snapping into mission mode.

Greg shook his head. "Nothing, I'm afraid. I was en route to the shop when it happened. Followed their vehicle as soon as I got through the crowds of paparazzi. But they pulled something. When I pulled the vehicle over, they weren't in it. Just gone. The driver doesn't have a clue where they went."

"They disappeared."

He nodded. "He had it all planned out. Two different towncars to distract the press, with a third vehicle hidden and ready to go. Got a description of it from one of the drivers and put out a BOLO, but nothing yet. And look, this is the last thing you want to hear, but I do have to be careful here. We're talking about a U.S. senator, and I have exactly zero proof that he did anything wrong. Willa never even confided in me—something you both should have encouraged her to do," he said, looking at me and Emerson in turn. "As it stands, I'm going to have to walk a very narrow line."

"She didn't want to get into trouble for breaking the law," I said. "It wasn't my story to tell."

"Dammit, Cole, do you really think I'd do anything that would jeopardize an abused woman? If so, you don't know me well. I don't care who her husband is. I don't abide by men abusing women. If she would have confided in me, I would have helped her. The legal way."

"Who says you could have?" I demanded. "Like you said, he's a U.S. senator. No offense, but he's got a lot more power than a county sheriff. She did things her way, and I wasn't about to take that away from her. He was a controlling ass. I sure as hell wasn't going to be."

He sighed. "You have a point there."

"So, what are you doing next?"

He gave me a long look. "I'm going to do what I do. Like I said, I have a BOLO out. I've got my men scouring the area. Jackson's doing some digging, trying to find out if anything in the area has been rented to the senator. We're keeping an eye on the airports. We've found other missing people before. We'll do our best to find her."

I shook my head. "This isn't just some other person. This is her. And a man with endless resources who will want revenge. Let me help."

He kept giving me that same look, an unreadable stare. "Officially, I'm telling you to go home and get some rest while I take care of this. Unofficially, I'm telling you that I'm going to do what I do. And... well..." He raised an eyebrow and turned around, walking off.

I got the message.

When he stalked off, Emerson moved to my side. "So, what's our first move?" he muttered under his breath.

"You don't have to do this," I said.

He snorted. "Like I'm going to let you have all the fun."

I gave him a grateful look and clapped him on the arm. "Alright. Do me a favor and keep Greg distracted for a bit."

"Sure. What for?"

"When I got here, I saw a map on Greg's desk, with the routes he's already checked and the area marked where they were last spotted. I need to get a better look at it. Then I'm going to have a quick talk with Jackson. Or if he doesn't want to talk, I'll take a look at his computer. Either way. Greg needs plausible deniability. Keep him out of my hair for ten minutes."

"Done."

Emerson grasped my hand and gave me a long look. I nodded and shook his hand back, then walked down the hall toward Greg's office to start narrowing down my search.

Hang on, Willa. I won't fail you this time.

Chapter Thirty-Six

Willa

I STAYED SILENT IN THE CAR AS DANIEL DROVE PAST THE road where Cole and I lived, heading to a more rural part of the mountain I had never even seen. I paid attention to every turn, memorizing the route in case I was somehow able to get away. The road turned to gravel and wound deep into the woods until we ended up at something that was barely more than a shack.

"Not quite your style," I commented as he stopped the car.

"Not at all," he said, chuckling. "But that makes it all the more likely we'll have the privacy we need. Besides, it seems this is right up *your* new style, based on what I've seen." He glanced over, looking at my outfit in disgust.

I stayed silent.

"I'm about to unlock your door, Wilhelmina. Running would be a very big mistake. Do you know why?"

"Because you have Cole," I said, repeating what I thought he wanted to hear.

"That's one reason, yes. But there's another. This cabin was owned by a fur trapper. I've been told he didn't always use the most ethical—or even legal—means of trapping. This property is practically booby-trapped. You run and the odds of your leg ending up in a steel trap are higher than you can possibly imagine. And if that happens, I'll be sorely tempted to simply leave you there to die. Not a pleasant death, now is it?"

Can't be any worse than what you have in mind for me, I thought. But I was smart enough to stay silent. I simply nodded, attempting to keep a remorseful look on my face.

He pushed a button, releasing the lock on my door, then sat there as if waiting to see if I would try running after all. When I didn't, he gave me a pleased smile. "Excellent," he said. "I see we're getting somewhere already." His phone buzzed in his pocket and he pulled it out, glancing quickly at the screen. "Go on inside, Wilhelmina. I'll be along shortly."

His words sparked fresh fear in me. Was it a trap? It had to be a trap of some sort. Why else would he let me out of his sight for even a moment? For all I knew, he was going to lock me in and set the place on fire.

But I nodded wordlessly and got out of the car. I trudged slowly toward the house, slumping as if dejected, using the time to scan my surroundings.

I glanced back at his car before going in to see if he was just waiting for something to happen—who knew? This place might blow the minute I opened the door. Though, admittedly, that wasn't Daniel's style. He liked to watch me suffer.

But he wasn't even looking at me. He was having an animated conversation with someone on the phone, and he appeared to be furious. I stood, hedging my bets, trying to read his lips. I didn't catch much, but two words were clear: *find him.*

I immediately turned to face the door, knowing I couldn't hide the shock on my face. *Find him.* He had to be talking about Cole.

Cole must be alive. He had escaped. *Of course* he had escaped. This was Cole we were talking about after all. Tears sprang to my eyes as I filled with newfound hope.

Hope and determination.

If Cole was alive, if he had somehow gotten away, there was absolutely no way I was going down without a fight. I quickly calculated my best odds. Run now or go inside and wait for Daniel? It was a gamble either way, but I felt better about going inside. There might be a weapon I could use to catch him off guard when he walked in—a chair, a board, *anything.*

So I opened the door tentatively and stepped inside, breathing a sigh of relief when nothing happened. No booby traps, no bombs. Fresh confidence filled my soul. I had three advantages Daniel didn't know about. First, Cole had taught me to fight. Daniel wouldn't be expecting that. Two, Daniel couldn't hold Cole over my head anymore. Third, I knew Daniel. I knew how he operated, knew how he lied. I needed to stop thinking he was always three steps ahead of me when the reality was that I could read him like a book. All those years of watching his every facial expression, trying to predict his every move—I still had that.

And now? I had a reason to fight.

The cabin was dark, lit only by the light coming in through the door, a single window, and cracks in the old plank walls. It smelled old and musty, like it hadn't been used in a very long time. It was a single room, without any modern amenities—nothing more than a basic shelter from the elements, really.

I scanned the room quickly, trying to get my bearings. Daniel had clearly set it up to terrify me. There was a dusty bed in one corner, with restraints obviously meant for me. There was a solitary wood chair in front of an old fireplace, beside a large stack of firewood. I nearly vomited when I saw what sat on the chair—the brand he had used on me before.

But worse than that, in the back corner, stood a table covered in photographs.

For a moment, I forgot about Daniel. I stepped forward, horrified by what I saw on the table. They were photos of me, taken when I was unconscious—trophies of his work. Images of me broken, battered, bruised, and burned.

Except one. One was of another girl. A girl who clearly hadn't survived the horrors she had been through.

I raised my hand to my mouth, fighting back the nausea and fear that threatened to overwhelm me. I had always known he was a monster, but this? Even I couldn't believe this. My newfound bravery started to crumble as I faced the evidence of how evil he really was.

The sound of the door made me jump. I turned, facing him, completely unprepared. I was sick. Sick from what I had seen, sick from what he had in store for me, and sick that I had wasted my opportunity to grab something.

But he wasn't on top of his game, either. He was flustered, angry. He tried to appear confident and in control, but the truth was in his eyes —it always was.

Even when I was the only one who could see it.

"I see you've had time to look around," he said, gesturing at the table.

I nodded, afraid to speak.

"Then you're well aware of what I'm capable of," he said. There was a hint of pride in his voice. It disgusted me. How had I ever fallen for this man and his lies?

I nodded again, taking a small step backward.

He took a deep breath, obviously trying to gather himself. "I'm prepared to give you a choice, Wilhelmina. A gesture of kindness since you've decided to show some submission for once. We can do things as I originally planned, or we can speed this up." He walked around the space, gesturing at it. "Neither one of us really wants to spend two weeks holed up in this place, now do we?"

"No," I said shakily, trying to stay focused on reading him.

"You've shown willingness to be put in your rightful place. Have you not?"

"I have." I nodded, hoping it wasn't a terrible mistake.

"Yes," he said with a small smile—a *relieved* smile. "Because of that, I will extend a choice to you. A chance for you to have some mercy. You should thank me for that, Wilhelmina. I certainly do not owe it to you."

"Thank you," I said, still nodding, trying to appear as submissive as possible—even as my mind raced a million miles an hour.

One thing was clear. Before the phone call, he had been excited about his plan, but his mood had changed radically. He no longer wanted to be here. And there was only one reason he would want to run away. Cole was free. Cole was looking for me.

Daniel Cavendish might enjoy hurting women, but there was no way he'd willingly face a man like Cole.

"So, your choice," he continued. "Option one, you remain stubborn and we stay here as planned, for as long as it takes to teach you your place. Or option two, you will show me that you've truly changed your ways."

My guard immediately came up. "How would I show you that?"

He gestured at the chair. "You shall brand yourself with my initials nineteen times, once for every month you deprived me of my rights as your husband. You will do the first one yourself, to prove your submission. I will put the next eighteen on you. Then, you will prove your submission there," he said, pointing toward the bed. "After I am satisfied that you've accepted your place, I will arrange for a private flight back to California." He gave me a small smile. "Just think. By tomorrow night, you'll be wearing silk again and this whole thing will be a nightmare we can put behind us."

Like hell. It was all I could do to bite back the scathing retort I wanted to give him. There would be time for that. I would make sure of it. But right now?

Right now was all about survival.

I swallowed back the bile and forced a small smile. "That seems gracious of you, Daniel."

He nodded. "Excellent. I'm glad we agree. Perhaps your time here in this wretched place did more good than I realized, showing you everything you were missing. Get to it then," he said, flicking his gaze toward the fireplace.

"You want me to–to build a fire?" I asked, legitimately unsure of what he was asking me to do.

He rolled his eyes. "No, darling, I thought we'd heat the brand up over cold firewood. Of course I want you to start a fire."

I glanced at the fireplace, deciding to take a chance. "I don't know how."

He glared at me. "What do you mean you don't know how?"

I shrugged, knowing I was risking his anger. It didn't matter though. I already knew that this would end with a fight at some point. In the meantime, I'd play what cards I could, trying to get an advantage. "I'll certainly try, Daniel, if that's what you want. But I've never built a fire before. Our fireplace back home was gas, remember? All I had to do was push a button. This," I said, gesturing at the firewood and putting on my best dumb female act, "is totally different. Do you have lighter fluid or something?"

He rolled his eyes dramatically. "Oh, Wilhelmina. You're lucky you're so beautiful. That's one thing I had forgotten about you. You're completely helpless when it comes to anything useful. Fine. I'll build the fire. But trust me when I say you'll pay for that as well."

"I understand. Thank you, Daniel," I said meekly as he rolled up his sleeves.

He turned his back to me as he started loading logs into the fireplace. I wanted to laugh out loud. I knew him, but he didn't know me at all—not anymore. Wilhelmina Cavendish was terrified of him. She wouldn't fight back.

But Willa Monroe?

Cole had taught me to be a fighter, and there was no way in hell I'd willingly let Daniel put a hand on me again.

Chapter Thirty-Seven

Cole

I BLEW OUT A BREATH OF FRUSTRATION AS GREG AND Jackson gave me the bad news. They didn't have a single lead. Jackson, apparently a wizard with a computer, hadn't been able to turn up a single rental agreement that would lead back to Senator Cavendish. They couldn't find anything even remotely suspicious—no records of cabins rented out to shell companies or anything similar. It wasn't tourist season yet, which meant most rentals were currently closed. The ones that were open were all accounted for.

They didn't have a clue where to start searching for Willa, and despite the time I had spent studying the maps in Greg's office, I didn't, either. I had to hand it to Daniel. He had managed to disappear without a trace.

"It's going to be okay, man," Emerson said.

"You don't know that," I growled out. "He has her. We don't know what she's going through right now." I shook my head and turned away, not wanting him to see the tears in my eyes.

Hang on, Willa. Don't go down without a fight. I'll find a way.

There were so many things I wanted to promise her. But I couldn't. Not until I found her.

"I wish we had more resources," I yelled, slamming my fist into the desk. Greg and Jackson were great, but a rural sheriff's department just didn't have the kind of technology or crew I was used to.

I needed a team, and I needed intel. As a civilian, I had neither, and it was killing me.

"Hey," Emerson said, grabbing my arm to stop my pacing. "Daphne's on her way up here. She may be able to help."

"How?" I asked, incredulous. "You're telling me she's capable of doing something Greg's best deputies can't? What, is she going to magically find her?"

A strange look crossed Emerson's face. "Well. Maybe."

"I don't have time for this," I said, stalking off to find Jackson. Maybe he had found something new in the five minutes since I had checked the last time. I hoped so, because otherwise, I was about to start knocking down the doors of every building in town.

CHAPTER THIRTY-EIGHT

Willa

I BIDED MY TIME WHILE DANIEL ATTEMPTED TO BUILD A FIRE, using every second to visualize what I was about to do. Fear tried to take hold of me, but I pushed it back, refusing to feel it. My plan might fail, and if it did, I would pay for it with all the pain Daniel could dish out. But I couldn't focus on that. I had to believe it would work—had to believe I was strong enough to succeed and win my freedom once again.

Daring and courageous became my mantra, Cole's voice echoing in my mind. He believed in me. He had trained me.

I would fight, and I would be free.

So when Daniel finally had a raging fire going and leaned over to begin heating up the brand he believed I was willing to place on my body—ha!—I made my move. I grabbed the solitary wood chair and lifted it over my head, bringing it down on him with every ounce of strength I had in me. He fell into the fire, screaming as the flames burned his face.

I grabbed him, holding my breath at the smell of burning flesh, and pulled his keys out of his pocket. He grabbed at me, but I was already running—not out the door, but to the table. I grabbed the pictures he had left there and stuffed them into my shirt. With those safe, I turned back to the door—and found him blocking it.

"You bitch," he spit out, lunging for me.

But I was ready for him. When he lunged forward, I gave him the best punch of my life, knocking him backwards. I quickly followed it up with a kick to his groin, one that would ensure he stayed down long enough for me to get to his car.

"I am *not* your bitch," I said, stepping past him as he groaned on the floor.

"You'll pay," he croaked out. "I swear I'll kill you. I'll hurt you so bad you'll beg me for death, and then I'll hurt you more."

"You're never going to hurt anyone again," I said, shaking my head. "I'll make sure of it. You're the one who is going to pay, Daniel."

I turned to run, but he grabbed my ankle, pulling me to the ground. I kicked back with my free foot but missed. Before I knew what was happening, he was on top of me, with his hands around my throat. I tried to pull his hands off but couldn't—even injured, he was too strong. Panic set in as I fought for air that wouldn't come, but through it came Cole's voice.

You've got this. You know what to do. Echoes of everything he had ever told me became my lifeline, a mantra that held back the panic and let my body take over. I *did* know what to do. We had practiced this together.

I grabbed Daniel's arms and thrust my hips up the way Cole had taught me, flipping Daniel off me. Then I grabbed my metal hair comb —the one Cole had given me for Christmas—and jabbed it into Daniel's neck. He howled, letting go of me as his hands automatically reached for the comb. I scrambled away, then ran, focused only on one thing: getting to the car.

He chased after me, but I was faster. I threw the car door open and jumped in, slamming it closed just as he reached me. His bloody hands pounded on the window, but I barely noticed. I threw the car into gear and took off for the fastest drive of my life, with the image of his rage in my rearview mirror.

Daniel's cell phone was still in the car, thank God. I picked it up and immediately dialed Cole's number. He answered on the first ring.

"Where is she?" he growled.

"It's me," I said, gripping the steering wheel as the tears threatened my vision. "I'm okay, Cole. Are you okay?"

"Willa," he said, his tone changing instantly. "Thank God. Oh, baby. Where are you?"

"I'm driving," I said. "I stole his car. Listen, I need you to get the sheriff. Daniel's hurt, but he's alive. I have evidence of everything he did to me. Tell Greg I'll press charges. He just needs to get here and get Daniel before he gets away."

"Give me directions," he said, all business.

I quickly rattled off everything I remembered from our route up the mountain.

"Got it," he said. "We're on our way. Drive straight to the sheriff's office. Daphne and Janet are here now."

"Okay. Cole?"

"Yeah, baby?"

"I love you." I was so grateful to be able to say those words to him again, so grateful we were both alive and out of Daniel's reach.

"I love you, too, baby. Drive fast and safe. But keep your eyes open, okay? Daniel might send someone after you like he did me."

"I will. I'm fifteen minutes away."

"Good. Love you."

The phone clicked off and I breathed a sigh of relief. We were going to be okay.

I pulled Daniel's car right up to the entrance of the sheriff's department, not bothering to park in the lot. They could write me a ticket, I didn't care. I just wanted to be inside, in Cole's arms.

The relief I felt when I ran through the doors almost knocked me off my feet. Here, finally, I was safe.

"Willa!" Daphne cried, running straight to me. She grabbed me and hugged me tight.

For once, I didn't mind. I hugged her back, letting the tears come now that I was safe.

"Thank God you're okay," Janet said, reaching out for a hug of her own. "Come on. I have orders to take you straight to Greg's private office.

"Where's Cole?" I asked as the women ushered me down the hallway.

Janet and Daphne exchanged glances.

"He went with Greg to find Daniel," Janet said. "Greg temporarily deputized him and Emerson both. Emerson's the best tracker in the region, and Cole's entire background is finding people."

"What?" I said, anxiety flooding my body. "No. I don't want him anywhere near Daniel. Daniel already tried to kill him once. And Emerson too? Oh, Daphne, I'm so sorry," I said, choking on a sob. "I never meant to get either of you involved in this."

Daphne squeezed my hand. "It's not your fault. And Cole had to go, Willa," she said quietly. "He needs to see for himself that Daniel doesn't get away. Otherwise, you'll both always be looking over your shoulder. They'll be okay. I can feel it."

Janet nodded. "Don't worry. Greg will handle everything. And they took every available deputy with them, except Jackson. They've got a great team. It's going to be fine." She did a great job of masking her worry, but I could see it in her eyes.

"That's right. I'm here to play bodyguard," Jackson piped up. I hadn't even noticed him walking behind us. "They'll be back before you know it. In the meantime," he said, stepping forward to open the door to Greg's office for us, "I was told you have evidence of Senator Cavendish's crimes against you. Whenever you're ready, I'll take your statement. Cole said you want to file charges. I can get that ball rolling for you."

"Yes," I said, nodding.

"We can give you some privacy," Daphne said, starting to walk away.

"No, it's okay," I said. "I'd actually feel better if you stay. Until Daniel's in custody, I don't want us spreading out. I don't know what he might do if he feels trapped and desperate."

She nodded, and Janet reached out to squeeze my hand, giving me a sympathetic look.

"Here's the evidence," I said, pulling the phone and the stack of photos out of my shirt and tossing them onto Greg's desk for Jackson to see. "His phone. I know he tried to get Cole taken out of the picture. I'm pretty sure he spoke to whoever was involved in that on this phone today. And he apparently took photos of me after his abuse, when I was unconscious. Trophies meant to scare me into submission today. But the joke's on him because I'm going to use them against him. We can hang him with these, right?"

Jackson's face went dark as he stared at the photographs. "Maybe," he finally said. "But he'll have the best defense money can buy. You can count on that. They'll try to explain it all away somehow, maybe even say you and Cole faked it all trying to frame him. It won't be pretty," he warned. "But we'll help build the best case against him we can. I'll get an evidence bag. We'll test the photographs for his prints first thing. That alone isn't a smoking gun, but every bit of evidence we can stack together helps."

I nodded. "His prints will be on them. I'm sure of that. And they're clearly taken in the home we shared, over the course of years. I know that's not proof, either, but like you said. Every little bit helps. I'll testify, obviously. And I may know someone else who will testify, too," I said, thinking of Suzanna. I took a deep breath. "There's something else you should know."

"What's that?" he asked, tearing his eyes away from the nightmare in front of him.

"There's a photo in there of someone else. A woman. I don't know who. She appears to be deceased," I said, my voice breaking. "I think Daniel killed her."

Jackson closed his eyes and let out a breath. "Alright. I promise you I'm going to do my best to help nail this son of a bitch, Willa. I'm really sorry you went through any of this. And sorry for everything you're going to go through now."

"Me too," I said, swallowing back the tears.

But none of what I was facing mattered. I didn't care if Daniel dragged my name through the mud in a drawn-out court case, just as long as at the end, I was free of him and Cole was okay.

I was still terrified that Daniel would win by taking Cole from me.

Chapter Thirty-Nine

Cole

The ride up the mountain was tense. None of us were quite sure what we would find up there, but it didn't matter as long as Willa was safe. That was the only thing I cared about.

Though I sure wouldn't mind getting my chance to give Daniel Cavendish a piece of his own medicine.

"Turn left," I directed as Greg sped up the mountain roads toward the isolated cabin Willa had told me about.

"I think I know where we're headed," he said grimly. "There's an old trapper's cabin at the end of this road. The owner died about a year ago, and the kids have been fighting ever since about whether to sell it or keep it. It's been practically abandoned. Great hiding spot."

I shook my head. "He can't hide anymore."

The first thing I spotted when Greg parked in front of the cabin was the open door—and the blood trail on the ground.

Blood that I hoped didn't belong to Willa.

"Remember your orders," Greg said gruffly as he got out of the truck, pistol drawn.

I remembered them: Let him and his deputies take the lead. Stay behind and let them search the cabin. Remember that Emerson and I were only there to help with tracking, if necessary, and weren't authorized to use force unless it was without a doubt a matter of life or death.

Yes, I remembered them. Hadn't decided yet whether or not I was going to follow them.

I TAPPED MY FOOT RESTLESSLY AS GREG AND HIS MEN breached the cabin while Emerson and I sat back in Greg's truck like chumps.

It wasn't long before Greg waved us over. In an instant, I was out of the truck and at his side.

"What's the situation?" I asked.

"He's gone," Greg said flatly. "Emerson, are you seeing what I'm seeing?

Emerson took a moment to look. "This blood leads to where the car looks to have been parked, based on the tire tracks. Then straight to the tree line over there. Cole, did Willa say anything about running and hiding before she got the car?"

I shook my head. "No."

"That's what I thought. So I'm pretty sure this blood is his," Emerson said. "I'm guessing he took off into the forest."

Greg's face was a mix of anger and disgust. "Damn."

"What's the problem?" I said. "We can easily track him down in the woods. This is a freaking senator who gets manicures and lives in designer suits. He's probably lost and crying like a baby less than a half a mile away."

Greg shook his head. "I don't like it." He called his deputies to gather around. "We're walking into a dangerous situation. Senator Cavendish could be armed and dangerous, but more than that, we all know who this land used to belong to and his complete disregard of Tennessee trapping laws. I would not be surprised in the least if there are bear traps set out there, and we can't count on them all having been set off. What I'm trying to say is you need to be on guard. I don't want anyone losing a leg today. We've got to strike a balance between moving fast and being extra cautious. You got me?"

Everyone nodded assent, though I didn't have the slightest interest in being cautious.

I just wanted to catch the guy.

AFTER A BRIEF ARGUMENT ON WHO WOULD TAKE THE LEAD— I wanted it, mostly to ensure I took the greatest danger from the traps— Emerson scored the lead position, due to his tracking skills.

"Don't you dare get hurt," I warned him. "Daphne will kill me."

"Hell yeah she will," he said, grinning. "Come on. Let's head out."

We fell in line behind Emerson as he followed the blood trail, walking carefully to avoid any old traps left behind. After about twenty minutes, the trail ended at a stream. Emerson looked around for a bit, then gave us the news. "Looks like he went into the water. I'll cross over and see if I can pick him up on the other side."

But after walking up and down the stream, looking for the trail, Emerson called out in frustration. "There's nothing over here. Best I can tell, he must have walked in the water for a while before getting out. Or if we're lucky, he drowned and is still in there. We'll either have to pick a direction, hope we're right and double back to check the other way if we're wrong. Or we split up to cover ground faster."

"We should split up," I said instantly.

Greg frowned. "I don't like it, but you're right. Alright, every-one," he called out, "we're crossing over. Miller and Sanderson, you'll go that way with Emerson. Parker, you're with me and Cole. Let's go."

With a quick nod toward Emerson, I took the lead, heading downstream.

My mind raced, calculating what Daniel was up to. Walking through the stream was smart on one hand. It eliminated his blood trail. But it was still the early days of spring, and the stream was ice cold. Despite being shallow, that kind of cold would sap his strength fast. He'd need to get out and warm up quickly. He had been wearing a suit when he took Willa—not appropriate gear for being out on the mountain this time of year.

He couldn't be far.

A few hundred yards past where Emerson had stopped searching, I heard a noise. It was faint, but there was something moving in the trees across the stream. I stopped suddenly, motioning for Greg and Parker to stop as well, raising my finger to my lips in a signal to be quiet.

Greg came up beside me. "It's probably an animal," he said, whispering.

"I want to check it out. I'll cross over and take a look."

Greg eyed the stream. "It's deeper here. You're going to get wet.

"All the more reason he may have gotten out instead of continuing on. Stay here. I'll check and give you a signal if I see any blood. Okay?"

He gave me a long look. "Alright. Make it quick and don't lose your footing. Last thing we need is to take time to build a fire to warm you up."

I couldn't help but laugh. "You do know what I used to do for a living right? I'll be fine. Hang tight."

I carefully worked my way across the stream. It was deeper, yes, but not terribly so. The water only came up to my knees. Still, it was frigid, and the fast moving water and slippery rocks were treacherous. Daniel wouldn't want to navigate it for long.

When I got to the edge of the stream, I paused, listening. The noises had stopped completely, making me think whoever—or whatever—was over here had seen me crossing.

A quick search on the other side of the bank and bingo—fresh blood.

I stood up and motioned for Greg, who immediately began to cross over with Parker in tow.

But I didn't wait.

Daniel was here and I wasn't going to let him get away.

I followed the trail—easy now, as he seemed to be bleeding more heavily than before—making quick time through the woods. He was heading to higher ground and moving fast. I knew he was aware I was following.

I didn't care.

Suddenly, the noises stopped. I immediately ducked behind a tree. A moving target was one thing; a stationary one was another. I needed to be on guard in case he had a gun or something else and was trying to get me in his sights. Ignoring Greg's rules, I drew my pistol and waited. But the noises started up again as Daniel resumed his climb up the mountain.

I stepped out from the tree, giving chase again, when suddenly I heard a piercing scream. No hesitation now—I ran straight for the sound, pistol in hand.

Branches hit my face and tore my jacket as I flew through the woods. The screams turned to moans of anguish. I followed the sound, not even taking time to watch the trail—it was faster to let the sound guide me, and I knew I was zeroed in on him.

When I ducked underneath a heavy branch, I saw him on the ground. Instant relief flooded my chest. The screams and moans were Daniel's, not any of our crew. He hadn't caught anyone, he had been caught—by an old bear trap by the looks of it.

"You have to help me!" he cried, grabbing frantically at his mangled leg. Blood dripped from where the jaws of the trap held it tight. "My leg. The pain is unbearable! Help me!"

"Help you?" I asked, incredulous as I stalked toward him. "Help *you?* Are you kidding me?"

"You," he said, recognition dawning in his eyes. "You're the one who's sleeping with my wife."

"She's not your wife anymore," I spat out. "You destroyed that the first time you hit her. And you're asking me to help *you* because *you're* in pain? You must have lost your freaking mind."

New fear sparked in his eyes. "I'm a U.S. senator," he said, swallowing hard. "You can't hurt me."

"Can't?" I let out a laugh as I squatted in front of him, just out of reach, allowing him to get a clear view of the pistol in my hand. "That's funny coming from you." My eyes narrowed. "I saw what you did to Willa. Saw the fear in her eyes. The scars you left on her. I've woken up next to her when she's screamed out in the night, shaking from nightmares of your abuse. And now, fate seems to have given me a gift," I said, using my gun to gesture at the trap holding his leg. "See, I love

Willa. And the greatest gift I could ever give her would be to make sure you're never able to come after her again."

"You wouldn't," he said, swallowing hard again. "You'd spend the rest of your life in prison."

"Would I though?" I said, cocking my head. "Looks to me like I don't have to 'do' anything except turn around and walk on out of here, telling my friends I couldn't find you after all. You'd make a nice meal for a coyote or a black bear. At least then you'd serve some purpose in life, feeding Mother Nature and all."

"You can't leave me out here to suffer," he said, shocked. "It's inhumane."

"*Inhumane?*" I shook my head, laughing in disbelief. "You burned Willa's ribs with a fireplace poker. Literally branded your initials into her skin. Isolated her from the world. Beat her countless times and forced yourself on her night after night. And you want to talk about *humanity?* You're a sick son of a bitch, Daniel Cavendish, and I don't owe you a damn thing."

He glared at me. "Her name is *Wilhelmina,* and she brought every bit of that on herself. You have no idea how stubborn and willful that woman is. Someone had to train her to know her place. She was my wife. I had every right to punish her as I saw fit. And it doesn't matter what you think. I made sure she'll wear my initials on her body for the rest of her life. She belongs to *me,* and I will get her back. And when I do, I swear she'll suffer more than either of you can even imagine. You think those beatings were bad? What I did to her before is nothing compared to what I'll do to her in the future, I assure you."

I nodded and stood up. "Thank you, Daniel. You get all that, Sheriff?"

Greg emerged from the trees. "Yep. I think that will do it."

Daniel's eyes went wide. "You tricked me."

"I didn't trick you into anything. It's not my fault you didn't pay attention to who was around before bragging about what you did to *Willa.* She's free of you now, but you? You'll never be free again."

Daniel's eyes were full of rage as he spat at me. "You have no idea who I am or what I'm capable of. I won't spend a single night in jail. You both better sleep with one eye open because I'm coming for you.

You'll never take her from me. I swear I'll kill you both. I will slice her open and make you watch. Her blood will drip from your hands, and then I'll—"

"Senator Cavendish," Greg said, interrupting him to slap on a pair of cuffs. "You're under arrest for the kidnapping of Wilhelmina Cavendish. You have the right to remain silent," Greg said, "and can I kindly suggest you stop running your mouth and make use of that right? Cole's getting pissed off, and I'd like to get you out of here in one piece. Well," he said, glancing at Daniel's mangled leg. "Maybe two pieces."

THE HOURS DRAGGED BY AS WE WORKED TO SAFELY evacuate Daniel. He had suffered burns on his face that would forever mar his pretty-boy image, and with the amount of damage he sustained, I expected he would lose his leg. But he would live.

It was more than he deserved.

But that didn't seem to matter when I finally got back to town and saw Willa. She was waiting for me, and as soon as I walked through the doors of the station, she ran and jumped into my arms.

"You're safe," she said, holding me like she would never let go.

"Me? What about you?" I said, chuckling. "I'm fine, baby. But you. I'm so sorry I failed you. Did he... Did he hurt you?"

"No," she said, shaking her head as I gently placed her back down on her feet. "He wanted to. But I could hear your voice telling me not to go down without a fight. So I didn't. I fought him, Cole, and I won. *I won.*"

"I'm so proud of you." I ran my hands through her hair, wanting to stare at her and make sure she was real, that this was real, that she was really here and we were okay. "So, so proud of you, baby."

"I broke a chair over his head. Then I punched him in the face and kicked him in the groin," she said, her eyes sparkling just a bit. "And when he came after me again, I used the moves you showed me to get away. Then I stabbed him in the neck with the comb you gave me."

"I bet that felt good," I said, unable to hold back my grin.

"It did," she said like she was confessing something terrible. "I'm not a violent person, Cole, but it felt so good to fight back and not let him do the things he wanted to do to me. I never would have done that if not for you. You didn't fail me. You saved me, Cole. You made me believe I was strong and that I didn't have to take it."

"You are strong," I said, pulling her tight into my arms. I never wanted to let her go again. "Daring and courageous. That's my girl."

"Yes," she whispered. "For the first time in a long time, I believe it." She pulled back and sighed. "I'm only sad about one thing."

"What's that, baby?"

"The hair comb," she said, laughing softly, even as tears pricked her eyes. "It's so silly. It served a great purpose today, and that should be enough. But it was the first gift you gave me, and I'm sad to have lost it."

"You mean this hair comb?" I asked, pulling it from my pocket and placing it in her hands.

Her eyes lit up. "What in the world?"

"Shhh," I said. "I swiped it from the scene. Don't tell Greg."

She grinned. "It will be our little secret."

Epilogue

Summer, the following year...

"An August bride," Daphne sighed, tucking one last flower into my hair. "Is there anything dreamier?"

"I still can't believe it," I said, practically glowing as I looked at my own reflection. I was wearing an ivory silk wedding dress I had made myself. Every hand-stitch had been a promise of our future together, and the dress would be an heirloom to pass down to my children and grandchildren. It was perfect and beautifully accented with wildflowers in my hair, which had been collected by Daphne and Fiona. I carried an artful bouquet of the same that Daphne had made for me. I was barefoot. Sun-bronzed. Happy.

Free.

Daniel had been convicted of a long list of crimes, including what he did to me. People had come out of the woodwork to testify on my behalf—previous household staff, an ER nurse who had patched me up once, and even my own father. I still wasn't ready to have anything to do with him, but I was grateful he had decided to do the right thing for once. Between the testimonies, the confession Greg overheard, and the evidence Jackson had put together, that case against Daniel had been airtight. Sadly, the other woman in the photographs had never been identified, so there would never be full closure or justice there. But thanks to his other convictions, I had been assured he would never see the light of day again.

After the trial, I had finally been granted a divorce. Because of the circumstances under which I had created my false identity and faked my death, no charges had been filed against me, leaving me free to start my life for real. When we found out I was in the clear, Cole asked what I wanted to do. I told him the first thing I wanted was a new name—I didn't want to ever be known as Wilhelmina Cavendish again. He asked if I was going to legally change my name to Willa Monroe, since that's what I had gone by since leaving Daniel, but I told him I'd prefer the name Willa Hawkins.

His face had lit up and he had surprised me by dropping to one knee and pulling a ring out of his pocket. He had been carrying it for weeks, just waiting for the right moment to ask me. It was the most unique ring I had ever seen, with two bands—a gold one with a beautiful diamond star and a silver one with a diamond moon. He said he had known instantly it was the one for me, because our lucky stars had brought us together again.

It was everything I could have ever wanted.

Daphne squeezed me. "I am so, so happy for you. You deserve every bit of happiness."

"As do you, my friend," I said, hugging her back.

Little Eileen toddled over to her mama, tugging on her dress. Daphne immediately scooped her up and covered her in kisses, while Janet swept over and tucked yet another wildflower into the flower crown Fiona had woven for the child. Daphne and Janet were both hopelessly in love with sweet Eileen. I smiled, full of joy for my dear friend. No envy this time. I knew there would be babies of my own soon enough.

In fact, there would be one in about seven months, according to

Fiona. As the person I had chosen to be my midwife, she was the only one who knew so far. Well, except for Daphne, who probably already knew but hadn't said anything. I would give her the news officially after the honeymoon, but I wanted to surprise Cole first. I smiled, imagining what an incredible dad he would be. It was an unexpected, perfect wedding gift for us both.

I walked out on Greg and Janet's back deck and looked up to the sky, already growing dark with the first stars beginning to dot the heavens. It felt only fitting that Cole and I would marry underneath the stars that had watched over us so many times before. It meant a late evening wedding, but that was okay—our only guests were the handful of people who truly mattered to us. Cole's parents and siblings, whom I absolutely adored. Daphne and Emerson and their sweet daughter. Greg and Janet and Fiona. Suzanna, whom Cole had flown in from California for the occasion. And of course Jackson, who had earned Cole's gratitude for a lifetime for the effort he had put into building a solid case against Daniel.

Our friends had become family. Family that was willing to stay up late just so we could marry underneath the night sky.

"You ready?" Greg smiled at me. He was walking me down the aisle, standing in as the father figure I no longer had.

"I'm ready," I said, returning his smile.

He gave me his arm and led me down the steps onto the grass, to the rose-covered pathway Janet had set up. Our friends stood as I looked down the aisle, with eyes for only one person.

Cole.

My best friend. My hero. My love.

I had come to Rosemary Mountain for refuge, but I found everything I had ever wanted.

Thank you for reading Cole and Willa's story!
If you enjoyed this book, I would so appreciate you taking the time to leave a review at your preferred vendor. Reviews are invaluable to authors. It truly means the world.

Adore Fiona? Me too! Sign up for my mailing list and receive a recipe for Fiona's Hawthorn Tea.

Acknowledgments

Writing this book was one of the most fun experiences of my life. Since I was writing about fresh characters, I allowed myself to diverge from the normal Rosemary Mountain mysteries and indulge in my favorite kind of romantic suspense. I took some chances and tried some new things. I hope you all enjoyed reading it as much as I enjoyed writing it.

I have what feels like a million people to thank this time, but as always, my first thanks goes to my husband, Brandon. Not only are you an incredible life partner, but you were invaluable during the process of writing this book. Thank you for "alpha" reading and helping me get inside the head of a veteran, as well as your constant support in this writing life. You are the best, and I love that this book was your favorite!

I would also like to thank my children, who are becoming such interesting, fun pre-teens. It's been a joy to watch you fall in love with writing this year. I'm cheering for you as you write your own stories!

I owe a huge debt of gratitude to "Uncle-E," PJ/TL (Ret.). Your willingness to share your stories about life as a PJ meant the world to me. Thank you for your service to our country, and for offering me a window into that world. I hope that my character Cole has done justice to how incredible the PJs are, and to what a struggle it can be to adjust to life as a civilian after service.

Thank you also to Adam and Whitney Farmer and the Jonesboro Grappling Association for hosting incredible free women's self-defense classes. I thoroughly enjoyed participating and appreciate both the writing inspiration and the service to our community!

Huge thanks to my beta team for this book: Jessica Haigler, Deondra Childers, Candice Jenee, and Courtney Maree. I love that you all bring such different perspectives to the mix, and I always appreciate your wise feedback!

Thanks also to Mickey Reed, my editor. You are an absolute jewel to work with and I am so happy to have found you!

The cover art for this book—and entire series—was created by Brooke Passmore of BY THE BROOKE Designs. Thank you for creating another lovely cover to represent Cole and Willa's story!

Special thanks also to Misty Perry, for introducing me to Uncle-E!

As always, I want to express gratitude to the local businesses who have wrapped their arms around me and made me feel so welcome in the Paragould, Arkansas community: Juniper Tree Meadery and Weber's Book House.

Finally, one last thank you to my friends, family, and community. Your support, encouragement, excitement, and understanding is something for which I will always be grateful!

About the Author

Nicole Gardner lives in NE Arkansas with her husband, their two sons, and their two crazy dogs. If she's not at her desk, you'll likely find her either in the garden, or creating teas and tinctures in the kitchen.

Nicole's background is in psychology. This fascination with human behavior and relationship dynamics plays a significant role in her writing and the way she shapes her characters.

www.nicolegardnerbooks.com